SUMMER WITH THE BILLIONAIRE BOYS CLUB

CARA MILLER

Want my unreleased 5000-word story
Introducing the Billionaire Boys Club
and other free gifts from time to time?

Then join my mailing list at

http://www.caramillerbooks.com/inner-circle/

Subscribe now and read it now!

You can also follow me on Twitter and Facebook

Summer with the Billionaire Boys Club

Books in the Billionaire Romance Series:

The Billionaire Boys Club
Surrender to the Billionaire Boys Club
Billionaire Boys Club in New York
Summer with the Billionaire Boys Club
Secrets of the Billionaire Boys Club
A Date with the Billionaire Boys Club
Billionaire Boys Club in Love
Fireworks with the Billionaire Boys Club
An Evening with the Billionaire Boys Club
A Very Billionaire Boys Club Christmas
An Invitation from the Billionaire Boys Club
Midnight with the Billionaire Boys Club
Dreaming with the Billionaire Boys Club
A Promise from the Billionaire Boys Club
Engaged to the Billionaire Boys Club
A Surprise from the Billionaire Boys Club
Romance with the Billionaire Boys Club
A Billionaire Boys Club Wedding

"So are we going to deny this too?" Tyler asked Kelsey.

She smiled at him.

"Yes." They were sitting in Cal Anderson Park, and it was past midnight. Couples passed by holding hands, and teenagers sat in the park, talking and laughing.

Tyler sighed. He surveyed Kelsey in the moonlight, which glinted off of her gold-sequined dress. Tyler reached out and ran his finger through her long blonde hair.

"We're going to pretend this didn't happen because I'm not ready, and you're not ready."

"Yes," Kelsey said.

"Because I'm too busy for a relationship and because you're dating Lucas Anderson."

Kelsey paused for a moment before answering.

"Yes," she said hesitantly.

"All right," Tyler said. "None of this happened." He put his hand behind Kelsey's neck, gently pulled her forward, and kissed her deeply.

Kelsey broke away. She had tears in her eyes. "We aren't doing this, Tyler," she said.

Tyler surveyed her with his eyes. Then he slowly nodded. "You're right," he said, abruptly standing up.

Kelsey's eyes followed him. "I am?" she said, unsure of herself.

"You are," Tyler replied firmly. "Do you want to go back to campus?"

"What?" Kelsey said.

"You're right. We can't do this," Tyler said.

Kelsey thought for a moment as she looked at him under the park lights.

"Why?" she finally asked.

Tyler looked at her startled, then looked away.

"Because we aren't going to," he said softly.

"Then don't kiss me again," Kelsey said, with firmness, although her heart broke as she said it.

Tyler looked at her and frowned. Then he laughed.

"I don't think you mean that," he said, shaking his head.

"I do. I can't take the back-and-forth. If you aren't serious, don't start."

"Is Lucas serious?" Tyler asked.

"More serious than you," Kelsey replied.

"Do you want that?" Tyler asked.

Kelsey was silent. She knew what she wanted. She was looking in his eyes. But she knew she couldn't have him. At least not now.

"I don't want to play games, Tyler."

"We aren't playing."

"I'm not. You are. Tomorrow, you'll be just the same as you always are. Behind your glass wall. I can see the real you, but you won't let me in. And that's fine. But don't keep teasing me."

"I'm a tease?" Tyler asked.

"You are."

"What do you want from me, Kelsey? I thought we had settled this in New York. Neither one of us wants to commit, so we won't," Tyler said.

"True," Kelsey agreed. "But I don't want to pretend any more."

"So we aren't friends?"

"Of course we're friends. Friends without kissing."

Tyler nodded. "Okay. I see your point. Fine. Spend your summer kissing Mr. Anderson."

Kelsey stood up angrily. She cursed herself for wobbling gently in her heels. "I'll kiss whomever I want, Mr. Olsen," she snapped.

"Why are you so difficult?" Tyler asked testily.

"Me?" Kelsey said in outrage. "I'm not the one who's avoiding commitment."

"If you don't commit, you can't break up," Tyler commented.

"If you don't take risks, you can't win," Kelsey replied.

"And what am I trying to win?" Tyler asked.

"Clearly, nothing," Kelsey said. "I don't want to fight with you. Please take me home."

Tyler frowned. "Give me your arm," he said. "I don't want you to fall," he added.

Kelsey sighed and gave him her arm. He slowly led her toward the car.

"I don't want to hurt you, Kelsey," Tyler said gently.

"You don't know what you want," Kelsey retorted angrily.

Tyler looked at her thoughtfully. "Truer words have never been spoken."

"What are you so afraid of?" Kelsey said, as Tyler opened the car door for her. She lowered herself into the passenger seat.

Tyler didn't answer the question. He was silent the entire ride home.

At breakfast the next morning, Kelsey walked into the dining hall and sat down with her tray. Ryan was alone, eating a piece of toast.

"Good morning." He smiled brightly.

"Morning," Kelsey said, sitting down.

"I didn't expect to see you so early," Ryan commented. "Where's Tyler?"

"Tyler? I don't know," Kelsey said, as Jessica sat next down next to her.

Ryan looked puzzled.

"Weren't you with him last night?" he asked, as Jessica sipped her coffee.

"I was," Kelsey said.

"He messaged me at four this morning and said he was at the condo," Ryan continued.

Jessica lifted an eyebrow.

"Not with me. He dropped me off at two," Kelsey commented, eating her eggs.

"Oh," Ryan said, looking away and studying his toast.

That evening, Kelsey, Ryan and Jessica sat down for dinner together. A few moments later, Tyler sat down with his tray.

"Hi," he said.

"You stole my car and my condo," Ryan said to him.

Tyler smiled. "I knew you wouldn't mind," he replied.

Zachary sat next to Tyler.

"Hey. Want to play squash later?" Tyler asked him.

"Sure," Zachary replied.

"Where have you been all day?" Ryan asked. "I haven't seen you since breakfast."

"Payne family gathering. Dad's brother is here," Zach said.

"How was it?" Tyler asked.

"Fine," Zach commented. "He was less of a jerk than usual."

"That's good," Tyler said.

"So why did you steal my condo if you weren't sleeping with Kelsey?" Ryan asked Tyler abruptly.

Kelsey choked on her food, and Tyler glared at Ryan.

"I didn't want to wake Zach," Tyler replied.

"What time did the Law Review party end?" Zach asked.

"I dropped Kelsey off around two," Tyler said, eating.

"But you didn't message me until four," Ryan commented.

Tyler looked at Ryan in annoyance. "And?"

"So what were you doing?" Ryan asked innocently.

"Thinking," Tyler replied. "You should try it."

"I see," Ryan said.

"You really need a different hobby. My life isn't that interesting," Tyler said to Ryan.

"It's like changing channels on the television," Ryan said. "I keep hoping it will get better."

Tyler laughed. He glanced at Kelsey.

"Me too," Tyler replied.

On Monday, Tyler greeted Kelsey as usual, but didn't make conversation. Kelsey didn't feel like things were tense. Instead, she felt like Tyler was thinking about something. She wanted to believe it was about what she had said Saturday night, but knowing Tyler, it was just as likely to be something about Law Review or his grades. It still felt odd though, so when Lucas sat next to her at the library on Monday evening, Kelsey found that she was particularly happy to see him.

"Hey there," Lucas said, slinging his backpack onto the table and sitting next to her. "Studying hard?"

"Of course," Kelsey smiled at him.

"You always are," Lucas commented. "You must already be ready for exams."

"Almost," Kelsey replied. She had already completed the contracts outline and was waiting for things to normalize with Tyler before she sent it to him. Tyler would cut it down to his usual 20-page outline.

Lucas's eyes sparkled as he looked at her. "So should we go on another pre-date?"

Kelsey grinned at him but shook her head. "It's too close to exams, Lucas," she said.

"Oh, c'mon. You're going to get straight A's anyway. You can go with me to get ice cream."

"Maybe," Kelsey said flirtatiously.

Lucas smiled at her. "Good. Perhaps you aren't such a grind," he commented.

"No, I am," Kelsey replied. "But ice cream sounds nice. When do you want to go?"

"Now?" Lucas said.

"I need to finish what I'm working on," Kelsey replied.

"Tomorrow? After dinner?"

"Okay," Kelsey said.

Lucas stood and lifted his backpack. "See you tomorrow," he said. Lucas leaned down and kissed her on her hair. Then he walked off.

Kelsey smiled to herself.

A moment later, Jennifer Lane walked over. "Hi, Kelsey," she said.

Kelsey looked up. "Hi, Jen," she replied. She didn't know Jennifer that well, but Jen was friends with Jessica, and Kelsey had spoken to her for a while at the Law Review party.

"Have you broken up with Tyler?" Jennifer asked, a bit abruptly.

"Tyler and I aren't going out," Kelsey replied, taken a bit aback.

"Oh, come on, Kelsey. We all saw you at the Law Review party. Are you really dumping a billionaire for Lucas Anderson?" Jennifer asked.

Kelsey wasn't sure what to say, so she was silent.

Jennifer answered her own question. "Wow. Lucas must really be special," she said. "Well, good luck." Jen waved and walked off.

Kelsey found herself frowning as she put the key into her door. Jessica was sitting at her desk studying, and looked up as Kelsey walked in.

"Hi, Kels," Jessica said. "How's it going?"

"Why is Jennifer Lane asking me about Tyler?" Kelsey asked her.

Jessica looked at her.

"Jen had a lot to say about the two of you at the party when I saw her after class," Jessica commented.

"Did she?" Kelsey said.

"Don't dance with him in front of the press," Jessica said wisely.

At dinner on Tuesday, Tyler walked over to the table where Kelsey was sitting and placed a folder on the table next to her tray. He sat down next to her.

"A peace offering," he said, looking at her.

Kelsey picked up the folder and opened it. Three documents were inside, the outlines for all of their classes except contracts.

"Thanks," Kelsey said. Tyler smiled at her. So this is what he had been working on for the past few days. She wasn't sure if she was relieved or disappointed that he hadn't been thinking about their relationship.

"I'm sorry. I didn't really think about your feelings," he said. "I know that you're dating Lucas, and I'll try to stay out of that from now on."

"It's okay," Kelsey said. She decided not to think about Tyler's comment, but instead looked through one of the short outlines. As always, Tyler had done amazing work.

"I hope that you'll still go with me to the picnic this summer, though," Tyler said.

"I wouldn't miss it," Kelsey said.

"Thank you. I've spent the last two days fending off Jennifer Lane.

She's trying to set me up with her sister."

"No wonder," Kelsey said out loud.

"No wonder what?" Tyler asked.

"Never mind," Kelsey grinned. Jessica and Ryan walked over carrying their trays and sat down.

"Not hungry?" Jessica asked Tyler.

"I was just going, Miss Hunter," Tyler said, standing and winking at Kelsey.

"What's all that?" Jessica asked Kelsey.

"Our exam outlines," Kelsey replied.

"I love you guys," Ryan said, picking one up and looking at it.

"Aren't you writing the one for contracts?" Jessica said to Kelsey.

"It's done. Tyler just needs to edit it," Kelsey replied.

"We're depending on you," Ryan said. "Since Eliot only calls on you and Tyler, we've been sleeping during Contracts."

Kelsey laughed. "Don't worry. I know it all." She probably should thank Eliot. Contracts was the first class that she had this much confidence in going into the exam. Of course, she had neglected every other class in the meantime.

Ryan and Jessica began to eat, and Tyler sat back down a few minutes later with his tray.

"I'll send you the Contracts outline tonight," Kelsey said to him.

"Okay, I'll cut it down from your usual 120 pages," Tyler teased.

"It's only 98," Kelsey replied, grinning.

"Thanks for doing all of our work," Jessica said.

"It's just an outline," Tyler said. "It won't help you if you don't know what's going on in class. Right, Ryan?"

"I've been studying," Ryan pouted. "I don't want to end up like Matt."

"Your father will be happy to hear that," Tyler replied.

"Maybe we should study together tonight after dinner," Jessica said.

"It's fine with me," Tyler said. "Okay, Kels?"

"I can't tonight," Kelsey said. The other three looked at her.

"Another hot date with Lucas Anderson?" Ryan asked her.

"We're going for ice cream," Kelsey replied.

"Of course you are," Ryan said.

"What does that mean?" Kelsey replied. Ryan shrugged innocently.

"It's okay, I'll fill you in on what we studied later," Jessica said. Kelsey nodded.

Tyler finished his dinner and stood up.

"I'm going to make copies of the outlines for you two," he said to Jessica and Ryan. "Meet you in Ryan's room?"

"Sure," Ryan said. "Where's Zach?"

"Medina," Tyler replied. "I think his mom is starting to panic about his grades after Matthew failed out, so it's time for a lecture."

"Better him than me," Ryan replied.

"See you later, Kels," Tyler said, taking his tray and walking off.

"Are you really getting serious about Lucas?" Ryan asked after Tyler was out of earshot.

"Of course she isn't," Jessica said dismissively.

Kelsey frowned. "Lucas is really nice."

"Lucas is a dweeb," Ryan retorted.

"Stay out of my life, Ryan," Kelsey said.

"Fine," Ryan replied. "But I'm not promising not to set Tyler up this summer."

"Like Tyler would date anyone," Jessica said to him.

"If Kelsey keeps going out with randoms, I think he might," Ryan said.

"Randoms?" Kelsey said.

"Lucas isn't exactly extraordinary," Ryan commented.

"We can't all be as annoying as you, Ryan," Kelsey retorted.

"Clearly, you're only dating Lucas to make Tyler jealous," Ryan said.

"That's not true. Lucas is a really nice guy."

"I'm sure," Ryan said with sarcasm.

"Go away, Ryan," Kelsey said.

The group sat in silence for a moment, then Ryan said, "Speak of the devil."

Kelsey looked up and saw Lucas walking over to the table. She smiled and Ryan rolled his eyes.

"Hi, Kelsey," Lucas said, taking Tyler's empty chair.

"Hi," Kelsey replied.

"Ready for ice cream?" he asked.

"I'm ready," Kelsey replied.

"Kelsey's giving up her studying for you tonight. Make sure you show her a good time," Ryan said to Lucas.

"We always have fun," Lucas said, looking at Kelsey. Lucas stood, as did Kelsey.

"Drop by Ryan's room when you get in," Jessica said to Kelsey. "We'll probably still be up."

"Okay," Kelsey agreed. Her dates with Lucas didn't usually last long, and she did need to catch up.

"Bye," Jessica said as Kelsey and Lucas walked away.

"Are you really giving up studying for me?" Lucas asked her as they left the dining hall.

"I'll study later," Kelsey replied.

"Wow, I'm honored," Lucas said. They walked out into the quad, which was still damp and cold. Seattle's summer wouldn't arrive for another six weeks. "So I heard you went to the Law Review party with Tyler Olsen."

"I did," Kelsey replied.

"Why did he ask you?"

"I guess he needed an escort," she replied.

"But you aren't dating him?" Lucas asked her.

"No. Tyler isn't interested in dating me," Kelsey replied.

"Why not?" Lucas asked in surprise.

"You'd have to ask him," Kelsey said.

"I thought he was smart," Lucas said. "I guess not."

"Not everyone who is smart wants to date me," Kelsey replied.

"If they knew anything they would," Lucas retorted.

"You're very sweet," Kelsey said.

Lucas smiled at her. "So what kind of ice cream do you want?" he asked, changing the subject.

"Mint," Kelsey said.

"Mint?" Lucas said.

"I haven't had it in a while," Kelsey said.

"I hate mint," Lucas commented.

"Really?"

"Ick," Lucas said.

"Okay, what kind do you want?" Kelsey asked. They had left campus and were heading to Madison Street.

"Strawberry probably, but maybe caramel," Lucas replied.

"Caramel is good too," Kelsey said.

"I don't believe that you actually like mint," Lucas said.

"What do you brush your teeth with?" Kelsey asked him.

"Fennel. Baking soda. Anything but mint," he replied.

Kelsey laughed. "We won't share our ice cream then," she said.

They walked onto Madison Street and down towards the ice cream shop. To Kelsey's surprise, Lucas took her hand into his own and held it.

"Do you want to study together next week?" Lucas asked Kelsey.

"I'd better not," Kelsey said. "I usually study with Jess." Kelsey had no intention of tutoring Lucas over the next two weeks to the detriment of her own grades, cute smile or not.

"I'm sure that you'll do great," Lucas said. "What will you do over your break between school and work? Go home?"

"I don't think so," Kelsey said. "It's going to be really busy at my parents' store, so I won't see much of them. I think I'll stick around here. How about you?"

"I'm going home for the week," Lucas said.

"Nice. Will you see your siblings?"

"Most of them live near my parents, so probably," Lucas replied. "I'm really looking forward to seeing my nieces and nephews."

"That should be fun."

"Yeah, it will be a good break after Darrow," Lucas agreed. They stopped in front of the ice cream shop and went inside. There was another couple there, so they looked at the flavors while they waited.

"I don't see mint," Kelsey said.

"No offense, but good," Lucas replied.

"I"ll get caramel instead," she said.

"Much better. Then we can share," Lucas said. The other couple finished and Kelsey and Lucas ordered, paying separately. They walked over to an empty table with their ice cream and sat down. Lucas had got strawberry again.

"Can I have a bite?" he asked Kelsey.

"Of course," Kelsey said. Lucas dipped his spoon into her ice cream and removed a large spoonful, which he ate.

Kelsey walked up the stairs of the dorm to Ryan's room. Per usual, her date with Lucas hadn't been a long one. They had eaten ice cream, then had sat in the Madison Park playground to talk.

A couple of small children, who obviously needed some running-around time after dinner, had been in the playground as well, supervised by their hovering parents. Because of the kids, Lucas and Kelsey's conversation had turned to their respective families in Shaker Heights and in Port Townsend. And over the half-hour of discussion, Kelsey began to question why she had agreed to date Lucas in the first place.

Lucas was a really nice guy. That was clear. But what was also clear to Kelsey was that his worldview was completely different from her own. Lucas had planned out his life already. He would graduate from law school, although he wasn't confident he'd make it through Darrow. Then he'd go work in construction law in one of the large Midwestern cities within a day's drive from his parents' Ohio home. He wanted lots of kids and a big house. Kelsey knew exactly what Lucas wanted. But she was less confident about her own desires.

She was still pondering this question as she headed down the hall. Ryan's door was open and she pushed it to enter. Tyler looked up. He was sitting on Ryan's bed, wearing rolled-up khaki pants and a navy cotton sweater. He was looking over one of the outlines, pen in hand.

"Hi, Kels," he said.

"Hi," Kelsey replied, sitting at the empty desk that had once been Brandon's.

"Ryan and Jess went to your room to get food," Tyler said. "We ate all of mine."

"That doesn't surprise me," Kelsey replied. "What have you been working on?"

"Contracts, so you wouldn't miss anything," Tyler replied. "How was your date?"

Kelsey surveyed Tyler's face, but once again, there was no emotion hidden there.

"Fine," Kelsey replied.

"Good," Tyler said.

Kelsey frowned. She knew she shouldn't care, but she was curious as to why Tyler wasn't concerned at all about her relationship with Lucas. So, throwing caution to the wind, she decided to ask him.

"What do you think of Lucas?" Kelsey asked.

"Do I have an opinion about Lucas Anderson?" Tyler asked her.

"You have an opinion about everything," Kelsey replied.

Tyler smiled. "Yes, I guess that's true," he replied. "Lucas seems fine."

"Fine?"

Tyler looked at Kelsey with his soft brown eyes. There was a sparkle of amusement in them.

"Lucas is a nice, pleasant guy who will move back to the Midwest, put up his own shingle, marry a pretty wife and have 2.8 adorable children," Tyler commented.

"Is there something wrong with that?" Kelsey asked.

"No," Tyler replied.

"But?"

"But what?" Tyler asked innocently.

"But you're not impressed."

"It's not a question of whether I'm impressed," Tyler said. "I'm not going out with him."

Kelsey narrowed her eyes at Tyler.

"So you think I can do better?"

"I know you can. But it doesn't matter. Lucas won't marry someone smarter than himself. His ego can't take it. I have a feeling he'll come to that conclusion on his own this summer," Tyler replied, smiling at her.

"You are so arrogant," Kelsey said.

"You asked me what I thought. I told you," Tyler replied. "Perhaps I'm wrong. Maybe Lucas has an engagement ring all picked out for you."

"And you're willing to risk it?" Kelsey asked him.

"Kelsey, if you decide to marry Lucas Anderson, I'll give you the lakefront house as a wedding gift," Tyler replied.

"You're so annoying," Kelsey said. But she smiled.

"Annoying, but correct?" Tyler replied.

"Yes," Kelsey conceded.

Tyler looked at Kelsey. "I wish my life wasn't such a mess. But while it is, I won't drag you into it."

"I know."

"But I want to," he replied.

"I know," Kelsey said.

"Don't marry Lucas Anderson," Tyler said.

"I won't," Kelsey replied.

"Okay." Tyler said. The two of them sat quietly for a moment, then the door burst open and Ryan and Jessica walked in.

"Kels, you're back!" Jessica said happily.

"I thought you just went upstairs," Tyler said, taking a bag from Ryan's arms.

"There wasn't enough to eat there, so we walked over to the cafe," Ryan replied. "How was your date?" he asked Kelsey.

Kelsey smiled at Tyler, who smiled back.

"It was fine," she replied.

Over the next few days, Kelsey and the rest of the Darrow first-year class finished their final classes of the year. Kelsey wasn't sorry to say goodbye to Eliot and contracts, but she knew that she would miss Keith, who would be graduating this year and starting a clerkship for a Washington State Supreme Court justice.

After their last classes on Friday, the first-year class was in a state of nervous excitement. Their first year of law school was over, and now they just had to get through exams. Then it was time to go off to internships, which almost every Darrow first-year had been offered.

Ryan leaned his head against Jessica's shoulder in the dining hall at dinner.

"I can't believe you're leaving me," he sighed.

"Only for a few weeks," Jessica said, stroking his hair.

"Months," Ryan corrected.

"You'll be fine. Kelsey, Tyler, and Zachary will all be here."

"But you won't," Ryan moaned.

"I don't leave for another week," Jessica said.

"Don't go," Ryan replied.

"Of course I'm going," Jessica replied.

"Won't you miss me?" Ryan asked her, sitting up.

"Of course I will. But it will be good for us to spend the summer apart."

"Why?" Ryan asked.

"We can sort out our feelings," Jessica replied.

"I know what I feel," Ryan said. "Don't you?"

Jessica was silent.

"We'll have fun this summer, Ryan," Tyler injected. "Maybe we can go on a road trip with Kelsey and Zach."

"You won't have time to leave Seattle," Ryan scoffed.

"We'll see," Tyler replied. "But we'll have fun anyway."

"I won't have any fun without Jessica," Ryan said, shaking his head.

"Of course you will," Jessica said. "What did you do before you met me?"

"Things I don't do any more," Ryan replied.

"Ryan..." Jessica began, but Ryan rested his head against her shoulder again.

"Don't go," he repeated, closing his eyes.

"Go and have a good time," Zachary said, looking up from his plate. "Honestly, Ryan, you're being ridiculous."

Ryan fixed Zach with his eyes. "You don't know what it's like to be in love. You don't care because you're always fighting with Kimmy."

"Not always. Anyway, don't you want Jessica to grow and have new experiences?"

"No," Ryan replied. "I want her to be here with me."

"Why didn't you go to New York?" Zachary asked.

"You know why. Lisa would have had a cow," Tyler replied. "Ryan's stuck in Seattle, just like I am."

"It's only for the summer, Ryan," Jessica said.

"I've seen you every day for months. I just can't imagine being without you," Ryan replied, head still resting on Jessica's shoulder.

"It will be fine," Jessica said.

"We'll all miss you, Jess," Kelsey said.

"You'll have a new roommate, too," Jessica said, as Ryan lifted his head up for the second time, and he reached for a celery stick. "I'm sure she'll be cool."

"Where are you living, Kels?" Zach asked.

"Lower Queen Anne," Kelsey said.

"We'll be neighbors," Ryan said, biting into the celery. Belltown, where his condo was located, was the next neighborhood over.

"Poor you," Jessica quipped.

Ryan glanced at her. "You'll miss me too. You just don't want to admit it," he pouted.

"You're right. I will," Jessica said.

"Then don't go. Work for Tactec this summer," Ryan said.

"Work for your dad? I don't think so," Jessica replied.

"Why not? Anyway, Legal isn't under my dad. Lisa's group runs it."

"Even worse. No offense, Tyler," Jessica said.

"None taken," Tyler replied. "Notice I'm not working there."

Jessica giggled.

Ryan sighed. "This sucks," he commented.

"You should be focusing on exams,"' Tyler said.

"I'll pass," Ryan replied.

"Is that all?" Jessica said.

"No. I'm going to try to get at least two B's," Ryan replied.

"You?" Zachary said.

"Yes, me. You should talk, Mr. Payne. I did better than you last semester," Ryan commented.

"I know. My mother won't let me forget. If the papers only knew the trouble that they caused for the rest of us by publishing your and Tyler's grades."

"Why do you tell your parents your grades at all?" Tyler asked.

"Because they're paying for me to be here. It's part of the deal," Zachary replied. "But if my grades don't get better, Dad says they're taking my tuition and going on an around-the-world cruise."

"Tell him I want a souvenir when they go," Tyler quipped.

"So funny, Tyler. I'll show all of you. Wait until grades come out," Zach said.

"You'd better get to work if you're going to beat Tyler," Ryan said.

"My parents' aren't expecting miracles," Zach said. "I just need to beat you."

"Sounds like a challenge," Tyler commented.

"Please. I'd like to see you try," Ryan said.

Zachary stood. "I'm going to study."

"I've been studying all semester, dude," Ryan replied. "One week isn't going to help you. We have four exams."

"I'll do what I can. It's a matter of honor," Zachary replied. He took his tray and left the dining hall.

"Well?" Kelsey asked Tyler, who shook his head.

"Not a chance. When I get back to the room, Zach will be sleeping," Tyler replied.

On Wednesday, Ryan walked over to the table with a dinner tray, just as dinner was about to end. He was wearing a sleek yet conservative navy Italian suit. Heads turned in the dining hall. Ryan wasn't wearing usual pre-exam wear.

"You look nice," Jessica said, glancing at him. "Where were you?"

"My lawyer's office," Ryan replied. He took off his jacket. hung it over the back of an empty chair, and rolled up his shirt sleeves. There was a bandage in the middle of one arm.

"And while you were there, you decided to give blood?" Jessica asked. Ryan frowned at sat down.

"You might as well tell her." Tyler said to Ryan.

"I had a paternity test," Ryan said simply.

Jessica looked at him, stunned. "What?" she said.

"It's not mine," Ryan replied.

"How can you be sure?" Jessica scoffed.

Ryan looked at her with his clear blue eyes. "Because I'm responsible," he replied simply.

"To be fair, Jess," Tyler interceded, as Jessica frowned, "it's not uncommon for people with money to get sued for paternity. There's some people who hope that you'll settle with them to avoid taking the test, and others just want to try their luck. I've been sued for paternity as well."

"You?" Kelsey said in surprise.

"Talked to the wrong girl," Tyler replied.

"This is why you have a Kelsey," Ryan commented. "Keeps the scammers away."

"Interesting," Jessica said doubtfully.

"Jess, it isn't mine," Ryan repeated.

"When will you know for sure?"

"I know for sure now. But I'll get the results of the test by Friday," Ryan said, taking a bite of his dinner.

Jessica surveyed Ryan as he ate.

"Okay," she finally said. "I trust you."

"Thank you," Ryan replied. He smiled at her.

"I don't trust him," Jessica said to Kelsey an hour later.

"Ryan? Why not?"

"Who gets sued for paternity?"

"You heard Tyler. Billionaires do."

"Suppose Ryan's a father?" Jessica asked.

"Then he'll have to deal with it," Kelsey replied.

"I don't think I could handle that," Jessica commented.

"Ryan doesn't think he's the father."

"Ryan still believes in the Easter bunny," Jessica snapped.

"Look, Jess. You'll know before exams. Don't let it stress you," Kelsey said soothingly.

"Why am I dating him?" Jessica sighed.

"Because you love him," Kelsey replied.

"I do. But this is insane. A paternity suit?"

"They live lives very different than ours. Come on, do you have your own lawyer? They get sued all the time."

"Maybe. You believe him?"

"Ryan? That he's not a father?"

"Yes."

"Yes. I believe him," Kelsey said.

Jessica sighed. "I don't know if I can."

"Then don't. Wait and see what the results are," Kelsey said.

"How can I have a future with a guy I don't trust?" Jessica asked.

"I don't know. Maybe you can't. But honestly Jess, I think it's on you to change," Kelsey replied.

"What do you mean?"

"Ryan hasn't actually done anything wrong since you started going out with him."

"How do you know?" Jessica challenged her.

"Well, if he has, he certainly hasn't been found out," Kelsey stated.

"That's what I'm worried about. That I just don't know about what's going on."

"Jess. Ryan's famous. Don't you think someone would know what he was up to, if he was up to anything?"

"He has enough money to keep things out of the paper if he wanted to."

"Sure. But he's never bothered to before. The internet is littered with the exploits of Ryan Perkins."

Jessica giggled. "That sounds like a book. 'The Exploits of Ryan Perkins.'"

"If things don't work out between you two, you can write it," Kelsey replied.

"Did you know that you eat Rice Krispies for breakfast every morning?" Jessica asked Ryan at lunch on Thursday.

"What?" Ryan said to her.

"You also never travel without Vitamin C tablets and Red Bull," Kelsey added.

"What are you reading?" he asked.

"Ryan Watch. A blog dedicated to all things Ryan Perkins. Wow, I didn't know you liked Golden Retrievers," Jessica said.

"That one's actually true," Ryan smiled.

"This is quite eye-opening," Jessica said. "I'm learning so much about you."

"Are you?" Ryan asked.

"This is insane. Who cares this much about anyone?" Jessica said.

"I wouldn't mind knowing that much about you," Ryan said.

Jessica glanced at him. "Yes, but you wouldn't blog about it. I mean, there's even a photo gallery."

"Cute," Ryan said.

"Did you know about this site?" Kelsey asked.

"Not in particular. But I knew there were sites like that."

"Sites? You mean there isn't just one psycho writing about you?" Jessica asked.

Ryan shrugged.

"Tyler, do you have a blog dedicated to you?" Kelsey asked as Tyler sat down.

"I hope not," Tyler said. "Why?"

"Have you read Ryan Watch, the blog about all things Ryan Perkins?" Jessica asked.

Tyler laughed. "No. I know enough about Ryan. Why are you reading it?"

"I just can't believe someone writes about Ryan," Jessica commented.

"He's famous," Tyler said.

"Ryan?" Kelsey asked.

"Money, models, and an insatiable attraction to trouble. His lifestyle sells magazines."

"I think I'm taking offense at that, Tyler," Ryan pouted.

"Please. It's all true," Tyler retorted.

"I haven't even gotten a ticket in the past year," Ryan replied.

Tyler looked at him doubtfully.

"Okay, in the past month," Ryan admitted.

"Exactly," Tyler said.

"I'm a changed man," Ryan commented.

"Maybe," Tyler replied.

"Do you really only use ginger toothpaste?" Jessica asked.

"No," Ryan replied. "Stop reading it, Jess."

"It's like driving past a car accident," Jessica said. "You can't help but notice it."

"But it isn't true. Here, give it to me," Ryan said, taking the tablet from Jessica's hands.

"Click on the celebrity girlfriends tab," Jessica said.

"There's several categories. Models, actresses, and singers," Kelsey added.

"It looks pretty complete to me," Tyler said, looking over Ryan's shoulder.

Ryan glared at him. "I don't even know her." he said, looking at the list and pointing.

"Maybe you should send in a correction," Kelsey said. Tyler laughed.

"Where do they even get this information? I don't like cottage cheese," Ryan said. He handed the tablet back to Jessica. "They're completely off base," he said.

"About your diet, perhaps," Jessica commented.

Ryan looked at her. "I haven't dated everyone on that list, you know."

"No?" Jessica asked.

"No," Ryan said.

Jessica looked at Tyler. "Really, Tyler?" she asked.

"Keep me out of this, Jess," Tyler said.

"What difference does it make? I'm dating you now," Ryan said.

"I suppose," Jessica said.

"I can't change the past, Jess," Ryan said.

"I know."

"Then what's the point of this discussion?" Ryan asked.

Jessica thought for a moment. "Maybe there isn't one."

"Good. Then we can drop it," Ryan replied.

Jessica was silent for a moment, then she looked at Ryan. "Why would anyone feel the need to change relationships that much?" she asked him.

Tyler glanced at Ryan, who sighed.

"I was waiting for you," Ryan said to Jessica.

"Right. Like I believe that," Jessica replied.

"Jess, what do you want me to say?" Ryan said. "I love you. You know that, right?"

"I know what you say," Jessica said.

"I say what I mean," Ryan replied.

"I guess."

"Why are you so insecure about us?" Ryan asked her.

"I don't know," Jessica said. "You don't think I have a reason to be?"

"No, I don't," Ryan replied.

"Interesting," Jessica said.

"Honestly, Jess. I can't believe that we're having this discussion," Ryan said. "I don't know how to prove that I'm committed to you."

"Me neither," Jessica replied. "Maybe you can't."

Ryan examined Jessica with his bright blue eyes, and sighed again. "I wish you trusted me," he said.

"Me too," Jessica said.

"Did you get your results?" Jessica said to Ryan over lunch on Friday.

"Results? We haven't taken exams yet," Ryan replied.

"The paternity test, Ryan," Jessica said in exasperation.

"Oh. Negative."

Jessica was silent.

Ryan glanced at her.

"Okay?" he asked her.

"I guess."

"You'd rather I was a father?" Ryan asked.

"I'd rather you didn't get sued."

"Never going to happen," Tyler interjected.

"Really? How many lawsuits are you involved in right now, Tyler?" Jessica asked doubtfully.

Tyler thought for a moment.

"Hang on," he said. He reached for his iPad and pulled up a document. Kelsey and Jessica watched as he scanned down a list and mentally counted.

"Twenty-three," he replied, setting the iPad aside.

"No way," Kelsey said.

"How is that possible?" Jessica asked in disbelief.

"Well, fifteen of them are related to the lawsuit between Tactec and

Keller. I'm not actually named in any of those, but obviously they are a concern. I'm named in six nuisance suits...."

"Nuisance suits?" Jessica interrupted.

"Frivolous stuff, Jess. One of my high school classmates sued me because I bumped into him in the hall. I was sued another time for insulting someone I had never met, in a state I've never been to."

"What nuisance suits are happening now?" Jessica said in interest.

"Who knows? Ask Jeffrey if you're interested."

"That leaves two others," Kelsey said to Tyler. "What are those?"

"I was in a car accident in Boston. The driver of the other car didn't get enough money from the insurance company, so he's suing me personally."

"I thought you couldn't drive outside of the Pacific Northwest," Kelsey said.

"I was a passenger. The other driver is alleging that I directed my driver to drive recklessly."

"Why don't you consider that a nuisance suit?" Kelsey asked.

"Because I actually had to be deposed," Tyler said.

"Why can't you drive outside of the region?" Jessica asked.

"It's Ryan's fault," Tyler said, glaring at Ryan.

Tyler continued. "Tactec security didn't want us to get our licenses at all, but Lisa insisted. She said it was a necessary part of growing up. Then Ryan got into a car accident his first week at Brown. They had to find legal counsel in Rhode Island, and manage it from Seattle. It was a giant mess. After that, they limited us to driving where Kinnon Martin had offices."

"That explains the Pacific Northwest," Kelsey said.

"Didn't Kinnon Martin have offices in Idaho?" Jessica asked.

"They did, but I've never been," Tyler said.

"Idaho's boring," Ryan commented. Everyone looked at him.

"And the last lawsuit?" Jessica asked, returning to the subject.

"I'm suing the blogger who put my grades on the internet."

"You aren't. That's so mean," Jessica said.

"It wasn't my idea, Jess. Having said that, I'm getting tired of everyone invading my privacy," Tyler said.

"You're a public figure," Jessica said.

"No, I'm not," Tyler replied.

"You're a billionaire," Jessica pointed out.

"It doesn't mean that I don't have a right to basic privacy," Tyler commented.

"It doesn't?" Jessica asked.

"No. I've never actively sought the public eye. No court would consider me a public figure," Tyler replied.

"But Ryan's a celebrity?" Kelsey asked.

"Nah," Ryan interjected.

"I would argue that in the past that Ryan found himself in newsworthy situations, but legally he isn't a public figure either."

"Ryan, are you suing?" Kelsey asked.

"You could sue the Ryan Watch blog," Jessica added. "Get them to shut down."

"Bob doesn't like to. He thinks it's a hassle. Anyway, the blog was kind of cool," Ryan said.

Jessica gave him a look. "Lisa and Bob must get sued a lot," she said.

Tyler shook his head. "Constantly. My father's suing my mother right now."

"No way. For what?" Jessica said.

"Intentional infliction of emotional distress," Tyler replied. "He decided to sue her for keeping me away from him for so long."

"How do you feel about that?" Kelsey asked.

"Weird," Tyler admitted. "I tried to talk him out of it when we were in New York, but he went ahead anyway."

"Wait, he just filed the lawsuit?" Jessica asked.

"There are four elements to the claim. An intentional act, outrageous behavior, the causing of distress, and severe emotional distress. Chris is claiming that the severe emotional distress happened after he spent the year with me and understood what he had missed over the years," Tyler explained.

"How much is is suing for?" Kelsey asked.

"Thirty million dollars," Tyler said. "Two million dollars for every year he missed between the ages of three and eighteen."

"Wow," Kelsey said.

"Do you think he'll win?" Jessica asked.

"I don't know. I'm thinking about trying to talk Lisa into settling after she stops being so angry. She was just served yesterday."

"Lisa's not going to settle," Ryan said. "She lives for litigation. And she hates to lose."

"I know," Tyler said. "But I'm going to try anyway. I think Chris's lawyer is planning on dragging me into it, and Mom's not going to want that."

"What about Chris?" Kelsey asked.

"Chris doesn't know what he's getting into," Tyler replied.

"But he's okay with you getting deposed?" Jessica said.

"Chris wants the money. And to see Lisa apologize," Tyler commented.

"Talking about things that are not going to happen," Ryan said. "Lisa is never, never going to apologize to Chris for anything. Ever."

"I'm hoping that she won't consider a large check an apology," Tyler replied.

"She's paid him off before," Ryan said.

"That she has," Tyler replied.

"How did this come up? Did you ask your dad, 'Are you planning on suing Mom today?'" Jessica asked.

"He told me. Chris didn't want me to read about it in the media."

"Wouldn't your mom tell you?" Jessica asked.

Tyler shook his head. "No. She tries to keep me out of her legal battles with Chris. At least now she does."

"He's sued her before?"

"Numerous times. But not in the past few years. Before, it was mostly to get her to comply with the visitation orders."

"Which never worked," Ryan said.

"No," Tyler said. "This is a supremely bad idea on Chris's part."

"Why is he doing this now?" Kelsey asked.

"I'm not sure. I think it might have to do with the trust. Chris saw that Lisa was giving out money and thought he should have a share."

"What does he think about you being a billionaire?" Jessica asked.

"Honestly? I think he's a little jealous," Tyler said.

"Your own father?" Kelsey asked.

"Artists aren't always great with money. Chris is firmly in that group. He works really hard and here's his son, who already has more money than he could ever spend in a lifetime," Tyler sighed. "I guess we'll see what happens."

Exam week was upon them, and for the first time, Kelsey felt pretty good about her chances. She and Tyler had already been notified by Keith of their pass grade in Legal Writing. Eliot's Contracts exam was on Monday, and when she left the exam, Kelsey knew that she had done well, thanks to Eliot's torture over the past year.

On Tuesday, the class took Schiavelli's Constitutional Law exam, and to Kelsey's amusement, and probably to the detriment of the grades of at least the male half of the class, Professor Schiavelli stood at the front of the classroom and looked her usual stunning self.

Wednesday they had a break. Kelsey and Tyler went for a long run down to Seward Park, Ryan and Jessica studied on the beach, and Zachary was called back to his parents' house in Medina for a reminder that he'd better improve his grades.

"No pressure," Zach said sarcastically at dinner that night.

On Thursday, the first year class had the Criminal Law exam. It had been one of Kelsey's favorite subjects, although she had no intention of practicing Criminal Law. She had wished that she had been able to pay more attention to the subject, but of course, Eliot made sure that Kelsey's full attention was on Contracts. Kelsey left the exam hoping for an A, but confident of at least a B.

Friday was their last exam, and it was Evidence. Jessica couldn't eat breakfast because she was so nervous, and Kelsey felt the pressure as well. Even with Tyler's very clear outline, Kelsey found Evidence complicated. When time was called and she put down her pen, she breathed a sigh of relief. Her first year of law school was over.

She and Jessica met up with the boys at lunch. As they were eating, the dining hall suddenly became more quiet than usual, especially for the last day of exams.

Kelsey looked up from her lunch. To her surprise, Lisa Olsen was walking across the dining room floor, Jeffrey at her heels. Kelsey looked across the table, but Tyler, Ryan, and Jessica were all focused on their food. Lisa sat down in the empty chair that Zachary had just vacated and Ryan and Jessica looked up.

"Hello, Tyler," she said brightly.

"Hi, Mom," Tyler replied, looking up.

"You don't seem surprised," Lisa commented. She glanced at Jeffrey.

"I'm rarely surprised with you," Tyler said.

"Good," Lisa said.

"Hi, Lisa," Ryan said.

"Hi, sweetie. Hello, ladies."

Kelsey and Jessica mumbled their hellos. They were both shocked by her presence, as was seemingly everyone else in the room but Tyler. Lisa adjusted the red cotton sweater that was tied around her slim shoulders and over her silk sleeveless dress. Jeffrey stood near, but not too near, the back of her chair.

"So why are you here?" Tyler asked.

"I thought that you had something to negotiate with me?" she said.

"Now?"

"No time like the present. Anyway, you aren't prepared. You just left your last exam in your first year of law school. And you're surrounded by your classmates. It's the perfect opportunity to negotiate. For me," She smiled at him.

"Fine," Tyler said. "I'm ready."

"Good. What are you proposing?"

"What are you willing to consider?" Tyler asked.

"I was thinking about spending 30 million dollars on legal fees to make sure that Christopher Davis doesn't get another penny from me," Lisa replied.

Tyler smiled. "Of course you are. Why not just pay him off?" he asked.

"Because I don't like him. And I've given him enough of my money," Lisa said.

"You know his lawyer is planning on deposing me," he said.

"How do you know that?" Lisa asked, frowning.

"Chris mentioned it."

"Was he trying to get you on his side?"

"I'm not taking sides," Tyler replied.

"No?" Lisa asked.

"No," Tyler replied.

"Why not?" Lisa asked.

"Because I don't think Chris should have sued you."

"So you're on my side?"

"And I don't think you should have kept me from him," Tyler continued.

"Ah. I see," Lisa commented. "So you're neutral. Then why do you think I should pay him off?"

"Because I don't want to be caught in the middle. I have better things to do."

"Chris has sued me before. It didn't affect you."

"It will this time. He knows my phone number," Tyler replied.

Lisa put her hand to her lip thoughtfully. Kelsey felt like she was almost blinded by the sparkling diamond bracelet on Lisa Olsen's wrist. The tables around them had gone back to their usual level of post-exam noise.

"If I were to settle, and I'm not saying I will, how much do you think it would take?" Lisa asked.

"Ten," Tyler said.

"Ten million? Forget it. I'd rather litigate," Lisa said.

"You'd always rather litigate. I'm asking you not to this time."

"A favor?"

"No, because then I'll owe you one," Tyler said.

Lisa beamed. "You know me well," she commented.

"Too well. I'm just asking you to consider settling so I don't have to deal with something else right now."

"Did you ask your father not to sue me?"

"I did."

"You knew he was about to, though?"

"He told me when I was in New York."

"Why is he doing this?" Lisa asked Tyler.

"I don't know."

"Chris didn't tell you?" Lisa said.

"No. He just told me that he was going to do it."

"He hasn't changed. Fine, Tyler. I'll give it some thought," she stood.

"Thank you."

"I'm not promising you anything."

"I know."

"In fact, I'm really leaning toward letting him go through with this. Then you can see what he's really like."

"Mom. Please."

"I didn't start this, Tyler."

"But you can end it."

"So can he."

"You know he won't," Tyler said.

Lisa looked at him in surprise. "You are getting to know your father," she commented.

"I know he's more inflexible than you," he said. "And that worries me."

Lisa smiled. "You're worried about him, aren't you? Because you know once I start, I won't retreat."

"Exactly."

Lisa sat back down and thought silently for a minute.

"I'm not going to settle. He's going to have to fight," she finally said, standing again.

"Mom…" Tyler began.

"I'm sorry, Tyler. I love you, but you can handle a deposition."

Tyler frowned. Lisa smiled at him. "You'll learn something. And so will he." She ran her hand through her dark hair. "When are you coming home next?" she asked.

"Not soon. Work starts on Monday," Tyler replied.

"When do you start, Ryan?" Lisa asked him.

"Next Thursday," Ryan replied.

"Let me know if you need anything," Lisa said to Ryan. "I'll be in the Legal Department on Friday."

"Okay. Thanks," Ryan said.

Lisa looked at the plates on the table. "Is this what you usually eat?" she asked.

"Yes," Tyler replied.

"No wonder you asked Margaret to send food over," Lisa said. "Okay, say hello to Bill Simon for me," Lisa laughed. "I'm sure he'll love that."

"I'm sure," Tyler replied with sarcasm.

Lisa walked over and kissed the top of Tyler's head. "Have a nice weekend, all of you. I'll see you boys at the board meeting."

"Bye, Lisa," Ryan said. She gave him a kiss too, then she and Jeffrey walked off, through the stares and whispers of the remaining students at Darrow Law.

"Well, that didn't work," Ryan said to Tyler.

"Did you see the gleam in her eyes?" Jessica said to Kelsey, who nodded apprehensively.

"Chris is dead," Tyler said. "She can't wait to go to court. It's not like I didn't warn him."

Ryan glanced at Tyler. "It's not your problem."

Tyler sighed.

"Put it out of your mind, bro. It's supposed to be nice tomorrow. Let's hang out at my pool." Ryan frowned. "And say goodbye to Jess." Jessica smiled at him and rubbed his shoulder gently. Ryan turned to her.

"I can't believe you're leaving me," he said.

"It will be fine," Jessica replied.

Late the next morning, Tyler pulled his car up to Bob's Medina house. Kelsey got out of the front seat, tote bag in tow. She had brought her Kindle, one of Jess' fashion magazines, and her red swimsuit, which was showing its age. She needed to buy a new one, but she had decided to put it off until later in the summer. Kelsey needed to save as much money as possible this summer so she wouldn't have to take out as many student loans in the fall. Tyler got out of the car, and grabbed his own bag out of the back seat.

Ryan's Porsche already sat in the driveway, as did Zachary's Land Rover. Kelsey followed Tyler on a path curving around the back of the house. After a surprisingly long walk, the path opened up to a large lawn, with an expansive view of Lake Washington. Ryan, Jessica, and Zachary were all lying on teak lounge chairs artfully arranged around a beautiful oval pool.

"Good morning, Kels," Zachary said. Kelsey had already seen Ryan when he had picked up Jessica.

"Hi, Zach," Kelsey said.

"Kelsey, you can change there." Tyler said gesturing to a Asian-style cabana in the direction of the house. Kelsey headed over as Tyler put his bag on one of the lounge chairs. Kelsey opened the door of the cabana and immediately felt like she had been transported to Thailand.

The airy cabana was gently lit, with fresh orchids and a silk-covered bench to sit on while changing. Kelsey put on her old bathing suit and immediately felt out of place in such an elegant room. She ignored the feeling, gathered her bag, and left the cabana. As she walked back toward the pool she passed by the outdoor shower, which had been decorated in a gold-and-turquoise mosaic.

Tyler was sitting on his lounge chair when she returned. He pulled a book out of his bag and placed it next to him on the chair. Ryan, who was lying on the chair next to him, looked at the cover.

"You aren't actually working today, are you Tyler?" Ryan asked.

Tyler glanced at him and picked up the book as he leaned back on the lounge. "Bill Simon told me to read three books before I started with him this summer. Thanks to Sophia, I've read none."

"Is there a quiz?" Jessica asked Tyler.

"Knowing what I do about Bill Simon, yes," Tyler replied.

"*Mergers and Acquisitions,*" Ryan said, reading the title. "Sounds riveting."

"Considering where your father is, you might want to get your own copy," Tyler replied.

"Where is Bob?" Zachary asked. Ryan looked at him blankly.

"He's in Boston looking at an electronic payment startup Tactec is considering buying," Tyler answered for Ryan.

"Why does Tyler know where your father is, but you don't?" Jessica asked Ryan.

"I knew Bob was somewhere," Ryan replied.

"What else do you have to read?" Kelsey asked Tyler, relaxing onto her own lounge next to Jessica.

"A book on valuation, and an overview of intellectual property law," Tyler replied.

"Can I borrow the intellectual property book when you're done?" Kelsey asked.

"Of course," Tyler replied.

"Are you really going to finish all three books by Monday?" Zachary asked.

"Doubtful, but I thought I'd better at least skim them," Tyler answered.

"Your summer is going to be awful," Zach said.

"At least I'm not working with my parents," Tyler retorted.

"I didn't say my summer was going to be any better," Zach said, putting his sunglasses over his eyes.

A few minutes later, a butler came out from the house with drinks. Per usual, Kelsey hadn't been asked what she wanted, but had got what she wanted all the same. Tyler's orange juice had been delivered to the small table next to him. Kelsey saw that Jessica had received a sparkling water and was interested to see that Zachary's usual drink was ginger ale. Kelsey took a sip of cranberry juice.

"Mr. Perkins, Miss Margaret would like to know what time you and your guests would like lunch," the butler asked.

"One o'clock?" Ryan said.

"Sure," Tyler said, without looking up from his book.

"Very good," the butler said, bowing politely and heading back to the house.

"Isn't Margaret your cook?" Jessica asked Tyler. "Why is she cooking for Ryan?"

"Because Tyler's here. Margaret always cooks for Tyler," Zachary said venomously.

Tyler smiled. "Don't be a hater just because Margaret loves me," Tyler said.

"Exactly. Enjoy your lunch," Ryan commented.

"I know I will," Jessica said. "She's a great chef. What are we having?"

"I requested Italian, in your honor," Ryan said.

"That's what I'm going to eat all summer, you know," Jessica said.

"I know. When you're sick of Italian food, you'll miss Seattle even more," Ryan replied.

"You've thought of everything," Jessica said with sarcasm.

"Everything except how to spend the summer with you," Ryan said. Jessica reached out and stroked his face with her hand. Ryan closed his eyes peacefully.

After an amazing lunch of homemade calzones, and a game in the pool where Jessica rode on Ryan's shoulders and Kelsey rode on Tyler's and they tried to knock each other over, the group of five had settled back into their places on the lounges. Tyler had returned to his book, Ryan lay in the sun, and Zachary was playing a game on his phone. Jessica surveyed the boys.

"Some days I feel like I'm watching a Ralph Lauren ad," Jessica mused.

"What do you mean?" Kelsey said, looking up from the magazine.

"Tyler's the preppy guy, Ryan's the fun loving, sandy-haired one, Zach's the good-looking Asian, and you're the hot blonde."

Kelsey giggled. "And who are you?"

"I don't think there are a lot of curly-haired Italians in Ralph Lauren ads," Jessica replied.

"Well, a gorgeous, young Sophia Loren really needs her own ad," Kelsey replied.

Jessica laughed. "What will I do without you this summer?" Jessica said.

"Just Skype me," Kelsey replied.

"You'll be too busy having fun here," Jessica replied. "In the meantime,

I'll be pulling Nick's gum out of my hair when I'm babysitting for the third weekend in a row."

"You'll have a good time too," Kelsey said.

"No, she won't," Ryan commented from behind his closed eyes. "She'll miss us too much."

"Are you wishing me bad luck?" Jessica asked him.

"Of course not," Ryan said.

"Ryan's just fussy," Zachary said.

"You'd be fussy too, if you wouldn't see your girlfriend for three months," Ryan said.

"I haven't seen Kim since Spring Break," Zachary pointed out.

"You don't love Kimmy the way I love Jessica," Ryan commented.

"Is this a contest, dude?" Zach asked.

"No," Ryan sighed. "Ok, I'm just fussy." He took Jessica's hand and kissed it.

"You're going have a great time living with Ryan too," Zachary said to Tyler.

"I'll be at work," Tyler replied, reading.

"Then Kelsey can come over and we can miss Jess together," Ryan said.

"Sounds like a good time," Jessica said sarcastically.

"I'm not letting you go to New York next summer," Ryan said, still holding her hand.

"It's not up to you," Jessica replied.

"It should be," Ryan pouted.

"Ryan, Jessica is leaving tomorrow. Deal with it," Tyler said to him.

"No," Ryan replied. "You don't have anything to complain about. Kelsey's staying here. You'll probably see her all the time, since her office is downtown. While you're having lunch with her, my Jessica will be thousands of miles away."

"Your Jessica?" Jessica repeated.

"I'd like to know who else's Jessica you are," Ryan replied grumpily.

"My own," Jessica said.

"Which is why she's going to New York," Zachary said.

"Don't remind me," Ryan said.

"When are you going to stop complaining?" Tyler asked in annoyance.

"September. When Jessica's back," Ryan replied.

At seven-thirty, the group ate a dinner of lasagna and garlic bread. Afterwards, Jessica and Ryan sat on the edge of the lake, holding hands and looking out at Seattle. Tyler had moved on to the book about valuation, Zach was sleeping, and Kelsey was reading a book about running on her Kindle.

Tyler set his book to the side. "What do you want to do this summer, Kels?" he asked her.

"Anything," Kelsey replied. "Do you think you'll have time to leave the office?" she teased.

Tyler laughed. "Probably not," he replied. "I'm trying to be hopeful."

"What we're doing today is nice," Kelsey said.

"Yeah, we don't have enough days like today," Tyler commented. The sun, which was low in the sky, still sent beams across the lake, making it shimmer. "Do you want me to help you move to Queen Anne tomorrow, or are you going to Sea-Tac with Jessica?"

"I don't think my presence at Sea-Tac is necessary," Kelsey said, looking at Jessica and Ryan. Jessica was resting her head on Ryan's shoulder.

"I don't know what he's going to do without her," Tyler commented. "He's right, though, I should be less hard on him. You're staying here."

"And that's a good thing?" Kelsey teased.

"Yes," Tyler replied seriously. "I mean, I'm sure Lucas Anderson thinks so," he added.

"Ha, ha,Tyler," Kelsey frowned.

Tyler grinned at her. "Just kidding, Princess," he said.

"Stop calling me that, Kelsey said.

"Never," Tyler replied.

Kelsey laughed. "Why are you such a pain?" she asked.

"I thought I was endearing," Tyler replied.

"Never," Kelsey smiled.

The next day, after a somber brunch and lots of hugs, Jessica left with Ryan for the airport. A few hours later, there was a knock on Kelsey's door.

"Come in," she called, and Tyler walked in, carrying a duffel bag.

"Are you ready?" he asked, looking around the now almost-bare room. "First year of law school is done," he said.

"Thank goodness," Kelsey replied, stuffing her quilt into a box. "That's not everything from your room?" she asked, spotting the duffel bag.

"It's what I'm taking to Ryan's tonight," Tyler replied.

"What about the rest of your stuff?" Kelsey asked him.

"Jeffrey will have it packed up," Tyler replied.

"You're so spoiled," Kelsey commented.

Tyler smiled at her. "Would you like to have your things moved for you?" he asked.

"No. I can do it myself," Kelsey replied.

"Okay," Tyler said.

"But I'll accept the ride downtown," Kelsey added.

"Oh. That's okay with you, Miss North? Not too much help, but just enough?"

"Exactly," Kelsey said, as haughtily as she could.

"I see," Tyler replied.

Kelsey grinned. "Okay, okay. Thanks for helping," she said.

"You're welcome," Tyler said.

"What time do you have to be at work tomorrow?" Kelsey asked, checking the drawers to make sure nothing had been accidentally left behind.

"Nine," Tyler replied. "I need all the time I can get. I haven't finished the third book."

"So you're staying up late then?"

"I think so. You, on the other hand, will be sleeping in," Tyler said.

"All week," Kelsey replied.

"Maybe I should have taken the job with Collins Nicol. I could spend the summer relaxing."

"You could. I won't be," Kelsey said.

"If you don't want to work, tell them you're Bob's stepdaughter. They'll never know, he's had so many," Tyler said.

"Yeah, that's not going to work," Kelsey said. She looked around the room and realized she was done. She was ready to leave the room where she had had so many memories, both good and bad, over her first year of law school.

"What can I take down?" Tyler asked her.

"Those," Kelsey said, pointing to her backpack and her own duffel bag. "But I'm ready. I'll go too." Tyler and Kelsey picked up her bags and the quilt box. Kelsey placed the keys on what had been Jessica's desk, looked around one last time, and they left the room.

Tyler drove Kelsey to her Lower Queen Anne apartment building.

Kelsey got the key from the superintendent, and Tyler helped her carry her things into her first-floor flat. Kelsey selected a bedroom and placed her bags inside. Then, taking her new keys with her, Kelsey headed out into her new neighborhood with Tyler.

"You're sure you have time for dinner?" Kelsey asked him.

"Yes. I don't know who I'm kidding. There's no way I'm going to get book three read tonight. I should get some sleep and hope that makes me alert enough for when Simon quizzes me tomorrow, " Tyler replied. They crossed a quiet street and kept walking down West Mercer. Tyler's phone buzzed, and he glanced at the messages and smiled.

"Ryan asked me to bring a big bag of chocolate home so he can drown his sorrows." Tyler shook his head. "And my summer with him as my roommate begins."

Kelsey giggled. "Jeffrey could rent you an apartment," she noted.

"It's good for me to live with Ryan. It will teach me patience," Tyler said.

"Have you lived with him before?"

"Just on vacation," Tyler replied as they crossed another street. "This place has good Thai," he said as they passed by a restaurant. Kelsey noted it. She might not have a lot of time to cook this summer. "What are you in the mood for?" Tyler asked her.

"Anything is fine," Kelsey replied.

"I was thinking Indian?" Tyler said.

"Sure, I haven't had that in a while," Kelsey said. They crossed a third street, and Kelsey noticed that with each passing street, the area was becoming more crowded with cars and stores.

"Vietnamese," Tyler said gesturing to another restaurant.

"You know Queen Anne well," Kelsey said.

"It's where I usually get take-out when I'm at Ryan's," he replied.

"Do you spend that much time at Ryan's?" Kelsey asked.

"I did. Before I met you," Tyler replied.

"Oh," Kelsey said. She felt herself blush.

"Be careful," Tyler said as they crossed a busy intersection. They waited for the light, then crossed a second street. "Excellent pizza," Tyler said to her, as they walked past a pizzeria. They walked a few more paces and entered an Indian restaurant.

"Two," Tyler said, as Kelsey looked at the elaborate decorations.

They had a delicious Indian dinner with tandoori chicken and lots of hot naan bread. Tyler paid the bill, and they walked back out into the cool June air. The weather was just as beautiful as yesterday, but just like the day before, things began to cool off as the evening arrived. Kelsey put her hands into jeans pockets as they walked back across West Mercer, still heading away from Kelsey's new home. After another block, they walked down a set of stairs into a large supermarket.

"There's a drugstore and a bunch of other stores upstairs," Tyler said as they walked past the sliding glass doors. "I think the drugstore's open 24 hours."

"Important when you arrive home at midnight with a headache after a day of work," Kelsey commented.

"Exactly," Tyler said. They walked past a huge deli, and headed toward the back of the store. "I'm here for Ryan's chocolate," he added.

"Poor Ryan," Kelsey said.

"You won't be saying that by the end of the summer. You'll be as annoyed as the rest of us," Tyler replied.

"I think it's sweet," Kelsey said.

"Right," Tyler replied. They walked into the candy aisle, and Tyler took a bag of chocolate off the shelf. "Do you want to get anything?"

Kelsey shook her head. "I'll set up the apartment tomorrow," she said. "Thanks for bringing me here. I wouldn't have known there was a supermarket so close."

"Actually, there's another down the block. This is the gourmet one," Tyler said.

"Even better," Kelsey said. They walked to the express checkout counter, paid for the candy, and left the store. As they headed back, Kelsey wrapped her arms around herself. Tyler glanced at her and took off the navy cotton sweater he was wearing over a polo shirt.

"Here," Tyler said to her, handing her the sweater.

"Thanks," Kelsey said, putting it on. "Aren't you cold?"

"No," Tyler said. "I'm fine." He was quiet as they waited for the light to change, then Tyler looked at Kelsey.

"Ryan says I'm jealous. That's why I'm so annoyed with him," Tyler said.

"Are you?" Kelsey asked. She felt a funny feeling in her heart when she asked the question.

"Sometimes I wish I were less analytical. Ryan just jumps into things, and he never considers the cost. So, maybe I am a little jealous. Not of his relationship, but his willingness to get hurt."

"Ryan is very brave," Kelsey said.

"Or crazy," Tyler said.

"Maybe both," Kelsey agreed.

"Per usual, I don't have time to think about this," he said. "And I said I'd leave you alone while you're dating Farm Boy."

"Now you're jealous of Lucas," Kelsey smiled.

"I'm never going to be at peace," Tyler said. But Kelsey didn't feel like he was only referring to his situation with her.

"If you're bored, you're dead," Kelsey said.

"I haven't heard that before," Tyler replied.

"One of my friends back home said it. Eric. I'm not sure he's the best life guru though. He could give the old Ryan a run for his money."

"What about you?"

"What about me?"

"Are you jealous of Jessica? Of her relationship with Ryan?"

"No," Kelsey said.

"Why?"

"Because one day it will be my turn. I can afford to be patient. It's not like I don't have anything else to do," Kelsey said as they walked.

"That's a very healthy attitude," Tyler said.

"I'm trying to be a healthy person," Kelsey replied.

"I could learn from you," Tyler said. "If I had time, that is."

"You could make time," Kelsey said.

"One day," Tyler replied. "We're here. This is your street." Kelsey glanced up. Her new apartment was a few steps away.

"Do you want to come in?" Kelsey asked him.

Tyler shook his head. "I'd better go home and read," he replied. "Come visit me at work?"

"Let's do lunch," Kelsey said, taking off his sweater and handing it to him.

"You're such a lawyer already," Tyler replied as he took the sweater.

"And which one of us is complaining about not having any time? I think you're the stereotypical lawyer around here," Kelsey replied.

Tyler laughed. "I'll take that as a compliment."

"It wasn't," Kelsey replied. They walked over to her door and Kelsey put the key in the lock.

"I'll see you soon. Goodbye, Kelsey," Tyler said to her as Kelsey opened the door.

"Goodbye, Tyler," Kelsey said. Tyler looked at her for the briefest of moments, then walked away.

Kelsey woke up at 9:15 the next morning. It took a moment for her to register where she was, but she smiled and stretched when she remembered she was on her first week of summer vacation. She considered going running, but decided to head out and get the few things that she needed instead.

After a shower and a cup of coffee bought at the gourmet grocery store Tyler had introduced her to last night, Kelsey walked around the neighborhood. She located the second supermarket, the post office, and several other restaurants and useful stores, including a bookstore and a movie theater.

She found the bus stop for her route into downtown Seattle, which she took after having lunch. The bus took her within two blocks of her new office, and Kelsey got off the bus and looked around. She located the gym where she had been given a summer membership, the food court where she would probably find herself since she wasn't likely to bring her lunch, and of course, Starbucks. Kelsey wondered if she would save any money this summer.

After exploring her work neighborhood, she decided to walk around. Although she had been to Seattle numerous times as a kid — and of course, she knew everything about Madison Park — downtown Seattle still felt like a bit of an unknown to her. She wanted to explore.

Kelsey began walking back towards the shopping district. Collins Nicol was on the southern edge of downtown, in Seattle's largest skyscraper. As she walked, Kelsey passed by the Seattle Public Library, where she stopped in and got a library card. She continued, walking past Tactec's Seattle offices, which were located in a different, but still impressive skyscraper. Kelsey knew that Tyler's new law firm was somewhere nearby.

As she strolled and got comfortable with the business area of the city, a place that she hadn't explored as a tourist from Port Townsend, Kelsey thought about Tyler. She wondered how often she would see him this summer, since they were both likely to be busy. Of course, Kelsey did expect that they would have lunch or dinner together at some point, but Kelsey also knew that she'd probably want to spend time with her new roommate, who she hoped would be fun, and of course her co-workers at Collins Nicol.

Kelsey was both excited and nervous about her summer. She felt the same butterflies that she had had when she had arrived at Darrow for the first time. Kelsey smiled when she looked back over her year. She had been terrified, but ultimately she had made it through her first year. She frowned with the sobering thought that others, like Dylan and Ashley, had not.

Kelsey still hadn't spoken to Dylan, over six months after he had left her home and gone into rehab. Ian, Dylan's brother, had stayed in touch and updated Kelsey on Dylan. She knew he had left rehab and was staying on the Oregon coast. But she knew nothing more. Dylan hadn't contacted her, and Kelsey thought she knew why. He was embarrassed.

Kelsey had been in the same place once, where she had to face the people who she loved and who she had disappointed. But she didn't have the luxury of some of them being hundreds of miles away. Dylan did, and he was using the distance to avoid her. Kelsey wondered when he would realize that she would welcome him back and contact her. She felt it would be a while. In the meantime, she would stay in touch with Ian, who Dylan couldn't ignore.

Kelsey looked up and found that she had reached Belltown, where Ryan's condo was located. She smiled at the thought of Ryan and Tyler living together. They were so different, yet so close. Kelsey wondered how long Tyler would last listening to Ryan whine about missing Jessica. No wonder he was planning to work a lot this summer.

Since Belltown was next to Lower Queen Anne, Kelsey decided to see how far it was to walk home. She knew that she could walk the distance to work, although she didn't expect to do so. But she was surprised that it hadn't felt like it had taken very long. Kelsey continued to walk, spotting the Space Needle and heading towards Queen Anne Hill. Within fifteen minutes, Kelsey began to recognize the edges of her new neighborhood. She stopped by the grocery store for dinner and a few supplies. Then she was home.

That evening, Kelsey chatted with Jessica on Skype.

"I told you I'd be babysitting," Jessica said to Kelsey, glumly.

"Already?" Kelsey said in surprise.

"Joey and Andrea aren't going to let this moment pass. I'm glad I didn't make any plans for myself this summer."

"Sorry, Jess."

"It's okay. I love my nephews," Jessica said in resignation.

"How was the trip to Sea-Tac?"

"Ryan was his usual crazy self. I will never understand him," Jessica said fondly. "He did manage to let me get on the plane though, so it was fine."

"Have you talked to him yet?"

"He called at eight a.m. this morning," Jessica said. "Maybe I need to get a new number." Kelsey smiled to herself. Eight a.m. New York City time meant that Ryan had got up at five a.m. in Seattle. She knew that as much as Jess complained, she really loved Ryan.

"And your flight was okay?"

"Yes, but I missed traveling in first class," Jessica said. "I swear, I can't believe how spoiled we were last school year."

"I know. Tyler bought dinner last night, and I enjoyed every bite, because although the restaurant's a few blocks away from me, I won't be able to afford to eat there."

"Just invite the boys to dinner. You know they'll pay."

"Jessica!" Kelsey protested.

"Oh, come on. Don't pretend you haven't thought of it," Jessica replied.

Kelsey giggled. "You're right. I have. That's terrible, isn't it?"

Jessica laughed with her. "Yes. But seriously, Kels, you guys should get together over the summer. We're all living together next year, and you know Tyler's going to miss you. If you don't make the effort to see him, he'll be working too much to see you. Everyone knows Bill Simon is a workaholic."

"I guess you're right. But now I'm going to feel guilty. Like I'm just calling Tyler to get a free meal," Kelsey said.

"Like Tyler cares," Jessica said. "Or Ryan, for that matter. It isn't their money."

"I guess," Kelsey said.

"So how's the new place?" Jessica asked her.

"It's great. The neighborhood's cute, although I don't know how much time I'll be spending here. I think I'll probably be in downtown more."

"Your roommate comes on Sunday?"

"Yeah. I left her the larger of the two bedrooms, so I hope she likes it."

"You still haven't talked to her?"

"Not yet. I get the sense she's as busy as Tyler."

"So you'll be alone this summer then?" Jessica teased.

"It looks like it."

"Hang out with Ryan. He'll have nothing to do. At least that's what he says, although I doubt it."

"I imagine that he won't get into too much, having Tyler as a roommate. There won't be any parties lasting until 4 a.m., for sure."

"I guess so," Jessica said thoughtfully. "Have you talked to Lucas? When's your date?"

"I'll see him at work. He went back home for the week."

"So what are you doing now?"

"I spent the day just wandering around downtown. I know how to get to work, where the gym is, and I got a library card."

"You aren't expecting to work much this summer," Jessica said.

"I figure that I'll have time on the weekends to relax," Kelsey said. "Nothing to study."

"No way. I bet you and your roommate will go out," Jessica replied. "Ryan says there's so much to do in Seattle during the summer."

"Maybe," Kelsey said.

"Go out. Have fun for me. I'll be here cleaning up fingerpaint," Jessica said.

Kelsey giggled.

On Tuesday, Kelsey took the bus up to the top of Queen Anne Hill, which was covered with the type of cute shops that Jessica loved to browse in, and to Kelsey's delight had a discount grocery store. She bought two bags of groceries, because it was all that she thought she could carry, and headed back home to cook dinner for the first time in months.

Wednesday, Kelsey chatted with her mother, who was still disappointed that Kelsey hadn't come home for the week. Then Kelsey went downtown for a haircut and to visit the dentist. Thursday, she went back downtown to buy stockings and a serious briefcase for work. She found the stockings easily, but had to visit a dozen stores to find a briefcase in her price range.

On Thursday evening, Kelsey stood in her kitchen making pasta, when she got a message from Tyler. She stirred the cream sauce, turned the pot down, and picked up her phone.

Hi, how's your vacation? Tyler had written.

Fine. How's work? Kelsey wrote.

Don't ask. When are you coming to visit me?

Tomorrow? Kelsey asked.

I'll look forward to it. Anytime. I'm always here.

Kelsey smiled. She could picture Tyler's face as he wrote the words, and was happy that he had written. Although she had been enjoying exploring Seattle, Kelsey had to admit that she missed him.

You aren't really, Kelsey replied.

You'll see, Tyler wrote. *See you tomorrow.*

Kelsey put the phone aside and stirred the sauce again, turning off the burner. She smiled to herself. Maybe Tyler missed her too.

Late on Friday afternoon, Kelsey arrived at Tyler's office. She had spent much of the morning organizing for work on Monday. Not only did she need work clothes, but she would also resume working out before work, so she needed a packed gym bag as well.

Kelsey walked past the flower shop and Starbucks in Tyler's building lobby, and pressed the elevator button to go to Tyler's office. After getting off the elevator on his floor, Kelsey walked into the offices of Simon and Associates.

"Can I help you?" the middle-aged receptionist asked Kelsey.

"Hi, I'm here to see Tyler Olsen." Kelsey replied.

"He's expecting you," the receptionist said. "Walk down the hall, Tyler's office is the last one."

"Thanks," Kelsey said.

Kelsey walked back to Tyler's office. She felt slightly out of place, since she was wearing khakis and a summer t-shirt, but she mused that she was still on vacation. She walked to the last office and looked into the glass wall. Tyler was wearing a navy blue suit, and looked every bit a serious lawyer. He was sitting at his desk, typing into a computer when she knocked on the door.

He beamed when he saw her. Kelsey walked into the office.

"It's nice to see you," he said. To Kelsey's surprise, he stood and gave her a hug.

"Is it okay that I came by? I won't stay long," Kelsey said.

"Stay as long as you want. Simon doesn't care. He encourages people to have their friends and family drop by. He knows it's the only time you'll see them," Tyler said, returning to his chair.

"You're joking," Kelsey said, sitting in one of the client chairs.

"I wish I were," Tyler replied. "Seriously, stay all night. If Simon finds out you're a law student, though, he'll probably put you to work."

"That's okay," Kelsey said.

"Have you enjoyed your vacation?" Tyler asked.

"It's been heaven," Kelsey said. "But I'm ready to get back to work. How has your week been?"

"Stressful," Tyler replied.

"How's Ryan?"

"Good. He's coming over in a few minutes."

"Really?"

"He just messaged me. He said he had something for me."

"Tactec's kitty-corner from here?"

"Cross two streets and you're there," Tyler replied.

"What are you working on?" Kelsey asked.

"An M&A brief," Tyler replied.

"Wow. Already?"

"It's a good thing I read the M&A book first," Tyler said. "So what have you been doing this week?"

"Looking around downtown, mostly. I haven't spent a lot of time in this part of the city."

"Really?" Tyler asked thoughtfully. "I guess there isn't a reason to come here unless you're working. What have you discovered?"

"I know how to get to work. I found the gym and Starbucks."

"The necessities," Tyler teased.

"Exactly," Kelsey said. "Oh, I did go to a grocery store you'd like. Lots of gourmet food. On the top of Queen Anne Hill. There's a branch near Darrow too. "

"I know the one. Jeffrey doesn't like going there."

"It's too cheap," Kelsey said.

"Exactly. He feels like he's losing class points. But I like their cereal. I think he sends Martin."

Kelsey laughed.

Tyler looked at her. "It's weird not seeing you every day," he said. The intercom buzzed.

"Tyler, Ryan Perkins is heading back."

"Thanks," Tyler answered.

"How's Ryan been?"

"Less annoying than I expected," Tyler replied. "You can tell him I said that."

Kelsey laughed again.

Ryan walked into Tyler's office holding a large envelope. "Hi, Kels," he said with delight. "I wasn't expecting to see you here."

"I wanted to see Tyler's office," Kelsey replied.

"Cool. This is for you," Ryan said, handing Tyler the envelope.

"What is it?"

"I don't know. I didn't open it. Lisa was in the office today and asked me to give it to you."

"How was her visit?"

Ryan sighed and sat in the other client chair. "It was great being the boss's son for one day. Then your mom came in and told them to give me more work. So now I'm swamped."

"Told you," Tyler said, opening the envelope. He pulled a slim binder out and opened the cover. He glanced quickly at the title page, then hurriedly flipped to the back.

"What is it?" Kelsey asked.

"Lisa's response to Chris' lawsuit. I want to see who her lawyer is," Tyler said. His face fell. "It's over."

"Who is it?" Ryan asked.

"The Barracuda," Tyler replied.

"Poor Chris," Ryan replied.

"The Barracuda?" Kelsey asked.

"Lisa has two sets of personal lawyers. A small law firm in Wallingford does most of her work, but she also has a guy who works out of Pioneer Square. He was the mastermind of Lisa's no-visitation policy when I was a kid, and that's who she's decided is working on the case."

"What does that mean for Chris?" Kelsey asked.

"You can tell how seriously Lisa is taking the case by which firm she hires. I bet she's kept the Barracuda on retainer just waiting for this moment."

"What's his real name?" Kelsey asked.

"Barry Cinelli," Tyler said, as he flipped through the binder. He stopped on a page, glanced at it, then continued flipping through.

"So what does Lisa say?" Ryan asked.

"She's filing a counterclaim against Chris," Tyler shook his head in amusement, and looked up. "She wants fifty million."

"No way," Kelsey said.

"I did warn him," Tyler commented.

"What's she claiming?" Ryan asked.

"What isn't she claiming? Barry's thrown in the kitchen sink. So far I've seen paragraphs about how Chris has violated the divorce decree, Lisa's own claim of intentional infliction of emotional distress, plus my personal favorite so far, tortious interference with business relationships."

"Tortious interference with business relationships?" Kelsey asked.

"Lisa's claiming that since Chris knows she's trying to conclude a deal with a family-owned company in Taiwan, he chose this moment to drag her to court and embarrass her. I'm not Chris has even heard of Taiwan, and he certainly doesn't know Lisa's doing a deal there," Tyler said, leaning back in his chair. He tossed the binder on his desk. "I think Barry took the torts outline and came up with a claim for each cause of action. I'll read it later."

Ryan smiled at him. "I guess you'll be hearing from Chris soon."

Tyler shook his head. "I'm turning off my phone. The only thing I have to say to Chris is 'I told you so.'"

"Why do they hate each other so much?" Kelsey asked Tyler.

"Actually, I think it's just a big game to Lisa at this point. Chris gets so worked up about everything, but he can never out-think Lisa, and I think that frustrates him. Lisa thinks it's a joke. I think she was serious when she said she'd spend 30 million dollars to make sure he doesn't get a penny," Tyler said. "My parents," he concluded.

"At least you have a good attitude about it," Kelsey said.

"They've been at each other's throats for over two decades," Tyler replied. "I'm used to it." He was thoughtful for a moment.

"Hasn't it been a while since they've been to court?" Ryan asked.

"A couple of years. Lisa finished paying the last of the penalties over the visitation violations at my Harvard graduation."

"At graduation?" Kelsey asked.

"She wanted to give it to him personally. I think she threw the envelope at him. It was the first time they had seen each other for years. Chris wasn't allowed to come to my high school graduation. Lisa had a restraining order against him."

Ryan laughed. "I love her. She's so evil."

"Just don't get on her wrong side," Tyler said.

"So are you going home soon?" Ryan asked.

"Are you kidding?" Tyler asked.

"No. I'm done for the day," Ryan replied.

Tyler looked at his phone. "It's 4:30," he said. "I thought Lisa said you had to work."

"Yeah, but it's Friday. You know everyone in Seattle leaves work early on Friday in the summer," Ryan replied.

"I don't," Tyler said.

"That's because you were stupid enough to work for Bill Simon," Ryan said.

"Stop reminding me," Tyler said. "It's only day five."

"Of ninety? One hundred?" Ryan teased.

"Shut up, Ryan," Tyler said.

"What are you doing now, Kelsey?" Ryan asked.

"I was going to head home and start getting my stuff ready for Monday," she replied.

"That's boring. I'll take you to dinner. We can talk about Jess," Ryan said.

"Bring something back for me," Tyler said.

"Doesn't Simon get food for you guys when you work late?" Ryan asked.

"Are you kidding? Bill Simon figures if you're still here after 5, it's your own fault," Tyler said. "All evening, a parade of food delivery guys walk through here. It's every man for himself."

"I thought pizza was the reward for working late in a law office,"

Kelsey said.

"Maybe it is everywhere else," Tyler said.

Ryan took off his jacket and slung it over a chair. "Come on, Kels. Let's go get take-out and come back and eat with Tyler. What are you in the mood for, bro?"

"Anything," Tyler replied.

"We'll go to the Market," Ryan said. "Come on, Kels."

Ryan and Kelsey walked out of Tyler's office and back down the hall. As they did, Kelsey realized that offices she thought had emptied for the sunny Friday were full again, their lawyers back at their desks. Perhaps a meeting had been going on. She and Ryan left the offices and went out to the elevator.

"That place is a sweatshop," Ryan said as they waited for the elevator. "I can't believe Simon doesn't feed them."

"Do you think Tyler will quit?" Kelsey asked.

"Tyler would sooner die from exhaustion than admit to Lisa he was wrong," Ryan replied. Kelsey nodded as they got on the elevator. She thought so too.

"How's Jess?" Kelsey asked.

Ryan smiled. "She's great. I talked to her this morning."

"Do you talk to her every morning?" Kelsey asked.

"I'm going to try," Ryan replied. They got off the elevator and walked outside. They turned left and began walking to Pike Place Market.

"How's your new place?" Ryan asked.

"It's really nice," Kelsey said. "I like the neighborhood a lot."

"How's your roommate?"

"I haven't met her yet. She's supposed to be here on Sunday," Kelsey replied.

"She won't be as nice as Jess," Ryan commented.

"No way," Kelsey replied.

Ryan and Kelsey walked to the market. On the way, they discussed potential gifts for Jessica's birthday, which was coming up in July. They bought fish and chips and headed back to Tyler's office. When they arrived, a middle-aged man was standing in the doorway.

"Bill Simon," Ryan whispered to Kelsey. They stood to the side of the corridor as Simon finished talking to Tyler. Simon left the doorway and headed back down the hall when he spotted Ryan.

"Hi, Ryan," Simon said, extending his hand.

"Hi," Ryan said politely.

"How's Bob?"

"Good," Ryan replied. "This is my friend, Kelsey North." Kelsey juggled the bags in her hand so she could shake Bill Simon's hand.

"Nice to meet you, Miss North," he said, shaking her hand. Then he walked on.

"My dad is playing golf with Simon next week," Ryan said. They walked into Tyler's office.

"More work?" Ryan asked.

"Of course," Tyler said. "What did you guys get?"

"Fish and chips," Ryan replied. He set the bag down on a small round table behind the client chairs, next to the door.

"Good, I'm starving. And I'll be here all night," Tyler said. He stood up and joined Kelsey and Ryan, who were opening the food.

"Where else would you be?" Ryan asked.

"So amusing, Ryan," Tyler said. He picked up a french fry and ate it.

"Do you have plates?" Kelsey asked.

"I think there are some in the kitchen," Tyler said. He left the office and returned with three paper plates.

"Not very environmentally friendly," Ryan said.

Tyler looked at him in amusement. "Do you want to wash dishes?" Tyler asked him.

"No," Ryan said, taking a paper plate. The three of them placed food on their plates, then sat down in the office chairs to eat. Kelsey smiled to herself as she ate, remembering her call with Jessica. Once again, she was enjoying a free meal, courtesy of Tyler and Ryan.

"This is great," Tyler said, standing up to get more fish. "Where did you go?"

"Lowell's," Ryan said, eating some cole slaw.

"Good choice," Tyler replied. "I'll have to remember this."

"Just ask me to pick it up for you. I'll be your delivery boy this summer," Ryan said.

Tyler laughed. "Don't joke with me, I might hire you."

"Have you left the office today?" Kelsey asked between bites.

"Only to get coffee," Tyler replied. "Around two."

"Isn't there a coffee machine?" Ryan asked.

"It was a chance to see the sun. I grabbed it," Tyler replied, biting into a slab of fish.

"I'm worrying about you already," Ryan said.

"Worry about yourself. You're on Lisa's radar now," Tyler replied.

"That's right, I forgot to tell you. I know why they changed the trust," Ryan said to Tyler. "Why they decided we should inherit instead of giving it to charity."

"Who told you?"

"Everyone in the Legal Department. After Hurricane Lisa left," Ryan said.

"Go on," Tyler said. Kelsey was curious too. A few years ago, Lisa Olsen had made a very public pledge to give the majority of her Tactec stock to charity. There had been more than a few outcries in the media about her turnabout, and her decision this year to give it to her son instead.

"So you know that Bob was never in favor of giving the money to charity in the first place, but of course whatever Lisa says goes."

"Of course," Tyler replied.

"But I heard that Lisa completely freaked out during the year that you spent in New York. Supposedly even Bob said it was one of the worst years of his professional life. She hated that you were with Chris, and made life hell for everyone," Ryan said. "She thought that she had lost you, that you were going to stay in New York with your father."

"I had considered doing just that," Tyler said.

"When you came back to go to Darrow, Lisa decided that she needed to find a way to make you stay. So she told Gates and the rest of the world to shove it."

"So it's my fault."

"Exactly. Thanks. I'm looking forward to spending my money," Ryan said.

"How did this come up?" Kelsey asked.

"Lisa was all sunshine and roses when she visited Legal today. Someone commented on what a change it was from before, and the entire story spilled out. It wasn't a secret. Everyone knew."

"Everyone but us," Tyler said.

"Naturally," Ryan said.

"So if I hadn't spent a year in New York with my father, I wouldn't be chained to Tactec for the rest of my life," Tyler commented.

"At least you're getting a few billion dollars out of the deal," Ryan said.

"You know it isn't worth it to me," Tyler replied.

"I know," Ryan said. "But since your sacrifice means that I get billions, too, I'd say that it is."

Tyler frowned at him. "Of course you would."

"Really, Tyler, only you would be upset about inheriting money," Ryan said.

"You know it's not the money, it's the lack of control over my own life. I hate that."

"You don't have any control over your life now, you work for Bill Simon," Ryan commented.

"I can quit. We're not going to be able to quit Tactec without a fight. Anyway, you don't care. Bob's perfectly happy with you being in Legal. Lisa is going to want me to be CEO."

"Just like Mommy," Ryan teased.

"I hate you," Tyler said.

Ryan grinned. He took another forkful of cole slaw, and Tyler ate a french fry. Kelsey looked at Tyler. He was so unhappy about the position he found himself in. Kelsey wondered if he would eventually find himself CEO of Tactec.

"You might as well get used to it. We'll be attending board meetings all summer," Ryan commented.

"I know," Tyler said. "What a nightmare." He looked at Kelsey."How is your dinner?"

Kelsey chewed the food in her mouth then answered, "Great."

"Good. So have you missed the drama that is my life, over the past week?" Tyler asked her.

Kelsey giggled. "I like to think of your life as interesting."

"How diplomatic of you," Tyler said. "For me, the word crazy comes to mind."

"You should meditate," Ryan said. Tyler looked at him in amusement.

"Are you kidding me?" Tyler said.

"The reason that you have such chaos in your life, is because your mind is unsettled. Meditation would calm you."

"Shut up, Ryan," Tyler said. Ryan shrugged.

"Will you work tomorrow?" Kelsey asked Tyler.

"Yes, that's why Simon was here. There's a filing on Tuesday."

"A filing?" Kelsey asked.

"Lawyer-speak for giving documents to the court," Tyler explained. "It means that we're either suing someone or responding to someone else's lawsuit. So we'll be spending the next few days writing briefs, doing research and making sure everything is formatted properly. Then we give it to the court by the deadline."

"Does someone take it to the courthouse?" Kelsey asked. Tyler shook his head.

"Everything is filed electronically now. Lisa talks about how everyone used to be running around the office making copies to give to the messenger service before the courthouse doors closed at five. Now our filing deadline is midnight."

"Lucky you," Ryan said.

"I know, it means I'll be here until midnight on Tuesday," Tyler replied, eating another french fry.

"Your life sucks," Ryan commented.

"At least I have my friends to support me," Tyler replied.

"I brought you dinner," Ryan pouted.

"That you did. And you will again. Thank you," Tyler said.

Saturday, Kelsey spent the day hanging out around the apartment. On Sunday, Tyler picked her up and she accompanied him to the Darrow Law School graduation. Sophia had asked him to attend, and Kelsey was happy to go to be able to say goodbye to Keith.

As Law Review editor, Sophia gave a speech. She chose to discuss the importance of loyalty and hard work in the legal profession. Tyler and Kelsey accompanied Sophia, her partner, and several of their friends to brunch after graduation, then Tyler drove Kelsey home.

Kelsey heard the doorbell ring on Sunday night. She stood up to answer it. When she opened the door, a girl with flaming red hair and a slim body looked at her, annoyed.

"What took you so long?" she snarled. She pulled a large purple suitcase on wheels behind her as she walked in and looked at Kelsey disdainfully. "You're Kelsey, right?"

"Right," Kelsey said doubtfully.

"I'm Brittany." She looked around the apartment. "What a dump." She glanced at Kelsey again. "Are you as blonde as your hair?"

"Excuse me?" Kelsey said.

"I guess so," Brittany laughed cruelly. "Where do you go to school?"

"Darrow," Kelsey replied.

"Darrow? Really? Who did you sleep with to get into Darrow?" Brittany asked.

Kelsey frowned at her.

"Where's my room?" Brittany asked.

"Over there," Kelsey pointed.

"I bet you took the larger one," Brittany groused. She dragged her suitcase across the living room floor and wheeled it into her room. Then she slammed the door.

Kelsey left the apartment early on Monday morning, wearing her gym clothes, with her suit neatly draped over her arm. Her new briefcase hung from her shoulder, next to a new black gym bag. Kelsey walked to the bus stop and took the bus downtown.

When she arrived downtown, she walked up the hill three blocks to her new gym. As with everything related to Collins Nicol, the gym was beautiful and modern, and Kelsey's membership was waiting for her at the front desk. Kelsey put her things into a locker and began her workout.

An hour and a half later, Kelsey was on her way to the office. She strode into the Columbia Center with confidence, wearing her new navy suit, with her hair in a professional bun. Her gym bag and briefcase were in her hand. She rode up the elevator to the fortieth floor, changed elevators and rode up to Collins Nicol. When she arrived, she went to the reception desk.

"Hi, I'm Kelsey North. I'm starting today," she said. The pretty blonde receptionist smiled.

"Hang on. I'll have someone take you to your office," she said to Kelsey. Kelsey waited for about 30 seconds, then a young man in a white shirt and blue-and-red striped tie walked up. He was carrying a clipboard.

"Hi. Kelsey?"

Kelsey nodded.

"Great, follow me." The young man walked Kelsey through the locked door on the side of the reception desk and through the maze of offices and cubicles. Kelsey tried to pay attention to where they were going as he made conversation with her.

"I'm Ted," he said. "You're a first-year summer associate? What school?"

"Darrow," Kelsey replied.

"We have seven from Darrow this year, four first-years and three second," Ted said. "What group will you be with?"

"Intellectual Property," Kelsey repled.

"That's a tough group to get into," Ted said admiringly. "Your grades must be stellar."

Kelsey felt her stomach flip. She still hadn't got last semester's grades, and although she thought she had done well, she wouldn't stop worrying until she received them.

"Here you are," Ted said. Kelsey walked into her new office. It was small, with a not-so-fabulous view of Interstate 5, but she couldn't complain. It was all hers.

"Your pass and keys are in the envelope on the desk," Ted said.

"Thanks," Kelsey said. Ted smiled at her and walked off. Kelsey put her bags next to the desk and picked up the schedule that was under the envelope. She looked at it carefully. At 10 a.m. there was a meeting for all of the new summer associates, then there was a welcome lunch, then at 2 p.m., Kelsey would meet the other Intellectual Property lawyers along with the other two second-year summer associates assigned to the group.

Kelsey looked out of her window, onto I-5 and to the south. She sighed. It was going to be a long day.

At 9:55, Kelsey made her way into the summer associate meeting. She was surprised to see over 30 students in the room. Obviously, Collins Nicol believed that they would be making some new hires over the next few years, probably thanks to Tactec. Brittany, who was wearing a black suit with a long, matronly skirt, pointedly ignored her. Kelsey was grateful. Lucas walked over with a girl with glasses and short brown hair. Kelsey recognized her from campus.

"Hey, Kelsey. Have you met Eliza?"

"I've seen you around," Eliza said, sticking out her hand. Kelsey shook it.

"Nice to meet you."

"How's your office?" Lucas asked.

"A beautiful view of I-5."

"Really?" Eliza said. "I have a view of the Sound."

"How about you, Lucas?"

"The stadiums."

"What group are you in, Eliza?" Kelsey asked her, as Eliza brushed her skirt with her hand.

"Trusts and Estates," Eliza said.

Suddenly, five attorneys walked into the large conference room.

"Let's get seats," Eliza said quietly. She, Kelsey, and Lucas sat in a row of seats near the back.

The room began to settle down as the summer associates quickly found seats and stopped talking. Brittany sat in the front row.

"I'd like to welcome all of you to Collins Nicol," said a man with silver hair, wearing a navy suit. "My name is Thomas Collins, and I'm the managing partner here."

Kelsey listened carefully. She knew that Thomas Collins was the third generation of Collins Nicol. The firm had been founded by his grandfather seventy years earlier. But Thomas Collins had built on his grandfather and father's legacies and turned it into the Seattle legal powerhouse it had become.

They sat through several speeches, all designed to welcome them to Collins Nicol and introduce them to the firm's culture. In the middle of the speech by one of the senior partners of the firm's Environmental Law group, the fourth first-year summer associate from Darrow sheepishly walked in. It was Lucas's former Legal writing partner, Alana Alexander.

Kelsey and Lucas walked into the welcome lunch, which was already in full swing, thanks to the Collins Nicol associates who saw it as an opportunity to have a free meal. They got in line behind two women wearing professional suits, who were talking and laughing about someone's poor showing in court.

"It looks good," Lucas said to Kelsey, interrupting her attempt to figure out which department the women were in. Kelsey nodded and glanced at the spread. It did look good. Clearly Collins Nicol had spared no expense.

"How's your apartment?" Lucas asked. "I don't think I've met your roommate yet."

"It's fine," Kelsey lied. In fact, a part of her was wondering how she was going to last an entire summer with Brittany. "How's yours?"

"It's really nice. I didn't think I'd like First Hill, but it isn't bad. And

Parker's a really nice guy. He goes to Oregon." They had reached the food, so Lucas reached for a pair of tongs to take some vegetables.

"That's great," Kelsey said, taking some vegetables of her own and putting them on her plate.

"Yeah, I think we'll have a good time this summer," Lucas said. Kelsey nodded and looked up. She saw an associate looking at her, then quickly looking away. She turned her eyes back to the food. Lucas put a roll on her plate.

"Thanks," Kelsey said to him.

Eliza caught up with them a few minutes later, and they ate standing next to a wall. Kelsey noticed that Brittany had chosen not to eat, but instead was making a point of introducing herself to everyone around her. She had to admit that Brittany certainly knew how to network.

After eating, meeting Eliza and Lucas's summer roommates, plus saying a quick hello to Alana, Kelsey headed back to her office to get ready for the Intellectual Property meeting. There was a folder on her desk when she returned. Kelsey glanced at the clock, realized she only had a few minutes to get to the IP meeting, so she took the folder and left the office.

As Kelsey walked to the conference room, she looked at the paperwork in her hands. There were two printed contracts, plus three letters. A Post-It note was attached which said, "Kelsey, please read. I will be assigning you a project based on these contracts tomorrow." It was signed David Lim, who Kelsey knew was one of the IP associates. She wondered if she would meet him at the meeting. Kelsey clutched the folder carefully and hurried to the conference room.

The Intellectual Property group meeting was long but, Kelsey thought, very informative. There were three IP partners at Collins Nicol. Kelsey knew that one of them had become Tactec's contact person after Tactec had moved their work from Kinnon Martins. Although Taylor, Smart, and Mayer had taken most of the IP work, Collins Nicol did a fair share, and wanted much, much more.

Tyler, in annoyance, had told Kelsey that after he had accepted the job with Bill Simon, the Collins Nicol summer associate coordinator had called him at least three times to get him to change his mind, and come to Collins Nicol instead. Collins Nicol was confident that if the son of Tactec's CEO worked for the firm, that they would have IP projects for years to come.

There were 16 IP associates, and three of them had been assigned to oversee the work of Kelsey and the two second-year summer associates in the IP group. Kelsey's mentor was a serious-looking young woman named Emily Pierce, who worked in trademarks. One of the second-year summer associates was also from Darrow, and his mentor was a copyright attorney named Jamie Harding. The last IP summer associate was a second-year from Harvard, and his mentor was Alex Carsten, a senior attorney specializing in licensing.

The head of Collins Nicol's IP group was friendly, chatty partner named Mary White. Kelsey knew from her research that Ms. White had been at Collins Nicol for over ten years, and had a long list of impressive clients, including many of Seattle's most successful startups.

It was strange to think that if Tyler had accepted the offer from Collins Nicol, that he would be here, sitting next to her and working alongside her for the summer. Then again, it was also possible that if Tyler was here that she wouldn't be. There was only one first-year summer associate in IP, and for all Kelsey knew, there might not have been room for two.

In fact, Kelsey mused, it had taken Collins Nicol a long time to get back to her, well after Tyler had turned them down. Tyler not only had his Tactec connection, he also had better grades. Kelsey sighed to herself. She didn't want to think about it.

After the meeting, several of the IP attorneys hung around to introduce themselves to the summer associates. Alex Carsten walked over to Kelsey.

"Alex Carsten," he said, extending his hand. Kelsey knew who he was, since he had given the meeting a brief but comprehensive overview of the current IP licensing issues that Collins Nicol's clients were facing.

"Kelsey North," Kelsey replied, shaking Alex Carsten's hand. He was tall, slim, and carried himself with confidence. Kelsey also had to admit he was more than a little handsome as well.

"First-year, Darrow, right?" he asked.

"Right," Kelsey replied.

"What was your major in undergrad?"

"Biology," Kelsey answered.

Kelsey knew that there were invariably one of two responses to her major. Sometimes, there was an uncomfortable giggle, as biology made people think of sex. Usually though, people were a little astonished. As far as Kelsey was concerned, neither response was the correct one.

After having a dreadful freshman year of high school, and a not much better first semester of sophomore year since she didn't have the base to build on, Kelsey had surprised everyone, including herself, by getting an A+ in her first biology class. From that moment on, Kelsey's parents, mentors, and biology teacher had united to prepare Kelsey to get into a college biology program. Portland State accepted her, and she had thrived there.

"Wow. I'm impressed. You should take the patent bar," he said.

"Really?" Kelsey asked. She knew that she was eligible thanks to her major, but really hadn't considered working on patents.

"Absolutely. Good patent lawyers are in strong demand," he replied. "And you'll make a lot of money."

"It's time to consider being a patent lawyer then," Kelsey commented. He laughed.

"My kind of woman," he said. "Collins Nicol doesn't have a patent department at the moment, although I think Thomas is considering trying to lure a few patent attorneys over from Lewis and Lindsay. Why did you apply to be in Intellectual Property?"

When Kelsey had applied to Collins Nicol, she had been asked the top three departments she would be interested in interning with. At many other law firms, the firm didn't ask, but decided which group students would be placed with. Many law students, who had no idea what they wanted to focus on, were grateful to simply be assigned to a group.

Kelsey thought for a moment, then answered.

"I thought it would be interesting," she said.

"That's it?" Alex asked in amusement.

Kelsey felt herself blush a little. She hadn't known how to answer the question.

"Well, in law school I worked on a right-of-publicity project, and I learned a lot. I think that's why I started considering it."

"I see. Most first-years don't know much about intellectual property, so they don't apply to the group. But we had three applications to join IP from Darrow first-years this summer. "

Kelsey knew that Tyler was one of them. She wondered who the other one was.

"Darrow always surprises us," Alex went on. "Last year, we only had a total of five applications from students at Darrow. This year, we have seven summer associates from the school."

Kelsey nodded. Since Kinnon Martins had dissolved, and Collins Nicol was growing, it was the logical destination for Darrow students who wanted to stay in Seattle. Only a few other law firms were as large in the Pacific Northwest.

"It was nice to meet you, Kelsey," Alex said. "Let me know if you need any help this summer."

"Thank you, Mr. Carsten," Kelsey said politely. He looked at her with a smile, then walked away.

Emily dropped by Kelsey's office late that afternoon to discuss the group and find out if Kelsey had any questions.

"As a first-year summer associate, you aren't expected to put in a lot of long hours," Emily had said. "So feel free to leave around five or six, unless one of the associates tells you otherwise. You won't gain brownie points burning the midnight oil. The hiring partners aren't fooled. They know you don't have that much to do. Just make sure you're here by nine in the morning."

Kelsey had appreciated the advice. Never having worked in a law firm, she wasn't sure what the protocol was, and she was quite sure that Tyler was not having a normal summer associate experience.

So over the next week, Kelsey got used to Collins Nicol. She had got her first assignments on Tuesday morning, and worked diligently to understand them on Tuesday afternoon and all day Wednesday. She had lunch on Thursday with Eliza, Lucas, and to Lucas' displeasure, Alana, who was working in Environmental. On Friday, Tyler called her to invite her to dinner, and she happily accepted.

Tyler and Kelsey walked into the boys' living room Friday evening. Ryan was sitting on the sofa, wearing jeans and a t-shirt, watching television. Tyler closed the door and looked at Ryan.

"What are you doing?" Tyler asked.

"Watching TV," Ryan replied.

"I can see that. You never watch TV," Tyler commented.

"I have to do something," Ryan replied. "Hi, Kelsey."

"Well, usually on a Friday, you go out," Tyler replied.

"Not any more," Ryan said. "Not without Jess. I'm staying out of trouble this summer."

"Really?" Tyler asked doubtfully.

"I'm not getting so much as a traffic ticket. I don't want to give Jessica any excuse to break up with me," Ryan replied.

"Jessica knows who she's dating," Tyler commented.

"Someone responsible," Ryan said.

"Right," Tyler laughed. He took off his jacket and slung it over the side of the sofa.

"Seriously, bro. I'm going to work, then I'm coming home and sitting here. Nothing else."

"Don't be ridiculous. Jessica isn't doing that," Kelsey said.

"She doesn't have anything to prove. I do," Ryan said.

"You have a point," Tyler said. "I'm going to change, Kelsey," he said, walking into the bedroom.

Kelsey sat next to Ryan on the sofa. "What are you watching?" she asked.

"'The Bachelor'," Ryan replied.

Kelsey laughed.

"What?" Ryan asked. "It's interesting."

"I think you need to go out," Kelsey commented.

"Nope," Ryan said. Tyler came out of his bedroom, wearing jeans and pulling a polo shirt over his chest.

"Ryan needs an intervention. He's watching 'The Bachelor'," Kelsey said to Tyler.

"Come out with us," Tyler said.

Ryan looked at him. "Have you seen it? It's really interesting," he said.

Tyler walked over to the television remote, picked it up, and turned the TV off.

"Come on. We're getting dinner."

Ryan frowned. "You're already ruining my resolve."

"You're going out with Kelsey and me. We'll keep you out of trouble," Tyler replied.

"Where are you going?"

"Just downtown," Tyler said.

"Okay," Ryan said. "But you're driving."

The three of them ended up at a brewpub downtown. Kelsey had left her jacket and briefcase in Tyler's car, but in her sheath dress and heels, she was still a contrast to Ryan and Tyler's casual attire. They were seated in a booth and given menus.

"How's Collins Nicol?" Ryan asked Kelsey.

"It's great. Everyone's really nice and the work is interesting," she replied, looking up from the menu. "Do you like working at Tactec?"

"It's fine," Ryan said.

"Do you still have a lot to do?" Kelsey asked.

"I'm working on the Kinnon Martins lawsuit," Ryan said.

"You'll be working on that for the whole summer. It will never die," Tyler commented.

"I know. You were right," Ryan said.

"What do they have you doing?" Kelsey asked.

"Reviewing documents. It's been pretty boring actually," Ryan replied. "But I don't have to work as late as Tyler. Actually, you're home early tonight," Ryan said to Tyler.

"Simon flew to Arizona," Tyler replied. "Everyone fled the second he left the office."

"How late do you usually work?" Kelsey asked.

"Eleven every other night this week. I think it's going to get worse soon," Tyler replied.

"Eleven p.m.? As a first-year summer associate?" Kelsey asked.

"Bill Simon is a workaholic," Tyler commented. He put the menu to the side. "I feel bad for his associates. They work until 2 a.m."

"Wow," Kelsey said.

"Why would anyone work for him?" Ryan asked.

"He's the best. It's like a crash course in the law," Tyler replied.

The waitress arrived and they placed their orders.

"People must burn out like crazy there, though," Kelsey said, resuming the conversation.

"The associate who's been there longest currently is going on three years," Tyler replied. "I think the record is five. It doesn't matter to me though. I'll be at Tactec in two years."

"Reviewing documents?" Ryan asked.

"No way. I need a better job than that. Why didn't you ask for something else to do, anyway?"

"Because I don't care," Ryan replied. "It's just for the summer."

"What are you working on, Kelsey?" Tyler asked.

"I'm writing a memo right now," she said. "It's due on Tuesday. How about you?"

"I have a memo to write too. I have to send it to Simon tomorrow though."

"On Saturday?" Kelsey asked.

"Remember, I'm still supposed to be in the office," Tyler replied. "He wants it by noon. I'll finish it when I get back."

"I'd quit," Ryan said, as the waitress brought over their drinks.

"If I quit, I'd have to work for Tactec. I'd rather have no life this summer," Tyler responded.

"It looks like you'll get your wish," Ryan pointed out.

"It will keep me in form for Law Review," Tyler commented.

"I'd quit that too," Ryan said. "It's not like you need Law Review to join Tactec's legal department."

"I earned Law Review. I'm not quitting," Tyler replied.

"You're really planning on having a miserable year," Ryan said. "A summer with Bill Simon, then back to Darrow for Law Review."

"I didn't go to Darrow to have fun. Unlike some people," Tyler commented.

"You're missing out," Ryan said.

"I'm sure," Tyler said.

"When is your next Tactec board meeting?" Kelsey asked them.

"The 15th of July, I think," Tyler said. "Simon said I'll need to make up the hours."

Ryan laughed. "So you'll work until 1 a.m?"

"Whatever," Tyler replied, laughing as well. "At least we live downtown. I can get home in five minutes."

"How's your new roommate, Kelsey?" Ryan asked.

"She stresses about everything," Kelsey replied. She decided to leave out the fact that on Thursday night Brittany had screamed at her for leaving a glass in the sink. "I miss Jess."

"I do too," Ryan sighed.

"What is there for your roommate to worry about? Didn't she just start at Collins Nicol with you this week?" Tyler asked.

"I think he's already panicking about the impression she's making. She wants to get an offer for next summer." Kelsey knew this because of a loud conversation that Brittany had had with her parents on the phone on Tuesday night.

"Is she in Intellectual Property with you?"

"No, thank goodness," Kelsey replied. "She's in Trusts and Estates."

"Where does she go to school?" Ryan asked.

"Stanford," Kelsey said.

"Why didn't she stay in California?" Tyler asked.

"She's from Tacoma," Kelsey replied as their dinner arrived. Ryan had ordered a salad with grilled chicken, Tyler a burger, and Kelsey, BBQ chicken pizza. Kelsey took a slice of pizza as Ryan examined the salad and removed a slice of tomato, which he ate. Tyler ate a french fry.

"Can you stand her for the summer?" Tyler asked Kelsey.

"I hope so," Kelsey said honestly. But already, in her first week, she had her doubts.

"You can hang out with us this summer," Tyler said.

"Tyler will be at the office," Ryan noted.

"Funny," Tyler said. "But true," he added. "Of course, Kels, you can always visit me at the office. I'd love the distraction."

"Maybe I'll drop by after I leave work sometime," Kelsey said.

"Perfect," Tyler said. "I'm confident I'll be there."

Ryan ate one of Tyler's french fries.

"What are you going to do this summer? Are you seriously planning to sit at home?" Tyler asked him.

"Why not?" Ryan asked.

"Because you'll be bored," Tyler replied.

"It won't kill me," Ryan said. "It's better than getting into trouble with Jessica."

"Maybe you need a hobby," Tyler said, taking a bite of the burger.

"My hobby is Jess."

"Who's across the country. Figure out something else to do," Tyler said.

"Like what?"

"What else do you like to do?"

Ryan smiled knowingly at Kelsey, and looked her up and down. She frowned at him.

"But that's off the table. I love Jess. So what else?" Ryan continued.

"People do lots of things," Tyler mused.

"Like?" Ryan said impatiently.

"Knit. Exercise. Cook. Lots of things," Kelsey replied.

"Jessica likes food," Ryan said.

"Who doesn't?" Tyler commented.

"I should learn to cook," Ryan said with determination.

Tyler looked at him in surprise. "Cook?"

"Sure, why not?" Ryan asked.

"No reason, I guess," Tyler replied.

"So what do I need to start?" Ryan asked Kelsey.

"I would start with a cookbook," Kelsey said. "Something simple."

"A cookbook. Do I need anything else?" Ryan asked.

"Food," Kelsey smiled.

"Okay," Ryan thought.

"Are you sure this is a good idea?" Tyler asked.

"I don't see why not," Ryan said. "We have to eat. Margaret isn't always there, and I get tired of take-out. I think it's a great idea. You can learn too."

"No, thank you. Anyway, I don't have time for any hobbies this summer," Tyler replied.

"Too bad for Kelsey," Ryan teased.

"Funny," Kelsey said.

"How's Lucas?" Tyler asked.

Kelsey looked at him. "He's fine," she answered coolly.

"Good," Tyler said.

"Have you gone on your date yet?" Ryan asked.

"Not yet," Kelsey replied.

"We want all the details," Ryan said.

"You won't get them," Kelsey replied.

"What is he working in? Construction?" Tyler asked.

Kelsey nodded.

"Sounds thrilling," Ryan said, taking another fry.

"I don't know. Beats reading memos written by Brandon's dad in 1996," Tyler replied.

They ate dinner, then took Tyler's car to the mall so Ryan could look at cookbooks. Kelsey watched as Ryan's stack of books got larger and larger.

"You can start with one, Ryan," Kelsey commented.

"Nah," Ryan replied.

As he paid for seven cookbooks, Ryan asked the clerk, "Is there another place to see cookbooks here?"

"I'm pretty sure that they have them at the cooking store upstairs. Next to the skybridge," the clerk replied, handing over Ryan's two bags of books.

"A cooking store? Great, thanks," Ryan replied.

"This isn't enough?" Tyler asked as the three of them walked out of the bookstore and into the mall basement.

"Jessica has refined tastes, so I want to be able to make interesting things for her. Anyway, I want to see what the cooking store has. I don't remember ever being in one," Ryan said as they headed up the escalator.

"Sure, whatever," Tyler said. The trio went up the series of escalators and up to the skybridge which connected the mall with the large department store across the street.

"Oh, wow," Ryan said as they saw the store. "This looks amazing." He walked in, book bags in both hands.

Ryan set his bags down in a corner of the store near the front, and they looked around the large store. There were pots, pans and a wide variety of things for the chef, in addition a small selection of books. Ryan poked through the gleaming measuring cups, smooth basting brushes and a host of other things. Kelsey picked up a set of teaspoons and her eyes widened.

"Expensive," she said, quickly placing them back down.

"So, Kelsey, what do I need?"

"Um, a few things. But you can get them a lot cheaper," Kelsey said.

"Some of this stuff is probably already in the condo," Tyler added.

"I'm starting first thing tomorrow, so what should we get?" Ryan said, ignoring them both.

"Let me think," Kelsey said. She picked up a set of measuring cups. "You'll need measuring cups and spoons."

"Okay," Ryan said, removing them from her hands. Kelsey glanced at the neat display and began pulling items. As she selected things, she gave them to Ryan.

"Is that it?" Ryan asked her. "There's so much for sale here."

"You don't need a lot of equipment for cooking. Anyway, you're just getting started. You can get more things as you go along."

"Makes sense," Ryan said. He handed the items in his hands to Tyler, who was standing looking bored.

"Hold these for me, bro," Ryan said. "I want to look around the store. Kelsey, would you mind getting anything else you think I need?"

"Sure, Ryan," Kelsey replied, amused. Ryan walked off, and Kelsey turned to Tyler. "Is he really going to do this?"

"You never know with Ryan," Tyler said. "But since it's this or watching TV, there's the possibility he's serious."

A half hour later, Ryan was skimming through the cookbooks at the door. A very large pile of items sat on the front counter, including a large bowl mixer, sets of oven mitts and a matching apron.

"Ryan, they're closing soon," Tyler yawned.

"It's not a problem, sir," the clerk said brightly. "Take your time."

"Thanks," Ryan said, not looking up from his book.

"At least we should get something for our trouble," he said to Kelsey. They walked over to the shelves which held ready-to-eat gourmet products.

Kelsey pulled down a jar. "Yuzu syrup?" she asked.

"I prefer maple. Which they seem to have as well," Tyler replied. "Actually, I was thinking chocolate." He pulled a bar of chocolate off of the shelf. "What do you think?"

"I think this cost more than my textbooks last semester," Kelsey replied, looking at the tag.

"Only one textbook. Anyway, it's on Bob," Tyler said. "Ryan, are you ready?"

"Yep," Ryan said, closing the book and taking it to the counter. "Do you guys want anything else?"

"Just to go," Tyler said.

"Be patient. Think of all of the good things I'll make for you this summer," Ryan replied. "You can ring it up," he said to the cashier.

"Yes, sir," she replied, and began to ring up the purchase cheerfully. Ryan picked up his book bags from the floor.

"Do you really need a mixer?" Tyler asked him.

"Of course," Ryan replied. "Kelsey said so."

"You probably don't need one tonight," Kelsey commented.

"Do you think that Margaret can come over?" Ryan asked Tyler. "Teach me a few of the basics?"

"Probably," Tyler said. "I don't think Lisa's entertaining a lot this summer."

Ryan pulled out his phone and typed as the cashier continued to ring up the purchase. Kelsey watched in amazement as the prices flashed on the cash register screen.

"Three thousand two hundred forty-three dollars and ninety-five cents," the cashier concluded. Ryan placed his phone on the counter, pulled out a debit card, and gave it to the cashier. He then picked up his phone and continued to type, completely unaffected by the amount.

Kelsey glanced at Tyler, who continued to look bored. The cashier was assisted by two staff members who wrapped the packages while Ryan signed the bill. Everything was neatly bagged as Ryan finished with his phone, and placed it back in his pocket.

"Margaret will be by at 10:30," Ryan commented to Tyler. "Hey, maybe I can learn to make Kelsey's mom's cookies."

"I'm sure you can with all of this stuff," Kelsey said.

"Here you are, sir," the cashier said, beginning to hand him what Kelsey thought was a surprisingly small number of bags for the price. She gave Tyler a large box which had been artfully tied to allow carrying with one hand. Kelsey took two small bags and Ryan took the rest.

"Thank you," Ryan said. They walked out of the store.

"Everything's closed," Tyler noted as they walked through the quiet mall, and toward the elevators.

"Not the movie theater," Ryan said.

"Okay, not that."

"So, Kels, am I all ready to be a chef?" Ryan asked her.

"I think so," Kelsey replied, trying to keep the sarcasm out of her voice.

"So why does she have to stay with you?" asked Jessica over the speakerphone the next day.

Kelsey had joined the boys for the Fourth of July. She had watched Margaret teach Ryan to scramble eggs, before Margaret left to prepare dinner for Lisa's senior executives for a fireworks cruise in the evening. Then Tyler had returned from work at 1:30, since he only worked half-days on Saturday.

"That's what I was wondering," Tyler said glumly.

"Zach doesn't want to pay for a hotel. He's still broke from spring break," Ryan explained.

Jessica sighed.

"Jess, nothing's going to happen. Tyler's here. Anyway, it's Zach's turn with Kimmy," Ryan said.

"Eww," Jessica said.

"That didn't sound good," Tyler commented.

Ryan laughed. "Sorry. It's only for a few days," he said.

"Fine," Jessica conceded. "Okay, I'll talk to you later. We're going to take the boys to see the fireworks."

"Have fun. I miss you," Ryan said sadly.

"Bye, guys," Jessica said, and she disconnected.

Ryan sat dejectedly on the sofa. "Now what?" he said, looking up at Tyler.

"It's the Fourth of July. Let's go have fun," Tyler replied, amused.

"Fine," Ryan said.

"Where are the fireworks?" Kelsey asked.

"Lake Union," Tyler said.

"Where are we going to watch them from?" Ryan asked.

"Lake Union," Tyler replied.

"Not Gasworks Park?" Ryan said.

"We'd have to be there now for a good view," Tyler replied. "But I know a guy."

"Who? Bob's boat is being serviced," Ryan said.

"Simon," Tyler said.

"Bill Simon has a boat? And he invited you?" Ryan said.

"Yes, and yes."

"Why? Does he want you to work even more hours?" Ryan asked.

"All the staff was invited. He lives on a houseboat on Lake Union."

"Like Sleepless in Seattle?" Kelsey asked.

"Right," Tyler said.

"Cool," Ryan said. "What time are we going?"

"The party starts at 7:30."

"That's hours from now," Ryan moaned, leaning back on the sofa.

"You're pathetic, you know that, right? Come on, we'll go for a walk. I'll even buy you dinner."

"Where?" Ryan asked.

"McDonald's," Tyler replied.

Ryan laughed.

The trio left the condo, and began walking towards South Lake Union. Kelsey glanced around in interest. She had been in a much different frame of mind the last time she had walked in this neighborhood.

Tyler glanced at her.

"You've been here before, Kels?" he asked, smiling. Of course he knew she had.

"I have," Kelsey replied, smiling back.

"When?" Ryan asked.

"The night you dumped me," Kelsey replied. Tyler laughed and Ryan's face fell.

"We're never going to get beyond that, are we?" Ryan asked her.

"We have," Kelsey replied. "I just haven't walked through here since."

"We'll have to make some better memories here," Tyler said.

"I have good memories too," Kelsey said, looking at Tyler. That evening Tyler had picked her up, one might even say rescued her, and taken her to dinner. In some ways, it was the start of their friendship.

"I'm glad," Tyler said.

"I'm always the villain," Ryan commented.

"You did a bad thing," Tyler said.

"I know," Ryan said.

"And you've apologized," Kelsey said.

Ryan sighed. "But it hangs over my relationship with Jessica."

"Actions have consequences," Tyler said.

"Mine rarely do," Ryan replied.

"That's because Bob always bails you out. It's time to be a man," Tyler replied.

"I'm trying," Ryan said.

"You're doing well," Kelsey commented.

"You think so?" Ryan said. "Thanks."

"Don't rest on your laurels," Tyler said.

"I won't," Ryan said thoughtfully. "Do you think Jess misses me?" he asked Kelsey.

"Of course," Kelsey replied.

"She doesn't seem to," Ryan said.

"Ryan, she's busy. She has to get used to work and being back home," Tyler said.

"Maybe," Ryan said. "She was in a hurry to get off the phone."

Kelsey thought about that. Jessica had been in more of a hurry than usual. Kelsey wondered if it was her nephews, or the fact that Kimmy was coming for a visit. Jess didn't like Kim and disliked the fact that Ryan had previously dated her.

Ryan sighed.

"Ryan, it's only week two. Are you going to be miserable all summer?" Tyler asked.

Ryan looked at Tyler with his bright blue eyes. "Yes," he replied.

"Fine. Just don't ruin mine," Tyler said.

They walked around the South Lake Union neighborhood. Tyler stopped for coffee, then they went to Cascade Playground. Ryan sat on the edge of the sandbox and dragged his foot through the sand, while Kelsey sat on the swing and Tyler pushed her.

"I feel like I'm five," Kelsey said, as Tyler pushed her high into the air. Her blonde hair blew in the wind.

Tyler pushed her even higher, and Kelsey giggled.

"When was the last time you were on a swing?" Tyler asked her, pushing her again.

"I don't remember," Kelsey said, closing her eyes to the breeze. Then she opened them, and jumped off the swing.

Tyler ran over to her, and she was laughing.

"Are you okay?" he asked in concern.

Kelsey nodded happily. "Come on, let's climb," she said. She pulled his hand and took him to the empty climbing area.

An hour later, they left the playground. Kelsey brushed a twig out of her hair.

"I hope tonight is casual," she said.

"You look fine," Tyler said, tossing his empty coffee cup into a bin.

"Why was the park so empty? It's a perfect day," Kelsey said.

"Too many homeless hanging out there, I expect," Tyler commented. Kelsey looked back. She had been having too much fun to notice, but it seemed that Tyler was right.

"Let's get something to eat," Ryan said. "I'm starving."

They walked over to the burger restaurant that they had gone to with Zachary and Jess at the end of last year, and ordered.

"Remember being here with Jess?" Ryan asked.

"I remember she wanted to kill you," Tyler replied.

"I miss her," Ryan said, ignoring Tyler's comment.

They ate, then slowly meandered toward the edge of Lake Union, stopping at REI, going to a used bookstore, and pausing at the new offices that Tactec was building in South Lake Union. After a visit to the Center for Wooden Boats and a quick ride on the South Lake Union streetcar, it was 6:30 and time for dinner.

Kelsey fixed her hair in the bathroom as the boys waited to be seated. She was beaming. It had been an amazing, carefree day. She had been able to forget Brittany, her grades and the fact that like Ryan, she missed Jess too. She looked in the mirror one last time and walked out. Tyler and Ryan were sitting on the outside deck over the lake.

"Nice view," Kelsey said.

"Simon's will be better," Tyler said. "He lives closer to Gasworks

Park."

Ryan sat quietly, looking at the view. He had been abnormally quiet for most of the day.

"Ryan?" Tyler said to him.

Ryan looked at Tyler. "What?"

"She'll be back soon," Tyler said. Ryan sighed and looked back at the water.

They arrived at Bill Simon's luxurious houseboat at 8 p.m. and the party was in full swing. The houseboat was very modern, with teak furnishings and stainless-steel appliances. There were three decks, all of which had a beautiful view of the lake. Tyler introduced Kelsey to his fellow associates, and to Kelsey's surprise, she spent quite a few moments talking to Bill Simon himself.

As it got darker, the party moved up to the rooftop deck which, as Tyler had said, had a perfect view of Gasworks Park. Gasworks Park was completely covered with people ready to watch the fireworks. Kelsey chatted with Bill Simon's most long-term associate, who confided that he would be quitting at the end of the summer and moving to Collins Nicol. She also found out that of the four summer associates that Bill Simon had hired, two had already quit.

Night fell, and Tyler and Ryan joined Kelsey on the deck.

"Having fun?" Tyler asked her.

"It's been great," Kelsey replied. "I heard you're developing quite a reputation already," she said.

"Hmm," Tyler said.

"Reputation for what?" Ryan asked her.

"Fighting with Simon," Kelsey said.

"You?" Ryan said in surprise.

"He's a pain," Tyler replied.

"Everyone's rooting for you. They figure Simon knows you aren't afraid of getting fired," Kelsey added.

"Great," Tyler said.

"What have you fought with Bill Simon over?" Ryan asked.

"We didn't fight. I did complain about the workload though."

"You?" Ryan repeated.

"My fellow first-year was crying in the bathroom on Monday night. She wasn't going to say anything, so I told Simon. It didn't matter, she quit on Wednesday."

"Are you kidding?" Kelsey said.

"She figures that she'll take some summer classes," Tyler said. "I don't blame her, I don't think she would have lasted another week."

"Has anyone else quit since you've been there?" Ryan asked.

"A second-year summer associate. He wouldn't have lasted another day," Tyler commented.

"Someone else is leaving," Kelsey said quietly.

"Who?" Tyler asked. Kelsey motioned to the boys to come closer and whispered the name into their ears.

"Who's that?" Ryan asked as Tyler smiled knowingly.

"Interesting. He told you?"

"He's going to Collins Nicol in the fall."

"He's the associate who's been there the longest." Tyler said, answering Ryan's question.

Kelsey glanced around to make sure she wasn't overheard.

"Doesn't he get tired of all of the turnover?" she asked.

"I guess not." Tyler said. "Look, they're about to start." he said. Kelsey and Ryan looked out over the water. To Kelsey's surprise, Tyler put his hands gently on her shoulders, and the fireworks began.

Kelsey slept over at the condo that night. She was grateful for the invitation, as it meant that she wouldn't accidentally wake Brittany up. Brittany was a very early and a very light sleeper, and Kelsey had quickly learned over the past week that coming home between 8 and 10 wasn't a great idea. Her concern was that Brittany had been kept up by the fireworks, and Kelsey would arrive home just in time to wake Brittany and get yelled at. Brittany had a very sharp tongue.

Happily though, she was in the condo, teaching Ryan how to make her mom's cookies. Tyler was sitting on the sofa, working on his laptop.

"Does it matter if your measurement is a little off?" Ryan asked Kelsey.

She reached out and wiped some flour off of his freckled nose. "It depends," Kelsey replied, dumping the chocolate chips into the already-stirred batter. "Ten percent or so won't matter for cookies, but try to get as close as you can. Cakes are a bit fussier."

Ryan nodded seriously. "Stir," Kelsey ordered, and Ryan began to stir the mixture. Kelsey poured in a pre-measured amount of dried cranberries.

"That's enough stirring, they'll get tough," Kelsey said. "Okay now, get your teaspoon. We'll measure them out."

Ryan peered at her. "Teaspoon? Margaret always measures cookies with this thing, um…." Ryan began to rummage through a drawer.

"A ice-cream scoop," Tyler said, without lifting his eyes.

"Right," Ryan said. Kelsey looked in the drawer he had opened and pulled out a melon baller.

"This?" she asked Ryan. Ryan nodded.

"It's a melon baller." she said. Tyler looked up and looked at the utensil in her hand.

"It isn't for ice cream?" Tyler asked.

"Only if you want really small scoops," Kelsey commented.

"Interesting," Tyler said, returning to his book.

"This will work fine," Kelsey said. "You'll get nice even cookies, which is great."

"Why?" Ryan asked.

"If they are all the same size, they will bake evenly," Kelsey said, scooping out a ball of dough and placing it neatly on the cookie sheet they had prepared earlier.

"Can I try?" Ryan asked.

"Of course," Kelsey said, handing him the scoop. Ryan carefully scooped out a second ball and put it on the cookie sheet.

"Put a little more space between them. They'll spread in the oven," Kelsey said, moving the ball with her fingers.

"How many should we put on the sheet?" Ryan asked.

"Twelve," Kelsey said confidently.

"You've done this before," Tyler commented.

"I can bake cookies," Kelsey said.

"I can eat them," Tyler grinned.

Ryan finished putting the balls of dough on the cookie sheet and set the melon baller down.

"Now what?" he asked expectantly.

"Now we bake them," Kelsey said with amusement.

"Right," Ryan said.

"Carefully pick up the sheet and place it in the center of the oven," she said.

"Why the center?" Ryan asked.

"The temperature should be more stable," Kelsey said.

"Okay," Ryan said. "No wonder you're a scientist."

Kelsey laughed as Ryan opened the door of the oven and placed the cookie sheet inside.

"It's not science. It's cooking," Kelsey replied.

"It seems like both to me," Ryan replied. "How long do these stay in?"

"Six to eight minutes," Kelsey said.

"Which?" Ryan asked.

"It depends on the oven. We'll check them at six and see if they're ready. If not, we'll check them again at eight."

"All right," Ryan said, setting the timer.

"Can you really only bake twelve at a time?" Tyler asked Kelsey. "It seems like it would take all day at that rate for Margaret to fill the cookie jar."

"At my house, we can fit up to four pans in our oven. Two on the top, two on the bottom. We rotate them halfway through."

"I see," Tyler said thoughtfully. "That seems more efficient."

"Should I be doing something now?" Ryan asked Kelsey.

"You can prepare the next cookie sheet," she said.

"Cooking is a lot of work," Tyler commented.

"It's worth it. It's for Jessica," Ryan said.

"It's an expression of love," Kelsey said, as Ryan began to carefully scoop out balls of dough for the second cookie sheet.

"Cooking?" Tyler said.

"Told you," Ryan said to him.

"Of course. That's the way your family provides for you," Kelsey said.

"My mother hasn't cooked in her life," Tyler said.

"Yes, well, your mother provides money for you. That's the way she shows her love."

"Plus she hired Margaret," Ryan added. "She does the cooking."

"Exactly. Haven't you ever had someone make a food gift for you? Homemade candy or cookies for Christmas?" Kelsey said.

"No," Tyler said.

"Really?" Kelsey said in surprise. As a teenager, she, Jasmine, and Morgan regularly baked cookies to give to friends and family at Christmas, being too broke to buy gifts.

"I don't think so," Tyler replied.

"Charlotte used to buy cookies from Neiman Marcus for Christmas," Ryan said.

"That doesn't count," Kelsey said. "Let's check the cookies."

Ryan looked in the oven and shook his head. "They aren't done."

"Let me see," Kelsey looked in. "They're done. Pull them out."

"They don't look like cookies," Ryan protested. Kelsey looked at him, put on a potholder and pulled the pan out of the oven. She set the pan on the metal cooling rack to the side of the sink.

"They'll continue to cook once they're out. See the edge? When it's brown there, we pull the pan out. If you leave the pan in until they look like cookies, they'll be burnt when you remove them."

"That's weird," Ryan said.

"Trust me. I've made lots of cookies," Kelsey said.

"Are all cookies like that?" Ryan asked.

"A lot are. Usually the recipe will tell you what to look for to figure out whether it's done or not," Kelsey replied.

"Do we take them off the sheet?"

"Not yet. Let them cool for a while. Go ahead and put the other pan in the oven," Kelsey said. Ryan placed the pan in the oven and reset the timer.

"So, I'm curious. What do you usually get as gifts?" Kelsey asked. Tyler's birthday was in September, and she was clueless as to what to buy for him.

"Money," Ryan said. "What else would we get?"

"Not from your parents," Kelsey said. "From your friends."

"Like who?"

"Like Kim. What would Kim give you as a gift?"

"Why would Kim give me a gift?" Ryan asked, confused.

"I don't know. For your birthday?" Kelsey said.

"Kim's never given me a gift," Ryan said.

"Okay, forget Kim. Zach."

"Zach says I'm too rich to buy gifts for," Ryan said.

"What?" Kelsey said in surprise.

"Everyone says that," Tyler said.

"What did you get for your birthday last year, Tyler?" Kelsey asked. "Ryan, check the cookies."

"My mother wrote me a check, and so did Bob. Ryan bought me a sweater. Which he's borrowed a dozen times."

"You never wear it," Ryan explained, removing the cookies from the oven, and placing the sheet on the rack.

"That's it?"

"That's all," Tyler said.

"That's crazy," Kelsey said. "What about you, Ryan?"

"You guys took me to dinner. And I got checks from Bob and Lisa," Ryan replied.

"What did you get for your birthday last year, Kelsey?" Tyler asked her. Kelsey thought for a moment.

"My parents gave me spending money, Jasmine bought me a purse, Morgan bought me a sweater, Dylan sent me a Portland State shirt, and I was in Port Townsend, so we had a party and I got a bunch of smaller things, jewelry, a couple of books, things like that," Kelsey replied.

"Wow," Ryan said. "I guess when you're poor, people buy you things."

Kelsey frowned, but then realized that maybe Ryan had a point.

"What do you want for your birthday this year?" Tyler asked her.

"Nothing special," Kelsey said. "How about you?"

"What do you mean?" Tyler asked.

"What do you want for your birthday?" Kelsey repeated.

"I have no idea," Tyler said.

"If Tyler wanted something, he'd just buy it," Ryan said.

"But the point of gifts is to show your appreciation for someone," Kelsey said.

"I never thought about it like that," Ryan said.

"Why do you buy gifts for people then?" Kelsey asked him.

"Because people expect me to," Ryan said. "Except for you and Jess. Then, I guess, it's because you two never want anything, and it annoys me."

Kelsey giggled. "What should we want?"

"The same things that everyone else asks for," Ryan said.

"People ask you to buy them things?" Kelsey said incredulously.

"Of course," Ryan said dismissively. "They know I have the money."

"Suppose you don't want to spend it on them?" Kelsey continued.

"Then I don't."

"I think Kelsey doesn't understand people's expectations when they find out your parents are billionaires," Tyler said.

"Clearly I don't," Kelsey said.

"You and Jess aren't the norm, trust me," Tyler said.

"So Kim asking for a trip to London, that's normal?" Kelsey commented.

"More normal," Ryan agreed.

"That's crazy," Kelsey repeated. "And really rude. How can people expect you to just buy them things?"

"I don't know, but they do," Ryan said. "Tyler, we did get that nice gift from the Hudsons. The candy after first semester."

"I wouldn't call that a gift. It was more like a bribe," Tyler said.

"I agree," Kelsey said. "They're still hoping that you buy a house in Medina."

"I guess," Ryan said. "Is the first batch of cookies done?"

"They could use a little more time cooling. Unless you want to try one warm," Kelsey said.

"I do," Tyler said.

"You didn't help," Ryan said petulantly.

"I gave you moral support," Tyler commented.

"Give Tyler a cookie," Kelsey said. Ryan slid a spatula under one of the cookies and lifted one. He put it on a plate and walked it over to Tyler.

Tyler bit into the cookie. "Good work, Mr. Perkins," he said, tasting it.

Ryan and Kelsey had warm cookies of their own.

"Nice," Kelsey said. She chewed and frowned.

"Is something wrong with it?" Ryan asked in concern.

"No," Kelsey said. "I'm really disturbed that people expect you to spend money on them."

"Why?" Ryan asked.

"It just seems… I don't know. Obnoxious," she said.

"Ryan, how many people asked you to pay their tuition at Darrow last year?" Tyler asked him, glancing at Kelsey.

"Three," Ryan replied, taking another cookie.

Kelsey's mouth fell open in shock.

"I only had two ask me," Tyler replied.

"What did you say?" Kelsey asked.

"I told them to contact the Tactec Foundation," Tyler replied.

"What's that?"

"The charity arm of the company. They get a hundred letters a day, asking for money," Tyler replied.

"Seriously?" Kelsey said.

"Sure. If the letter is compelling enough, they have an account to fund personal requests," Tyler said.

"Did they know about you paying for Brandon? Were they friends?" Kelsey asked.

"No, they were strangers. And Brandon didn't tell anyone," Tyler said.

"I just can't imagine having the nerve to ask someone to pay my tuition," Kelsey said, taking another cookie and shaking her head.

"It would surprise you what people have the nerve to ask for," Tyler said.

"Kelsey, should I plate the rest of the first batch?" Ryan asked her.

"Sure, go ahead," Kelsey said. Ryan lifted the spatula and began to put the cookies onto a plate. "How does that not bother you?" Kelsey asked.

"People asking for money?" Tyler said.

"Yes," Kelsey replied.

"I guess I never thought about it," Tyler replied. "It seems normal."

"Unbelievable," Kelsey concluded. Ryan handed her the plate with cookies and Kelsey walked it to Tyler, removing one for herself. "All right, I have a different question for you," she said, sitting next to Tyler.

"Okay," Tyler said, taking a cookie and breaking it in half.

"How many people do you consider friends? I mean real friends, the kind who would help you if you were in a really bad place? Because I'm thinking that it must be difficult to separate the scammers from the people who really want to know you."

"Isn't that true for you?" Tyler asked her, as Ryan walked over and sat down.

"What do you mean?" Kelsey asked.

"You're a girl, how can you tell the difference between guys who want to know you and guys who just want to get you into bed?" Tyler continued. Ryan frowned at him.

"It's different," Kelsey said.

"Why?" Ryan asked.

"Because I think that most guys actually think that they have something to offer. What are people who ask you for money offering you?"

"You have a point," Tyler replied. "Okay, true friends. Besides the people in this room, Zach."

"I think Zach would happily pass by me in the gutter," Ryan commented. "Kimmy."

"Who would run me over with her car," Tyler said.

Ryan laughed. "Kimmy's my ride-or-die girl," he said.

"True. As much as I don't like her, I will admit that even if you went broke, Kim would be there for you. Most people wouldn't do that," Tyler said.

"Who else?" Kelsey asked.

"Brandon," Ryan said.

"Yes," Tyler agreed.

"Really?" Kelsey said in surprise.

"Although he has trouble dealing with you and Jess, Brandon is very loyal," Tyler replied.

"Except when he's suing us," Ryan commented.

"Technically, we started that," Tyler said, finishing his cookie.

"Who else?" Kelsey said. "Matthew?"

"No," Tyler said. "Matthew likes money, not us."

"Is that it? Two people each?" Ryan and Tyler looked at each other.

"I can't think of anyone else," Ryan said.

"How many can you think of for yourself?" Tyler asked.

Kelsey thought for a moment. Since she had been forced to test this theory during junior high and high school, she had a clear vision of how many people had run away from her demons, and how many had stayed to help fight them.

"I can think of at least ten," Kelsey said. At the top of her list would be Jasmine and Morgan, then Ben and another hometown friend, Matt, and at least a half dozen former teachers and counselors who had become confidants over time. Jess was an obvious new addition. She wasn't sure about Dylan, who was dealing with demons of his own.

"Wow," Ryan said to her. "That must be nice."

"Until I met the two of you, I had never really thought about how money would affect your relationships."

"It's both good and bad," Tyler said.

"I'm getting that," Kelsey said thoughtfully.

Although Kelsey managed to get through Sunday night without a run-in with Brittany, she wasn't in a hurry to go home on Monday evening after work. So when Tyler messaged her to have dinner with him, she jumped at the chance. When she arrived at Tyler's office, he was typing into his computer.

"Hi, Kels. I'm almost done."

"Okay," Kelsey said, sitting in one of the client chairs and putting her briefcase in the other. She took the pins out of her hair and let it cascade over her shoulders. When she looked up, Tyler was looking at her.

"Done?" she asked. Tyler nodded silently. He cleared his throat and said, "I'm not looking forward to going home tonight."

Kelsey laughed. Ryan had gone to pick up Kim from the airport.

"I swear, Simon picked this week to go to Arizona on purpose. I don't have a good excuse not to leave on time. What do you want for dinner?"

"Anything," Kelsey said. She had gone on a coffee date with Lucas at 3 p.m., and had eaten a yogurt then, so she wasn't starving now.

"Let's go to the Market and find something there then," Tyler said standing.

"Great," Kelsey replied, joining him. She picked up her bag and they left the office. As they stood waiting for the elevator, Kelsey spoke to Tyler.

"How did Ryan meet Kim?" she asked.

"He met her at a party in New York. Kim's from Cranston, Rhode Island, which is right down the road from Ryan's university. So Ryan gave her a ride home one night. Kim wasn't working much and Ryan wasn't attending classes often, so they hung out together."

"I thought Kim was a model when Ryan met her?" Kelsey asked as they got on the elevator.

"Kim was a model, but she wasn't famous. She was one of the many girls who try modeling, but go nowhere. When Kim met Ryan, she thought her agency was going to give her only a couple more months before they decided she didn't have what it takes, and send her back," Tyler said. "Until Ryan turned her into a superstar." he added.

"What did Ryan do?" Kelsey asked.

"He was Ryan," Tyler laughed. "Ryan took Kim shopping at the local mall, and Kim being Kim, she bought everything. To be fair, Kim was also broke and probably needed everything that she bought at the time. One thing in particular she bought was lingerie. Tons of it." Tyler and Kelsey got off of the elevator, and headed to Tyler's car.

"Ryan is generous, but he has rules. And his rule at the time was that he would buy anything for a girl, but she had to model it for him. So Kim followed the rule. And about 100 photos of Kim in lingerie ended up in Ryan's Instagram feed one weekend." Tyler opened the door of the Audi, and they got in.

"Did Kim know?" Kelsey asked.

"Of course, she didn't care. She figured that if she couldn't have a career in modeling, she might as well have a last photo shoot. Anyway, I'm sure it comes as no surprise to you that Ryan knows a lot of important people in the fashion world, and lots of them are on Instagram. The publicity was explosive for Kim. She went from nobody to being fashion's 'It Girl' overnight," Tyler said as he drove out of the lot and down the street.

"Kim was eating breakfast with Ryan at Brown that next Monday morning when her agency called her and told her to run back to New York because their phones were going crazy with bookings for her. Kim's been busy ever since."

"So Kim owes her career to Ryan," Kelsey said.

"She does."

"That was pretty clever of Ryan."

"It wasn't deliberate. I think Ryan was surprised that anyone was looking at his Instagram feed, to be honest. He almost never posts anything on it any more," Tyler said. He swung his car into a parking garage and parked the car. "Do you want to put your bag in the trunk?" he asked.

Kelsey shook her head. "I'll carry it. My wallet's inside." They got out of the car and headed to the exit. "So why is Kim here?" Kelsey asked.

"She doesn't have any bookings this week, and she decided to come for a visit. Her next shoot is in Hawaii, otherwise, she'd go visit her sister on the East Coast. Lucky us."

Kelsey giggled as they walked toward the market. "Why do you dislike her so much?" she asked.

"You've met her," Tyler replied.

"I guess," Kelsey said.

"Kim is spoiled. And putting her and Ryan together is just asking for trouble."

"Oh, oh. What about Ryan's promise to Jess?" Kelsey asked in concern.

"Ryan will stay out of trouble this week," Tyler said confidently. "Although Kim's going to do her best to destroy his resolve."

They walked through Pike Place Market and decided to have seafood.

After dinner, they strolled back to Tyler's car.

"Let me avoid Kim for a few more minutes," Tyler said, steering Kelsey into Target. He stopped at the grocery store and bought four pints of peanut butter ice cream.

"What are you doing?" Kelsey asked him, as he paid and got his bag.

"If I have to live with her, I'm going to annoy her," Tyler commented, as they left the store. Kelsey, who was still puzzled, followed him out.

As they got into the car, Kelsey remembered that she had forgotten to ask Tyler to loan her the intellectual property book Simon had given him. Things were heating up at work and she was hoping that it would clarify a few things.

"Tyler, when you have time, can you please give me the IP book Simon suggested?" she asked, as Tyler drove out of the lot.

"You can have it now if you like," Tyler replied. "I just have to drop by home."

"Next time I see you is fine," Kelsey said.

"No, let's get it now. You can help me greet Miss Chan," Tyler said. He drove to the building, and he and Kelsey rode up the elevator. Tyler sighed deeply, then opened the door to the condo.

"Hey, bro," Ryan said from the kitchen.

Kim, who was draped on the sofa, turned to see who had entered. Her long black hair swung to the side. "Tyler," she said coldly.

"Kimberly," he replied.

"Hi," Kelsey said.

"You're still dating him? You have a high tolerance for boredom," Kim said to her.

"Nice to see you too, Kim," Tyler said, glaring at her and walking to the kitchen. He put the bag on the counter.

Kim moved her legs so Kelsey could sit, and Kelsey did.

"We just got here," Ryan said to Tyler.

"Excellent. I wouldn't want to miss a minute," Tyler replied sarcastically. "I'll get the book, Kels," he said, walking into his room.

"So Ryan Bear, are you still dating the fat girl?" Kim asked him.

"Jessica's not fat," Kelsey said in outrage.

"In my world, she is," Kim replied.

"In your world, wearing pretty clothes is more important than learning things," Tyler said, leaving his room with the IP book in his hand.

"You aren't smart just because you went to Harvard," Kim commented.

"No, I went to Harvard because I'm smart," Tyler replied. "Ready, Kels?"

Kelsey stood in reply.

"I can see you haven't changed at all, Tyler," Kim said, tossing her hair and looking at him.

"Neither have you," he replied.

"I can see this is going to be an interesting week," Kelsey said.

"I certainly hope not," Tyler replied. "Ryan, I'm taking Kelsey home. Do you need anything from the store on Queen Anne?"

"Dried cranberries," Ryan said.

"What are you making?" Kelsey asked.

"More cookies. I said I'd bring some into work," Ryan replied.

Kim pouted. "I wish I could have one, Ryan Bear."

"Stay focused, Kimmy," Ryan replied.

"You could," Tyler said to her.

"I've got a shoot next week. I can't have anything," Kim snapped.

"Aw, too bad," Tyler said. "Hold on," he said, handing Kelsey the book, and walking back to the kitchen. Deliberately slowly, it seemed to Kelsey, Tyler took the four pints of ice cream out of the Target bag and put them into the freezer.

"Peanut butter?" Ryan said to him. "You don't even like peanut butter ice cream."

"I do this week," Tyler replied.

"I hate you, Tyler," Kim said, folding her arms in a huff.

"I'm glad," Tyler replied. "Let's go, Kels," he said, and they left.

On Tuesday morning, Kelsey got a message from Ryan inviting her and Tyler to lunch. So at noon, she walked over to Second and Cherry and waited for them. They arrived about two minutes after she did.

"So where are we going?" Tyler asked.

"You'll see," Ryan replied. "It's right here."

"Where's Kim?" Kelsey asked.

"At her boxing class," Ryan replied. He led them down a set of stairs and they joined a long line of business people wearing suits.

"Thank goodness," Tyler said.

"How was last night?" Kelsey asked him.

"I went straight to bed," Tyler replied.

"Heads up," Ryan said. "It's almost time to order."

"What?" Tyler said. Kelsey noted that the line was moving quite fast.

"You've been warned," Ryan said to Tyler, cutting in front of Tyler.

"What will you have?" the counter worker said to Ryan.

"Egg salad on wheat, with tomato," Ryan said promptly.

"Next," the worker said, looking at Tyler while she made Ryan's sandwich.

"Get turkey," Ryan said to him.

"I don't want turkey," Tyler said irritably.

"Then what do you want? You're holding up the line," said a tall, Asian man from behind the counter, who was ringing up customers.

"Tuna," Tyler said.

"White or wheat?"

"White," Tyler said.

"Next."

"Turkey on wheat," Kelsey said. She loved turkey and didn't want to be scolded. Brittany had done plenty of that lately.

They made their way through the line, and Ryan left Tyler to pay while he went to get a seat.

The tall cashier, said to Tyler, "So you're paying for this lovely lady too, right?"

Kelsey blushed.

"Right," Tyler said.

"She wants cake," the cashier said.

"Do you?" Tyler said.

"Of course she does," the cashier said, putting a slice on Kelsey's tray. "That will be twenty ninety-five." Tyler paid, and he and Kelsey took their trays over to Ryan, who was smiling at Tyler from a nearby table.

"Wasn't that fun?" Ryan said, taking his sandwich.

"Are we on a reality show?" Tyler asked him.

"Look around. We're surrounded by lawyers. I thought you'd like it," Ryan said.

Kelsey looked around as she bit into her turkey sandwich. It was delicious. Ryan did seem to be right — everyone in the room was wearing a suit, more than a few were reading briefs, and the conversations were littered with references to judges and filing dates.

"I guess we are near the courthouse," Tyler said, taking a bite.

"How is it?" Ryan asked.

"Great," Tyler said.

"Told you," Ryan replied, having a bite of his own. They ate their lunch, watching the other patrons in interest. The line moved like clockwork, as people ate, talked, and stood up from their tables to head back to work. After they finished their sandwiches, they shared the piece of chocolate loaf cake that Kelsey had received.

"I'm glad you wanted cake," Tyler said to her, breaking off a piece.

"Told you," called the cashier from behind his register.

On Wednesday, Kelsey attended the summer associate luncheon. She sat between Eliza and Lucas, who she hadn't seen since Monday.

"So, should we have our date on Friday night?" he asked her.

Kelsey smiled. "Sure," she replied.

Although Kelsey had been spending a lot of time with Tyler and Ryan, she had been looking forward to going on the date with Lucas. Despite Tyler's prediction that she wasn't serious about him, Kelsey did find Lucas attractive in his own way.

"Six?"

"Okay," Kelsey replied.

Lucas grinned at her. "So you didn't get a fail letter yesterday, right?" he asked.

"No," Kelsey replied. She hadn't expected one, although she still was concerned about her grades.

"Me either. I'm really happy," Lucas commented.

Kelsey looked at Lucas with a bit of surprise.

"Did you expect one?" she asked him.

"I was really worried about Con Law," he confided. "But I survived."

"I'm glad," Kelsey said honestly. Certainly, Lucas wasn't pushing himself academically.

"Let's get something nice," Lucas said. "I'll come get you at your office."

"Okay," Kelsey said giving him a smile.

After lunch, Eliza left her seat to go talk to an associate in her group, and Alex Carsten came over and sat next to Kelsey.

"How's it going, Kelsey?" he asked.

"Good," Kelsey replied. Lucas was talking to a fellow summer associate in the seat next to him.

"I understand you're working on a brief for Mary?"

"I am." Kelsey was quite nervous, since Mary was the senior partner in the IP group. She really wanted to do a good job.

"What's it about?" Alex asked her. He leaned back in his chair comfortably, as if he had all day to hear her response.

"About trademarking a color," Kelsey replied.

"Oh, that should be interesting. Have you heard of the guy who makes the shoes with the red sole?"

"Christian Louboutin?" Kelsey said.

"Wow, we have a fashionista," Alex said.

"Not really," Kelsey said, although she had to admit that thanks to getting dressed up at Tyler's behest, she knew more about fashion than she ever thought she would.

"Make sure you look at his trademark case, particularly the amicus curiae brief from Tiffany's on their blue color," Alex said.

"Okay, thanks," Kelsey said.

"You'll do fine. How are things otherwise?"

"Good," Kelsey said.

"Do you like your view?" Alex teased.

"It's great," Kelsey said sarcastically. The only saving grace was that she was too high up to notice the sound of the traffic on I-5.

"The most creative group in the firm and we have the worst offices," Alex commented. Kelsey smiled. Alex's view was only slightly better than her own. "Okay, keep me posted, Kelsey. Let me know if you need any help."

"Thanks, Alex," she said.

"Oh, good. You aren't calling me Mr. Carsten anymore," he said. "See you." He left. Kelsey looked around. Many of the summer associates had headed back to their offices. Lucas was still sitting next to her, though.

"Who is that?" Lucas asked.

"Alex Carsten. He's a senior associate in the IP group."

"Your mentor?" Lucas asked.

"No."

"What did he want?"

"Just to know what I was working on."

"I see," Lucas said. "I'll walk you back to your desk," he said, smiling.

On Thursday night, Kelsey had dinner with Tyler. Once again, he was avoiding Kimmy, and Kelsey was happy to avoid Brittany. Zachary had taken Kim out on Wednesday night, and Tyler had enjoyed his first evening at home since the weekend.

"Sorry," Tyler said to Kelsey as they stood outside the condo door.

"It's okay," Kelsey replied. "It's my fault." Tyler opened the door.

"Kim, put some clothes on!" Tyler said in exasperation as he walked into the living room with Kelsey. Kim was sitting on the sofa wearing a bra and panties, talking to Ryan.

"Such a prude," Kim said to him, getting up and walking into the guest bedroom. Tyler rolled his eyes, and Ryan grinned at him.

"How many more nights?" Tyler asked him. Kim returned wearing Tyler's Williams College shirt and a pair of shorts.

"Stay out of my clothes, Kim," Tyler said as Kelsey walked over to the coffee table and set out her tablet.

"You said to put something on," she shrugged, sitting back down next to Ryan.

"So who's hot right now?" Ryan asked her.

"Are you getting rid of your girlfriend?" Kim asked brightly.

"Of course not," Ryan pouted. "But I need to take someone to the Tactec picnic this summer. Jessica won't fly back."

"You can take me," Kim said.

No, Tyler mouthed to Kelsey, who giggled. He sat down across from her.

"I thought of that, but Zach said you'll be in the Azores on a shoot that weekend."

"Oh. Sports Illustrated. Sorry," Kim said, playing with her hair. "Who's hot?" she thought for a moment. "I know. There's this new girl. Dara Smith. Super hot. Everyone says she's the next Body."

"Really?"

"I don't know her well. I met her on a shoot in March. But she'd probably do."

"Have I seen her?"

"I don't think so. She walked a couple of shows last season, but nothing important," Kim said. She looked over at Tyler and Kelsey. "Are you doing homework? Isn't school out for the summer?"

"We're working, Kim," Tyler replied. "We go to jobs."

Kim tossed her hair. "Anyway, Ryan bear, I think you should ask her. I'll get her number for you, and I'll try to think of some other girls. But I can't imagine she's that busy right now. She's really new. And who'd turn down the opportunity to go out with Ryan Perkins?"

"Who indeed?" Ryan said.

"Hi, Kelsey." Kelsey looked up from her memo. Alex Carsten was standing at her office door.

"Hi, Alex. How are you?" Alex walked into the room and sat in one of the client chairs.

"I'm good. So what are you working on?"

"A memo for David Lim."

"What does David have you doing?"

"I'm researching causes of action for one of his clients. A band who didn't get their royalties?"

"David's lost cause. You're the designated summer associate for his busy-work this year, I see."

"What do you mean?"

"David knows all of the terrible metal bands in Seattle, and every year at least one of them complains to him because they didn't get the sixty cents of royalties that they earned for their 'album'. David always assigns the case to an unlucky summer associate. This year that associate is you."

"Why unlucky?"

"I guess you have a point. You might learn something. Like don't be friends with people who need free legal work."

Kelsey laughed.

"So what else is on your desk?" Alex asked her.

"I'm finishing the research for Shelby Johnson on calculating the damages in a software misappropriation case."

"How's that going?"

"There's a lot of case law federally, but almost nothing in Washington State."

"That's because Washington courts are full of cases about farmland and stolen cows," Alex commented.

"But we have all of these software companies here," Kelsey commented.

"Most of whom haven't been around long enough to sue each other," Alex said. "It's true everywhere really. Technology is moving much faster than the law."

"That's what I like about intellectual property. It feels very cutting-edge. Like you're helping to make the law, not just follow it."

"True." Alex said. "So do you need any help with anything?"

"I don't think so, although I appreciate the offer," Kelsey replied. Alex was really nice.

"All right," Alex said, standing. "Let me know. I'm down the hall."

"Thanks, Alex," Kelsey said.

"Anytime," he said, leaving her office.

On Friday night, Lucas arrived at Kelsey's office door holding a red rose.

"Knock, knock," he said.

"Hi, Lucas," Kelsey said.

"Ready to go?"

"I am," Kelsey said. She took her wallet out of her desk drawer and stood.

"Wow, you look great," Lucas said. Instead of her more usual blue suits and sheath dresses, Kelsey had decided to take a risk, and was wearing a flared dress with a black sleeveless top and bright pink skirt. She had gotten at least four compliments on it from staff members. Even Alex Carsten had commented on it.

"Thanks," Kelsey replied. She took the rose, and she and Lucas walked out of the door. "Where to?"

"Let's get burgers," Lucas said.

Unwilling to wait for one of the gourmet burger places that had sprung up in the Pioneer Square district that bordered their workplace, Lucas steered Kelsey into an uncrowded sports bar.

"Get what you'd like. It's on me," Lucas said.

"Thanks," Kelsey said, smoothing her dress. She felt completely out of place with what she was wearing, but Lucas didn't seem to notice. Kelsey looked at the grease-covered menu. All of the basics were there: burgers, fries, and the usual selection of drinks.

Kelsey smiled to herself. It was exactly the kind of place that she had been used to eating in when she was in college, but lately she had been running with a different crowd. One that thought that a thirty-dollar entree was a great bargain.

"What are you thinking?" Lucas asked her.

"I'm thinking bacon," Kelsey said. She knew she'd have to be careful with her dress, though.

"A bacon burger sounds good," Lucas said. "Want to split some fries?"

"Sure," Kelsey replied. The server came over and took their order. As she walked away, Lucas took Kelsey's hands and held them across the table.

"Finally. I get a real date with Kelsey North."

"We've gone out half a dozen times," Kelsey said.

"Only this counts as a date," Lucas said. Kelsey looked around at the decor of the bar. Frankly, it wasn't really first-date material. Her rose seemed particularly out of place. But Lucas seemed pleased. "How was your day?"

"It was good," Kelsey said. "I finished my brief for Shelby."

"Yeah," Lucas said. "I finished a bunch of stuff too. Now I can enjoy the weekend. I'm taking your advice and heading down to Portland with my roommate and a couple of guys from Darrow."

"Really? What are you going to do?" Kelsey asked.

"Don't know," Lucas said. "Hit some bars, the usual stuff."

"Have a good time. Portland's great," Kelsey said.

"What will you do this weekend while I'm gone?" Lucas said.

"No idea," she said. Kim was still in town, to Tyler's dismay, so Kelsey figured he would call her after he left work tomorrow and suggest something to keep himself out of the house. Since Kelsey liked to keep herself out of her own house, she would most likely join him.

"Girl stuff," Lucas said, dropping Kelsey's hands as the server put the drinks on the table. Kelsey picked up her cola and took a drink. It was watery.

Lucas spent the next hour talking about his experiences at Collins Nicol. As Kelsey ate her overcooked burger and her soggy fries, she heard about how Lucas didn't like his mentor, how the managing partner of the construction law group was too fussy, and a long commentary about how the unfair grading system in law school led to stupid people being hired as law firm associates.

By the end of the date, Kelsey had decided that perhaps Lucas had had a very bad day.

Lucas held her hand as they left the bar and walked out into the streets of Pioneer Square. The last time she had been here, she had just been dropped off by Tyler's chauffeur. How things had changed.

"Want to get a drink?" Lucas asked her. Kelsey shook her head. "Good, I'm glad you don't drink," Lucas commented. "It isn't very lady-like."

Kelsey didn't know what to say to that, so she said nothing.

"Dessert then?" Lucas asked.

"That sounds good," Kelsey replied. She and Lucas walked down the street to a candy store which catered to tourists. Kelsey ordered a handful of chocolate-dipped strawberries, while Lucas got a slice of fudge. They left the store with their purchases.

"Where to?" Kelsey asked him. Lucas smiled at her, then kissed her gently on the lips.

"Follow me," he said. Then dessert in hand, they walked down First Avenue, as the soft summer sun began to set.

Monday afternoon, Kelsey sat at her desk, working on David Lim's brief. As Alex had predicted, the case was a loser for the band.

"Hi." Kelsey looked up and Lucas was standing at the door.

"Hi," Kelsey smiled back. She hadn't seen him since Friday night, when they had walked downtown, eaten dessert, and chatted about Portland. Somehow during the walk, Lucas had managed to let Kelsey forget the dreadful dinner conversation. She thought that the chocolate, three kisses, and his cute smile helped. "How was Portland?"

"Awesome," Lucas said, sitting in one of the client chairs. "We had a great time. Did you do girl stuff here?" he asked.

Kelsey shook her head. "Not really," she replied.

"What did you do?" Lucas asked.

"I went swimming," Kelsey replied.

"All by yourself?"

"No, with Tyler Olsen," Kelsey said.

Lucas looked at her puzzled. "Tyler?"

"Yeah," Kelsey said. Bill Simon had returned, so Tyler had worked all day Saturday, but as usual his Sunday was free. He had driven her up to the Queen Anne Pool. They had spent a relaxing Sunday swimming, then they had dinner at a small bistro.

"You've seen Tyler this summer?"

"Of course."

"Does he know we're going out?"

"You asked me out in front of him, remember?" Kelsey said. She glanced at her computer. A message from David Lim had popped up on her screen.

"I do," Lucas said, frowning. "I have to go," he said standing.

Kelsey looked up. "Okay," she said.

"Do you want to go to dinner tomorrow?" Lucas asked her. "Six again?"

"I'd like that," Kelsey replied.

"I'll see you then," Lucas said in a distracted voice, and he left.

Kelsey and Lucas spent a nice evening at a small Italian restaurant in Pioneer Square the following evening. The food was better, but still not great. Lucas, on the other hand, seemed quite pleased with his day, unlike their previous date. They had another long walk in the setting summer sun, and a couple more soft, innocent kisses.

Tyler was supposed to work all weekend, so Ryan asked her if she wanted to go to one of Seattle's summer festivals with him on Sunday. A large number of food trucks were going to be set up near where they had walked in South Lake Union, and Ryan wanted to see if he could get some new recipes.

On Friday, as Lucas dropped Kelsey off at her bus stop after another dinner date, this time at a chain restaurant in downtown, he smiled at her. Kelsey smiled back.

"So, you aren't seeing Tyler this weekend, right?" he asked. Lucas was going camping with his friends all weekend.

"No," Kelsey answered, puzzled at the question.

"Great," Lucas said kissing her. "Enjoy your weekend. Stay out of trouble."

"Okay," Kelsey said. "See you Monday."

Lucas waved at her and crossed the street to get to his own bus stop. Still confused, Kelsey looked up as her bus arrived, and she got on.

On Sunday morning, as Kelsey arrived at the meeting place for Ryan, she was pleasantly surprised to see Tyler. Both boys were wearing jeans and t-shirts, as was Kelsey.

"Hi, Kels," Tyler said with pleasure.

"I wasn't expecting you," she said. "But I'm glad you could make it."

"We got the filing done early. We'll do the finishing touches on Monday," Tyler explained.

"Let's go try things," Ryan said. "What first?"

"Should we just go in order?" Kelsey asked. "Truck by truck?"

"Sounds good," Tyler said.

They had arrived early, but already there were lines at some of the trucks. Ryan had his phone out, ready to take notes if he saw anything he wanted to re-create at home.

"So how are you?" Tyler asked. "I haven't seen you all week."

"I know. I've been busy," Kelsey said. She had worked late on Monday and Wednesday on David Lim's project, then on Thursday she had been called into a meeting that went on late. She was too tired to drop by Tyler's office, and she figured that he was busy anyway, so she had gone straight home. Saturday, she had gone shopping on Capitol Hill, then locked herself in her room to avoid Brittany.

"Busy with Lucas?" Tyler asked.

"A little," Kelsey replied.

"Be careful," Tyler said.

"Of Lucas?" Kelsey asked.

"Just be careful," Tyler replied.

"Bro, have you had bacon jam?" Ryan asked Tyler.

"Bacon what?" Tyler replied. He and Kelsey walked over to Ryan to look. As they did, Kelsey wondered what was going on with the boys in her life. They were certainly acting strange.

"We should try it," Ryan said to them. The food truck was offering a grilled cheese and bacon jam sandwich.

"Why not?" Tyler asked. He pulled out his wallet and ordered one. When it was grilled, the three of them tasted it.

"Really good," Ryan said. "Do you think we could make this, Kelsey?"

"It can't be that difficult," Kelsey said. She pulled out her phone and did a Google search. "Look, here's a recipe for bacon jam. Grilled cheese sandwiches are easy."

"I know how to make grilled cheese," Tyler said.

"You can cook something?" Ryan asked.

"I am a pasta and grilled cheese sandwich expert," Tyler commented.

"Not together, I hope," Kelsey said.

"Not usually, Miss North." Tyler grinned.

"Did Chris teach you?" Kelsey asked.

"Please do not mention my father," Tyler said, taking another bite of sandwich.

"What happened?" Kelsey asked him, as Ryan licked jam off his fingers.

"He requested that I testify on his behalf, so he wouldn't have to subpoena me. I told him that not only would he have to subpoena me, I was going to fight it."

"And how did he take that?" Kelsey asked.

"Not well," Tyler replied.

"Sorry."

"It's wasn't the best of weeks," Tyler said. "What do you want to try next?"

Kelsey looked around at the food trucks on offer. "Maybe the chili," she said.

"Ryan, we're getting in line for chili." Tyler said. Ryan, who was taking a photo of a menu, nodded.

"At least Kim is gone," Kelsey said as they got in line.

"I'm so glad. By the way, do you want some peanut butter ice cream? I only managed to eat one carton in front of her," Tyler said.

"I really can't believe you did that," Kelsey said. "It is her job to be thin after all."

"She called Jess fat. She deserved it," Tyler replied.

"Okay, that's true. It's her favorite?" Kelsey asked.

"She loves it. According to Ryan, she hasn't had it in three years."

"You are evil," Kelsey giggled.

"I know. Chris said I inherited my mother's personality when I told him I was fighting the subpoena."

"I'm assuming he didn't mean that as a compliment," Kelsey said.

"You guessed right," Tyler replied.

"When did this happen?" Kelsey asked.

"Thursday night. I was at work when he called. I mean, of course I was. I knew this was going to happen."

Kelsey frowned. She felt bad for Tyler. He had finally got to know his father, and now he was once again in the middle of a battle between his parents.

"It will be okay," Kelsey said to comfort him.

But Tyler looked at her. "It won't be," he replied without emotion. "What kind of chili do you want?"

Kelsey looked at the board. There were at least a dozen choices, from habanero to venison. "Texas style?" Kelsey said.

"I was thinking that too," Tyler replied. He ordered and paid for the chili as Ryan walked over.

"Do you think Jess would like poutine?" Ryan asked her.

"Jess likes fries and cheese, so yeah, I think the added gravy would be a plus," Kelsey said, taking the plastic spoon Tyler offered her.

Kelsey tasted the hot chili. It was very spicy.

Tyler saw the look on her face. "Hang on," he said. Kelsey fanned her mouth with her hand until Tyler returned with a cup of cold water. Kelsey drank it quickly.

"Hot?" Ryan asked.

"Obviously," Kelsey replied.

Tyler tasted the chili. "Do you want to try it, Ryan?"

Ryan shook his head no. "Let's walk over there," he said, pointing to a

Thai food truck. Kelsey and Tyler followed him.

"Do you want any more chili?" Tyler asked Kelsey.

"Not unless you have a fire hose waiting," Kelsey replied. Her mouth was still burning. "How can you eat that?"

"I like it," Tyler replied. They arrived at the food truck and Ryan ordered a plate of pad thai, which he shared with Kelsey and Tyler, once Tyler had finished the chili.

"Jess likes Thai," Ryan said thoughtfully. "Maybe I should get a Thai cookbook," he said.

"Indian too," Tyler said.

Ryan glared at him. "You want me to learn how to make Indian so I can cook for you."

"So?" Tyler replied.

"Jess likes Indian too," Kelsey piped in.

"See. I'm suggesting it for Jessica," Tyler said.

"Really, Kelsey?" Ryan asked her, his blue eyes surveying her for any sign of a lie.

"Really. We don't order it because there isn't a place near school, but I know she likes it," Kelsey replied.

"Okay. If it's for Jess," Ryan said, noting it in his phone.

"Thanks," Tyler whispered to Kelsey, who giggled.

"You must be getting good, if Tyler's making requests," Kelsey commented as they threw away the empty pad thai plate and walked on.

"I'm trying," Ryan said.

"Your cooking is certainly better than the dining hall at Darrow," Tyler commented.

"That's a really low bar," Kelsey said.

"True. I want to be as good as Margaret," Ryan said.

Tyler shook his head. "That will be a while. Margaret's got decades of experience."

"Then I can cook for Jess and our grandkids," Ryan said. "I'll have lots of experience by then."

"Hope springs eternal," Tyler commented.

"Jess is going to marry me. Wait and see," Ryan pouted.

"We'll see," Tyler said. "What are we eating next?"

The trio ate their way through over a dozen trucks, stopping for all types of cuisines including fresh fish tacos, Belgian waffles and green tea ice cream. As they slowly began walking back toward downtown, Ryan looked through his notes.

"Kelsey, which do you think I should work on first? Thai, Indian, or Greek?"

"I think that Thai would be the easiest," Kelsey replied.

"Really?" Ryan asked doubtfully.

"Sure. The ingredients aren't going to be hard to get here and I don't think that the preparation is difficult," Kelsey replied.

"Why won't it be hard to find things like…" Ryan consulted his notebook, "... lemongrass?"

"Seattle has a huge Vietnamese community. Thailand's right next door to Vietnam. They probably use a lot of the same stuff. Anyway, just ask Margaret. Lisa loves Thai food, and Margaret makes it sometimes," Tyler replied.

"That makes sense. I'll start with pad thai," Ryan said. "I need a cookbook though."

"Another one?" Tyler said. "You have two dozen at home."

"You can never have enough cookbooks," Ryan admonished him.

"Perhaps you can buy them on Kindle?" Tyler said.

"Of course not," Ryan said dismissively. "Let's go to the Market."

A few minutes later, they walked toward Pike Place Market. Ryan led them into a cooking store.

"Hi, Ryan," one of the clerks said as he walked in. Kelsey glanced at Tyler in surprise. Obviously this wasn't Ryan's first time here.

"Hi, Teresa," Ryan replied. "I need a Thai cookbook." he said.

"Sure," she said, "Follow me."

"We'll be outside," Tyler said to him. Kelsey and Tyler exited the door of the store and sat on the steps outside. Kelsey looked at the view of hundreds of tourists and locals, milling around. She loved coming to Pike Place Market.

"He's really serious about this," Kelsey said to Tyler.

"Very. He makes breakfast every morning, gets recipes from his co-workers, and comes home and cooks every night. I'm not sure I've ever seen him so focused on anything," Tyler said. "Except Jessica, of course."

"Does he still talk to her every day?"

"Most days," Tyler said.

"Jess is really busy with her family, I think," Kelsey said. In fact, Kelsey knew that in addition to working and babysitting her nephews, she was also very busy trying to fend off potential dates her sister-in-law was setting her up on. She had already failed twice, and gone out with two people Jess had described as 'complete losers'."

"Are you having a good summer?" Tyler asked Kelsey.

"I am," she replied. In fact, the only dark spot was Brittany.

Tyler nodded thoughtfully.

"You don't seem to be, though," Kelsey said.

"I like spending time with you," Tyler replied. "It's okay. I'm trying to think of my time with Bill Simon as a learning experience. And I enjoy Ryan's cooking. I guess I'm just worried about my parents."

"Why? They've sued each other before," Kelsey said.

"I feel torn this time. Lisa didn't do anything. In the past, it was always easy for me to blame Lisa, and be on Chris's side. Particularly since I didn't know him," Tyler said.

"She kept him away from you."

"She's not now. Chris is just making a money grab, and I don't like it. But Chris isn't listening to me," Tyler mused. "I just don't want to be in the middle of this. I'm going to have to work with my mother on a daily basis in two years, and I don't want our relationship to be worse than it is. On the other hand, I'm just beginning to know Chris, and now I'm wondering if my mother was right about him all along."

Kelsey gently patted Tyler's back.

"I hate this," he said. Tyler sighed. They sat quietly for a minute, then Tyler said, "I really missed having you around this week."

Kelsey looked at him in surprise. "You could have called me."

"I know. I figured that you were busy," Tyler replied.

"I would have made time for you, Tyler," Kelsey said. "I thought I was giving you a break."

"I don't need a break from you," Tyler replied.

"I'll make a point of dropping by more," Kelsey promised. "And of course, I'll see you next weekend." The Tactec picnic was on Saturday.

Tyler laughed. "I know. Sorry."

"We'll have fun."

"I'm not sure that's possible," Tyler said.

"I always have fun with you," Kelsey said.

"Really?" Tyler said doubtfully.

"Always," Kelsey replied.

"Okay," Tyler replied.

"I hate that you're dating Lucas, you know that right?" he said.

"I know."

"That's why you're doing it?" he asked her.

"No," Kelsey replied.

"No? That's even worse," Tyler said.

"Let's not talk about Lucas," Kelsey said.

"Okay," Tyler said again.

"What are you filing on Monday?"

"A trial brief in an IP case," Tyler replied.

"Simon has you working on IP now?" Kelsey asked.

"Simon has me working on everything," Tyler replied. "What are you working on?"

"Nothing at the moment, I'll get a new project on Monday," Kelsey replied.

"What were you last working on?"

"A brief on music royalties and the calculation of damages in a IP case," Kelsey replied.

"Do you like Collins Nicol?" Tyler asked her.

"I do. It's a good place. I'm hoping they'll give me an offer for next year," Kelsey replied.

"I'm sure they will once they see your grades," Tyler said.

"Grades come out tomorrow," Kelsey said. She had temporarily forgotten.

"Are you worried?" Tyler teased.

"I'm always worried," Kelsey replied.

Tyler laughed. "You'll have at least two A's."

"Two?" Kelsey said. She was pretty confident about Contracts, thanks to Eliot's constant attention.

"Con Law. Every boy, and I mean every one of them, is going to drag the curve to the floor."

Kelsey giggled. Professor Schiavelli was beautiful, and she knew from talking to her male classmates that her beauty was incredibly distracting to the students learning Con Law. And of course, Schiavelli had stood at the front of the class during the exam.

"I hadn't thought of that," she said. "That's comforting."

"You'll be fine," Tyler said. He looked at the door behind him. "Where's Ryan?" he said. "He's been in there forever."

"Should we check?"

"It's okay. It's nice to be able to talk to you. Ryan's just going to ask you more cooking questions when he comes out."

"That's true. How's Zach?"

"He's good. He took Kim out twice when she was here, and I talked to him then. He's nervous about grades though. And of course, he should be."

"Did he study at all?"

"No. There's another lecture in his future when Ryan's grades get published," Tyler said. "He's certainly going be at the bottom of

Schiavelli's class."

Kelsey giggled. "Zach likes her too?"

"Let's just say Kim has a rival."

"How about Ryan? How do you think he's going do?"

"I think he's going to get his two B's. He was studying a lot last semester. He wants to make Jessica proud," Tyler said. The door opened behind them, and Ryan, carrying a large paper bag, walked out.

'Where are we going to put those?" Tyler asked him.

"We'll find a space," Ryan said. "Come on, Teresa told me where I can get lemongrass." Kelsey and Tyler followed Ryan down the hill, and walked towards the park.

"Where are we going?" Tyler asked him.

"Teresa says there's an amazing spice shop not far from the Hillclimb. She said it's a must visit for any real cook."

"And that would be you?" Tyler said.

"Exactly. Don't dawdle," Ryan replied.

Ryan led them south on Western Avenue, and looked around carefully until he found the spice shop that Teresa had suggested. They walked in and their noses filled with exotic scents.

"Wow," Ryan said. The wall of the store was lined with at least 100 jars of spices and they were surrounded by tables filled with spice blends, cookbooks, and cooking tools. "We'll be here for a while," Ryan commented.

"If you don't want to stay, there's a gelato place on the Hillclimb," Tyler said to Kelsey.

"Sounds good," Kelsey said.

"Ryan, message me when you're done," Tyler said. Ryan, waved his hand distractedly as he headed down the stairs of the store to look around.

"Come on, let's go," Tyler said in amusement.

He and Kelsey walked to the Pike Place Hillclimb and walked down the stairs to the restaurant. They ordered cones and sat on the patio.

"Do you want to try mine?" Kelsey asked.

"We'll trade," Tyler said, offering her his chocolate hazelnut gelato.

Kelsey took Tyler's cone and gave him her strawberry and cream cone in return. He took a lick and gave it back.

"Tired of peanut butter ice cream?" Kelsey teased him, tasting his gelato before returning his cone.

"Very," Tyler said. "Your strawberry gelato is good though," he added.

"I think you're going to be eating pretty well over the next few weeks, thanks to Ryan," Kelsey said. Tyler was right, the gelato was cold, sweet and delicious.

"It looks like it. Margaret is supposed to come back for a lesson this week, so if nothing else, she'll bring food," Tyler replied.

They sat quietly, eating their gelato in the sunshine. Kelsey mulled over the things that Tyler had mentioned this afternoon, but her mind focused on his comments about Lucas.

Why was she dating him? Was it to push Tyler into asking her out? Was it because she really was falling for Lucas? Or was he just a summer distraction?

Kelsey watched Tyler's brown eyes follow a passing hummingbird. After several dates with Lucas, she knew that despite the cute smile, Lucas wasn't for her. She knew it, Tyler knew it, but Lucas didn't seem to.

She enjoyed being with him, though, so she wasn't sure what to do next. Was she leading him on, or was he comfortable with their casual relationship? Kelsey had no idea. As she ate her gelato, and looked at the boy who was much more to her than a summer fling, she wondered what to do.

At 3 p.m. on Monday, Kelsey's phone rang. She picked it up.

"Hello?"

"Kelsey?"

"Hi, Dad," Kelsey said. She held her breath. Today was the day that her grades would arrive from Darrow. She had had them sent home.

"Kelsey, your mother and I are quite disappointed. Your grades came today," her father said in serious voice.

Kelsey smiled. She had got straight A's. Her father would never joke with her otherwise.

"Really? Are they that bad?" Kelsey decided to play along.

"Dreadful," her father continued. "Contracts. A critical class for any lawyer. And you got a D?"

"Impossible," Kelsey said.

"Why?" her father asked.

"Darrow doesn't give out D's," she replied.

"Oh," her father said. "All right, I misread that one. You got an A. But what's this? A C?"

"A C?" Kelsey asked.

"Darrow does give out C's, right?"

"Oh, yes. They do."

"Well, Professor Spaghetti seems to have given you one," her father said.

"Nope," Kelsey replied.

"How can you be so confident?"

"Professor Schiavelli could be a supermodel. All of the boys will have dragged down the curve. The lowest I could have gotten was a B. Every boy in class will have done worse than me." Except Tyler, Kelsey thought to herself.

"Fine. You got me. Congratulations on your straight A's. We're very proud of you, Kels."

"Thanks, Dad," Kelsey said joyfully.

"How are you?"

"I'm great."

"How are you enjoying Seattle?"

"It's wonderful."

"Are you having fun with your friends?"

"I am. It's really nice here in the summer," Kelsey replied.

"It is," her father said.

"How's Port Townsend?"

"Missing you," her father said.

"I miss you too," Kelsey said sadly.

"Okay, I won't keep you away from work. Have a good week, okay?"

"I will. Love you, Dad," Kelsey said.

"I love you too, Kels," her father said, and disconnected.

Kelsey was so happy. She looked on Google, but to her surprise, Tyler and Ryan's grades hadn't been posted online. She assumed Tyler's lawsuit against the blogger who had posted them last semester had warned others away. Kelsey picked up her phone and sent him a message.

Did you get your grades? she asked.

Straight A's. You?

Same.

Congratulations, Miss North.

How did Ryan do?

One C, two B's and an A.

In what? Kelsey typed in surprise. Ryan had got an A?

Schiavelli.

No way.

Ryan's seen a lot of beautiful women. I guess he wasn't distracted. Tyler replied. *How about your boyfriend?*

Kelsey looked at the phone for a moment, puzzled. Then she frowned.

Ha, ha. she wrote.

Just wondering. Tyler wrote. Kelsey could picture the smug look on his face. Lucas wasn't a great student.

I'll see you later.

Okay. See you later, Princess. Tyler wrote. Kelsey smiled and put the phone aside.

"Ready, Kelsey?" Lucas asked her the next evening. Kelsey looked up from her desk.

"I'm ready," she replied.

"You look great," Lucas said to her. If nothing else, dating Lucas was certainly good for her self-esteem.

"Thanks," she said standing. She smoothed out her red sheath dress and put on her jacket. She picked up her bag, walked out from behind her desk and joined Lucas.

The two of them left the office, and in the elevator Lucas took her hand.

"So I thought we'd just eat downstairs tonight," he said. "Happy hour is over, but I'm sure we can find something good."

Good, as Kelsey had learned over the past couple of weeks, meant inexpensive. It was okay, though because Kelsey knew the value of the salary she and Lucas were earning over the next couple of months. Although the amount would mean nothing to Tyler and Ryan, it would help to defray the cost of the next semester at Darrow.

"That would be great," Kelsey said. She loved the classic look of the seafood-and-steak restaurant in their building, and she had always wanted to try it. They got out of their elevator on the 40th floor lobby, switched to the express elevator to the main lobby, and headed the rest of the way down.

"How was your day?" Lucas asked in the elevator.

"It was good. I got a new assignment, and it looks pretty interesting. I'm working on a software contract. How about you?"

"I'm still working on the memo about the lien. Boring," Lucas said.

"Oh," Kelsey said. Lucas had been working on the same memo for days. When he had first described it, it sounded simple. She wondered why it was taking so long. They reached the lobby, and holding hands, they walked over to the escalators and headed downstairs. Lucas gave her a kiss.

"So," Lucas asked as they reached the top of the last set of escalators and got on, "What do you want to do this weekend?"

"This weekend? Today's the 21st, right?"`

"Right. I know because Jeff's going to court on the 24th and he's going to kill me if this memo isn't done," Lucas commented. They got off the escalator and walked toward the door closest to the restaurant.

"I can't go out this weekend," Kelsey said as they walked outside. The evening air was perfect as they strolled the few steps to the restaurant.

"Why not?" Lucas asked. "You don't have to work, do you?"

"No, of course not," Kelsey said. "I told Tyler I'd go to the Tactec picnic."

"Tyler again?"

"Yeah," Kelsey said.

"Tell him you can't go," Lucas ordered. They walked past the outside tables and into the restaurant. "Two for dinner," Lucas said to the server.

"One moment," the server said, walking off. The restaurant was crowded with office workers who were finishing their evening with drinks and dinner.

"I can't do that," Kelsey said to Lucas. "I promised him I'd go to the picnic with him ages ago."

"You're dating me now," Lucas replied. "You can't go."

Kelsey looked at Lucas in surprise. Then she laughed.

"You're joking with me, right?" Kelsey said.

"No," Lucas said seriously. "You can't go."

"I'm going," Kelsey said to him.

"No, you aren't. Not if you're dating me," Lucas replied.

"Your table is ready," the server said to Lucas. He looked at Kelsey, and she dropped his hand.

"Then I guess I'm not dating you," Kelsey said, and she walked out of the restaurant.

Kelsey walked slowly down Fifth Avenue. She couldn't believe what had just happened with Lucas. She knew that he was traditional, but this was beyond words. Lucas knew that she was friends with Tyler, as well as plenty of other guys. What was he thinking?

She walked in the gentle sun, enjoying the rays shining on her. She didn't feel anything but outrage. How dare Lucas order her around? Once again, Tyler had been right. She stopped suddenly in the street.

Why had Tyler warned her? What did he know about Lucas that she didn't?

Kelsey pulled out her phone. She decided that she wanted to find out. Now.

Are you at the office? she typed.

Of course. Where else would I be? :) Tyler replied.

Can I talk to you? Kelsey asked. It was almost seven p.m., so she hoped that Tyler could take a break.

Sure, just come by. Tyler replied.

I'll be there in five. Kelsey replied. She had been to Tyler's office enough this summer to know that he always welcomed a visit from her, and never saw it as an interruption in his day. Kelsey walked down to Second Avenue, and into Tyler's building. She reached the offices of Simon and Associates and was surprised to see that the door was open and the receptionist was still working at her desk. The receptionists at Collins Nicol were always gone by 5:15.

"Hi, I'm here to see Tyler," Kelsey said to her.

"You know where his office is?" the receptionist asked, not unkindly. Kelsey nodded.

"Just go back," the receptionist said, waving her hand and turning back to her work. As Kelsey walked down the hall, she could tell that the office was on a deadline. Almost every room had a frantic-looking associate sitting in front of their computer, typing away. She walked to Tyler's office where he was doing the same, although he didn't look frantic. He looked up.

"That was quick," he said. "What's up?" he asked. But before she could answer Tyler, a male voice spoke behind her.

"Done yet, Olsen?" Kelsey turned around, and looked into Bill Simon's eyes.

"Fifteen minutes," Tyler replied, looking back down.

"You have ten," Bill replied. "Hello, Miss North," he said, as he left the room.

"Give me a minute, Kels," Tyler sighed. Kelsey stood next to the window, and watched the summer sun over Elliot Bay. She wondered if Tyler ever noticed the view. Tyler typed furiously into his computer for a few minutes, then he said, "Nice to see you."

Kelsey looked over at him. "You too," she replied.

"I'm looking forward to having Saturday off," Tyler replied. He stretched gently in his chair. "You should have dinner with Ryan sometime. He wants someone to experiment on with his cooking. He's moved on to fish."

Kelsey smiled. "Really?"

"It doesn't keep well in the fridge, so I haven't given his latest meals good reviews. Ryan swears that it tastes better right out of the pan."

"Maybe I'll stop by," she said.

"He would like that," Tyler replied. "How are you?"

"I just broke up with Lucas."

Tyler smiled. "So you're good, then?"

"Funny, Tyler."

"Sorry, but I told you he was trouble."

"That's why I'm here. Why did you tell me that? What happened between you and him?"

Tyler pondered Kelsey for a moment, then he sighed.

"It wasn't a big deal," he replied.

"Tell me," Kelsey said forcefully.

"Sit. Please," Tyler replied.

Kelsey sat in one of the two client chairs and placed her bag into the second.

"Lucas came into the office last week and told me to leave you alone," Tyler said.

"What?" Kelsey said.

"Simon threw him out and told me to report it to Tactec security."

"No way. Lucas?"

"I was surprised too," Tyler said. "I didn't expect that." Tyler looked at Kelsey. "Mom wanted me to get a restraining order, but I told her that Simon told Lucas not to come back or he'd call Collins Nicol. I figured he didn't want to lose his job."

"Did he threaten you?" Kelsey asked in concern.

"Not exactly."

"So why did you need to report it to Tactec?" Kelsey said knowingly.

Tyler was silent.

"Tyler, I'm sorry," Kelsey said.

"It's not your fault. I guess I thought you should be careful, though," Tyler replied. "Why did you break up?"

"He ordered me not to go to the Tactec picnic."

Tyler laughed. "I cannot imagine ordering you to do anything," he commented.

"It didn't go well," Kelsey replied, smiling.

"Obviously," Tyler said. "You don't have to go, you know."

"I know. But I wasn't going to let Lucas decide for me."

"I'm surprised he tried. I guess he hasn't learned anything about you over the past couple of months," Tyler said.

"I guess not," Kelsey said. She leaned back in her chair. "So how late will you be here? It looks like you've got a big deadline."

"We always have a big deadline," Tyler said dismissively. "To answer your question though, I'll probably be here at least until midnight. That's the filing deadline."

"Have you eaten?"

"Not yet. Ryan offered to bring lukewarm fish, but I thought I'd order pizza. Should I order for two?"

"Are you inviting me for dinner?" Kelsey teased.

"Absolutely. You can help me work," Tyler said.

"If I'm going to help you work, I want something better than pizza," Kelsey replied.

"Done," Tyler replied. "What do you want?"

Kelsey thought for a moment. After eating on her budget and Lucas's, she had only one criteria for a meal paid for by billionaire Tyler Olsen.

"Something expensive," she said.

A few hours later, after finishing the finest sushi Kelsey had eaten in Seattle, Kelsey sat cross-legged on the floor reading a case on Tyler's iPad. Her jacket was draped over her lap. Bill Simon walked in.

"Have I hired a new summer associate?" he asked Kelsey, smiling.

"Not yet," Tyler replied. "She's really smart, though. You should steal her away from Collins Nicol."

"Another summer associate from Collins Nicol?" Bill asked Tyler.

"Kelsey's the girl I'm supposed to stay away from," Tyler replied.

"You aren't doing a very good job of staying away," Bill replied.

"I don't take orders well," Tyler replied.

"That I know," Simon countered. "Where's my brief?"

"On the way. I'm looking for a few more cases," Tyler replied.

"You or Miss North?"

"One guess," Tyler replied.

"Make sure you pay her," Simon said and he left the room.

"You can pay me in sushi," Kelsey said.

"My hourly is less than the cost of the sushi we just ate," Tyler replied.

"That's why you can pay me in sushi," Kelsey commented.

Tyler laughed. "Good call. I make nothing."

"I think you can use this one," Kelsey said, standing carefully and handing Tyler the iPad. He took it and looked at the case.

"Thanks, Counsel," Tyler said. He set the iPad on the side of the desk and began typing again.

"What else can I do?" Kelsey asked.

"Just wait for me at this point. I'll drive you home."

"You don't have to do that," Kelsey said automatically. She knew it was pointless, Tyler would never let her go home alone this late.

"It's late," Tyler replied. "I'll be done soon."

"Okay. Thanks," Kelsey said.

"Thank you," Tyler said. "I appreciate your help."

Kelsey looked at her phone. It was 11:30.

Fifteen minutes later, Bill Simon looked in on Tyler again.

"Is it okay?" Tyler asked him.

"It will do. Christine is editing it. Why did you cite Alice v. CLS Bank International?"

"I thought it was relevant," Tyler replied.

"It wasn't," Bill Simon commented and walked out.

"I don't have to worry about inflating my ego here," Tyler said, rubbing his eyes tiredly.

"What time did you get here this morning?" Kelsey asked.

"Six," Tyler replied.

"And you haven't left?"

"Nope. Want to go?" Tyler asked her.

"Simon isn't coming back?" she asked.

"Only to complain. I'm done for the night," he replied.

"Do you want to wait until they file? The deadline's only a few minutes away," Kelsey said.

"You're so diligent," Tyler said.

"So are you."

"Not in this office. I thought Sophia was bad. But I've reached my limit with Simon."

"You haven't quit yet."

"If I left on my own, I'd never hear the end of it from my mother. I'm staying until Simon throws me out. Which should be in a day or two."

"Doubtful," Kelsey replied, amused.

"Wishful thinking," Tyler said, yawning. He turned his chair, glanced out at the dark night and turned back.

"What time do you want me for the picnic?" Kelsey asked.

"Early. We need to drive to Redmond and Lisa wants Ryan and me to be there to greet everyone. Just stay over at our house on Friday night."

"It's in Redmond?"

"Tactec is renting Marymoor Park. We can stay for the concert afterwards if you want."

"Who is it?"

'"Some band from the eighties. General Public, I think. Lisa likes them."

"It's up to you," Kelsey replied.

An associate in a navy suit and fashionable glasses came to Tyler's door and he looked up.

"We've filed. Go home and get some sleep. By the way, good job on the draft," the associate said.

"Thanks, Christine," Tyler said.

Christine left and Tyler stood.

"Let's go," he said to Kelsey. She stood and put on her jacket. Tyler picked up her bag and they left the office.

On Wednesday, Kelsey was happy not to run into Lucas. At Collins Nicol, their respective offices were far apart. When they returned to Darrow, she didn't think she'd be as lucky.

Kelsey was surprised at how little she cared about breaking up with Lucas. She guessed it was because she knew all along that he wasn't the one. It probably also helped that she had spent time with Tyler last night.

"Miss North?" One of the support staff stood in her doorway, holding a bouquet of pink roses.

Kelsey sighed. She hoped this wasn't Lucas's way of making up, because she wasn't interested.

"Yes. Thank you," Kelsey said. The young man placed the roses on her desk and she picked up the card. Kelsey smiled. The card was in Tyler's handwriting. She glanced at the envelope. The flowers were from the flower shop in the lobby of Tyler's building.

Thanks for your help. Let me know when you want your pay in sushi. See you this weekend.
Love, Tyler

Kelsey pulled out one of the roses and sniffed it. She placed the card back into its envelope and placed it back in the flowers.

Thursday afternoon, Kelsey ran into Lucas at the Starbucks on the 40th floor.

"Nice roses," he sniped. "Back with the billionaire?"

Kelsey ignored him.

"I knew I couldn't compete with that amount of money," Lucas continued. Kelsey seethed, but remained silent. She took her iced green tea when it was finished, and walked past Lucas without a word.

Friday night, Kelsey arrived at Ryan's condo after work.

"Tyler has a filing. He'll be back after midnight," Ryan said, as she sat on the sofa and draped her jacket over the sofa arm. "What do you want for dinner?"

"Anything. Ryan. I can cook," Kelsey said.

"Don't be silly. How about risotto?" Ryan asked.

"Risotto sounds amazing," Kelsey said.

"Great, I'll get started," Ryan replied.

"Tyler said you've been making fish," Kelsey commented.

"Would you prefer that?" Ryan asked.

"No, just making conversation," Kelsey replied.

"I'm out of fish. I cooked salmon last night," Ryan said, taking down a skillet. "I figured I wouldn't have time to cook this weekend, so no point in buying more until Monday. It wouldn't be fresh."

"So how are you?" Kelsey asked him, as Ryan placed some butter in the pan, and began to melt it. He hadn't measured it. Ryan had become quite confident in the kitchen, Kelsey noted.

"Good," Ryan said.

"Looking forward to tomorrow?" Kelsey teased.

"Not really," Ryan replied. "So Tyler told me you broke up with the dweeb."

"His name is Lucas," Kelsey replied.

"Whatever," Ryan said. He swirled the butter in the pan and turned down the heat. He began chopping an onion. "Good, I'm glad he's history."

"What do you care?"

"You should be with Tyler," Ryan said. He put the chopped onion in the pan and stirred it with a wooden spoon. He took some garlic off of the counter and began to chop it as well.

"Tell Tyler," Kelsey said.

"He knows what I think," Ryan said.

"Why are you telling me this?" Kelsey said to him.

Ryan glanced at her as he tossed the chopped garlic into the onions, and once again gave it a stir.

"I thought you should know."

"I know what you think," Kelsey said back to him.

She also knew what Jessica thought. This morning when she had spoken to her, Jessica had told Kelsey that she although she hadn't said anything before, she thought it was wrong for Kelsey to have dated Lucas.

"Really, Kels. I know you say you aren't dating Tyler, but it isn't true. It's like you were dating two guys at once," Jessica had said.

"And? What's wrong with dating two people at the same time if they both are okay with it?" Kelsey had responded.

"Is that the kind of girl you are? Anyway, Lucas wasn't okay with it," Jessica replied.

"So I broke it off."

"You shouldn't have been dating him in the first place," Jessica had concluded.

Kelsey wondered whether Ryan had talked to Jessica after she had. She decided not to ask him. Ryan probably had a different opinion than Jess about the ethics of dating two people at a time anyway.

"So what should I do, Ryan? Wait forever?" Kelsey challenged him.

Ryan glanced at her with his bright blue eyes. He gently stirred the onions and garlic. He frowned.

"No," he admitted. "Just don't pick a jerk next time."

"Pick someone I'd like to marry then. Someone really great," Kelsey teased.

"If you want Tyler to ask you out, you'll have to pick someone who seems like a real threat. Lucas wasn't that," Ryan commented.

"So you want me to pick someone I really like so Tyler asks me out, then I should break up with the new guy and go out with Tyler," Kelsey said.

"Right."

"Do you know how insane that sounds?" Kelsey said.

Ryan stirred the skillet. "Do you like Tyler?" he asked her.

"You know I do," Kelsey said. However, she knew that Ryan didn't know how much she did. Zachary wouldn't have told Ryan, although it was possible that he had told Tyler about her feelings, which she had admitted to Zach at the ballpark.

"Do you want to marry him?" Ryan asked.

"I don't know about that," Kelsey said in surprise.

"I know I want to marry Jess," Ryan commented. "Why don't you know if you want to marry Tyler?"

"Because he hasn't asked me out."

"I don't get that."

"Ryan, I'm not thinking of actual commitment, when I can't even get the temporary commitment of a date," Kelsey said.

Ryan laughed. "Why are you stuck on this? You know he likes you."

"I guess I don't understand why he won't ask me out on a real date. Guys ask me out all of the time, and it's not a big deal. Tyler knows I'll say yes."

"That's what he's afraid of," Ryan said, stirring. The scent of the onions and garlic made Kelsey hungry.

"He's afraid I'll say yes," Kelsey said. "Ryan, sometimes you make no sense," she added in exasperation.

"You're the one for him," Ryan said looking at the skillet and stirring briskly. "Chris was the one for Lisa."

Kelsey looked at Ryan in interest.

"Lisa built Tactec for Chris," Ryan continued, "then he was gone. That's why Tyler can't, won't move forward with you. He's afraid you'll leave him too."

Kelsey pondered this. "So what you're saying is that if Tyler asks me out, it means he wants to marry me."

"That's the end game for him," Ryan said.

"That's the end game for everyone in a serious relationship," Kelsey said. "But breaking up is the risk in any relationship."

"Tyler doesn't like risk," Ryan commented. "He wants to know that you're as serious about him as he is about you. And your dating randoms isn't helping with that. If you dated someone decent, he might be worried enough to act."

"I don't care," Kelsey said. "It's not up to you. Or to Jess. Or to Tyler. I want what I want. And if I don't get a real commitment from him, I'm not going to pretend that I have one. And in the meantime, I'll date who I please."

"He loves you," Ryan said.

"Not enough," Kelsey replied firmly.

He turned off the heat and put the spoon aside. He turned and looked at Kelsey.

"What is he waiting for?" she asked Ryan.

"Courage," Ryan replied softly. "The courage to be willing to lose you."

Kelsey got dressed in the master bedroom the next morning. She was wearing a dress of white lace, which was so intricately made that even without the designer label, she realized that it must have cost thousands of dollars. It had been waiting for her in the closet, along with the accessories to match.

One thing that she appreciated about Jeffrey, was that he had realized after the first event that Kelsey didn't care what she wore, and therefore she had never been faced with having to decide between two dresses. Every event since the Tactec Holiday party, Kelsey had been given one perfect outfit, and her role was simply to put it on. That she could handle.

Kelsey had put her conversation with Ryan out of her mind. She had gone to bed before Tyler had arrived last night, to make sure she got enough rest. Today was going to be a long day.

"Kelsey, can you please get the door? It's Dara." Ryan called out from the bathroom. Kelsey stood up and walked to the door, straightening her dress as she walked. She opened the door to the most beautiful girl she had ever seen.

At least three inches taller than Kelsey, with big hazel eyes and a beautiful smile, Dara Smith glided into the room, a garment bag folded over one impossibly slim arm and a tote bag over the other shoulder. She wore jeans and a tightly fitted white t shirt.

"I'm Dara. Is Ryan here?" she asked Kelsey.

"Hi, Dara," Ryan called. "I'll be out in a minute."

"I'm Kelsey," Kelsey said.

"Lovely to meet you," Dara said.

Ryan walked out wearing a bathrobe and drying his hair with a towel.

"Hi, Dara," he said. She kissed him on the cheek. Kelsey knew that Ryan had met her for the first time over coffee yesterday so he could prepare her for the event. Tyler had joined them and had told Kelsey that Dara seemed nice.

"Where do I change?" Dara asked.

"You can take my bedroom," Ryan said. "My jacket's in the hall."

Dara smiled. "Let's take a selfie," she said, pulling out her phone.

"Like this?" Ryan asked.

"Of course. You look cute fresh out of the shower," Dara said. She posed next to Ryan, puckering up as if for a kiss and Ryan laughed. Dara snapped the photo. "Okay, I'll get ready," she said, walking into the bedroom.

Ryan returned to the bathroom, and Tyler walked out of his bedroom, wearing his suit pants and dress shirt. "Is Dara here?"

"She is," Kelsey said. "Wow."

Tyler laughed. "She's not my type."

"Really? I would think she's every guy's type," Kelsey said. "Make sure I'm not in any photos with her."

"You can hold your own, Miss North," Tyler said, tying the loose tie around his neck into a neat windsor knot.

"Kelsey?" Dara said, walking out of Ryan's bedroom, wearing his blue plaid bathrobe.

"Yes?" Kelsey asked, turning to her.

"Did you bring a blow dryer? I brought the wrong adapter for mine," Dara said.

"Sure, I'll get it for you," Kelsey said. She walked over to her tote bag and began rummaging around. Every since she had started being Tyler's standing date, she had acquired a hair dryer, curling iron and a slightly larger cosmetic bag. She planned to put it in Tyler's car in case she needed a touch-up during the picnic.

"What's up?" Ryan asked, walking out of the bathroom wearing his suit pants, and unbuttoning the cuffs of the shirt he was going to wear.

"Selfie," Dara said, posing next to his bare chest. They smiled and Dara took the photo. Kelsey handed Dara the hair dryer.

"Thanks," Dara said, walking back into Ryan's bedroom. Ryan finished unbuttoning the shirt and slipped it over his shoulders.

"She's as bad as Jess. Do you really need a picture of everything you do?" Ryan commented to Tyler as the hair dryer began to blow.

"Seemingly so," Tyler said, looking into the mirror. He turned back. "I'll put on my jacket when you two are ready."

"Sorry, sorry," Ryan said. He walked back into the bathroom.

"You're the only one ready to go," Tyler said to Kelsey.

"Maybe I'm the only one not dreading it?" Kelsey teased. She reached up and straightened his tie.

"Probably," Tyler said. "Thanks," he looked at her. "You look perfect. Really beautiful."

Kelsey blushed. "Thank you," she said. She picked up her purse.

Ryan returned from the bathroom, shirt on and tie undone. He walked over to the mirror and began to tie his tie.

"Do you want to grab a snack?" Tyler asked Kelsey. "There won't be a lot of food at this picnic for us. We'll be too busy smiling."

"It's okay," Kelsey said.

"We'll eat after," Tyler commented.

Dara walked out of the bedroom. She wore a soft yellow sundress, little makeup and looked absolutely stunning. No wonder they called her the 'Body' as Kim had put it. Kelsey was sure Dara would be a supermodel within weeks. She just needed the right person to see her.

"I'm ready," Dara said to them, swinging a tiny yellow purse.

"Just a moment," Ryan said. He walked into the hall closet and retrieved his jacket.

"Let's go," he said, and the group left the condo.

Tyler and Ryan drove the girls separately. Ryan's car sped away as soon as they hit I-5.

"So how long did you spend with Dara yesterday?" Kelsey asked Tyler.

"Ten minutes, I think. I made Ryan and Dara come to the Starbucks in my building because I barely had time to leave the office."

"On a Friday?"

"Fridays are the worst if Simon's in town. He's always trying to get an advantage in his cases. He likes to file on Fridays because his clients stay out of the news. Plus I think he enjoys making opposing counsel work over the weekend."

"I didn't know that," Kelsey said impressed. "You are learning things by working for Simon."

"He's a genius. Which isn't working in my favor these days," Tyler said. He merged onto 520 and headed toward the Eastside.

"I know. I'm feeling bad for you," Kelsey said.

"How's Collins Nicol?"

"Absolutely fine."

"Did Lucas like the flowers?" Tyler asked mischievously.

Kelsey looked at Tyler, who was smiling.

"How do you know that he saw them?"

"Because I paid the delivery guy to accidentally take them to his office first," Tyler replied.

"You didn't," Kelsey said.

"No one is mean to my Kelsey," Tyler replied.

Kelsey giggled. "I don't believe you, Tyler Olsen."

"I have to have fun when I can," he replied.

"He wasn't pleased," Kelsey said.

"Excellent," Tyler said. "Let me know if he doesn't leave you alone. He had his chance."

"Is every guy I date merely a placeholder until you're ready to ask me out?" Kelsey asked.

Tyler glanced at her, then put his eyes firmly on the road.

"Yes," he replied seriously.

"You are the most arrogant person I have ever met," Kelsey replied.

"Thank you," Tyler said, a smile playing on his lips.

"Why do I put up with you?" Kelsey said.

"No idea. But I'm glad you do," Tyler replied. He reached out and brushed her blonde hair gently with his hand.

"My last name had to be North," Kelsey said.

"Mine was supposed to be Davis, so it might not have mattered," Tyler commented. "Anyway, the real problem is that you came to Darrow. It wasn't like I was going to miss meeting you. The class is only 78 people now."

"I suppose," Kelsey mused. "Wait, more people failed out? There were more than eighty before exams."

"Sophia said at least three more students failed. Dean Wilson is rather unhappy with admissions right now. He attributes the failure rate to them not being rigorous enough about admits."

Kelsey laughed. "Of course it can't have anything to do with the professors being too harsh."

"Dean Wilson was once a professor. They can do no wrong," Tyler replied.

"So how is Sophia?"

"She's fine. She says Massachusetts is too hot and boring. I assured her one of those things would change by November."

"Have you spoken to anyone else since we left?"

"Keith said hello. He likes Olympia and he's enjoying his clerkship.

There seems to be a special clerk at the Supreme Court that is making the experience even better. Her name is Ellie. Otherwise, I've just talked to Brandon. Matt's still in hiding."

"How's the Tactec lawsuit?"

"Dragging. You should ask Ryan. He knows everything about it now. I haven't been paying attention. It won't affect the company's bottom line."

"How's Zach?"

"Miserable. He hates working at his parents' office."

"Will Kim come back this summer?"

"I hope not," Tyler replied.

Kelsey giggled.

"How's Jess?" Tyler asked.

"Ryan talks to her almost every day. You don't know?" Kelsey asked.

"All Ryan talks about is how much he misses her," Tyler replied.

"He's so cute," Kelsey said. "Jess is fine. She misses all of us too. I think she'll stay in Seattle next year. Her parents are driving her crazy and her sister-in-law is busy setting her up on dates." Kelsey thought about that in light of what Jessica had said about dating two people at once. She supposed Jessica would say in her defense that she didn't want to go on the dates at all.

"Really? They still don't know about Ryan?"

"Not a word."

"It must be strange to have a private life," Tyler said.

"Yours seems pretty private. At least compared to Ryan's. Jess still reads the 'Ryan Watch' blog."

Tyler laughed. "Why? It's all lies."

"I have no idea."

"Maybe she feels closer to him by having a weekly fictional update of what he's supposed to be doing," Tyler commented. "Do you read it?"

"I'd like to think I have a life," Kelsey commented. "Anyway, I'm not dating Ryan." Kelsey shook her head. "Jess reads all of that stuff. I guess it comes with being the daughter of dentists."

"What do you mean?"

"All the celebrity magazines in the waiting room," Kelsey explained.

"As long as she doesn't believe it, it's fine," Tyler said.

"How you manage to keep your life private?"

"I'm boring. Ask Kimmy," Tyler replied. "Also, my mother loves to sue on my behalf. She went after a tabloid with a vengeance after a picture of me was published when I was in college. I think that it's had a chilling effect on anyone who wants to write about me."

Kelsey nodded. It explained why although she had seen photos of Tyler in the media, she had never, not once, seen an article mentioning him that wasn't about Tactec or the trust.

"Do you ever Google yourself?" Tyler asked.

"Jasmine did after the Tactec holiday party, but I wasn't identified in any of the photos. I was 'and guest.'"

"Is that good or bad?" Tyler asked her.

"Good. I don't need any press," Kelsey said. She was famous enough in her hometown for all of the wrong reasons.

"I worry about that sometimes. You being linked with me."

"Why?"

"I don't want you to lose the freedom you have as a private citizen. It's precious."

"You have yours."

"I won't for long," Tyler said. "My mother has no privacy at all. I expect the same once I leave Darrow and go work for Tactec."

"Because you'll become a public figure?" Kelsey asked.

"I have a feeling I might."

"I don't know. I mean, no one is blogging about your mother's favorite flavor of toothpaste. They write about what she does with the business."

"I suppose. They wrote about her relationship with Tim Meyer."

"But he's also her lawyer," Kelsey said. "So maybe that's different?"

"Maybe. You aren't concerned?"

"No," Kelsey said. But to be honest, she really hadn't considered it. Suppose someone began to look into her former life. What would that look like in the tabloids? She put the thought out of her mind. The people who loved her already knew her at her worst. It didn't matter what strangers thought. Of course, she hadn't told Tyler about her past. She wondered what he would think. She decided not to think about it. Her life certainly hadn't been as colorful as Ryan's.

"I'm glad. There will be lots of photos and reporters today, so I hope that you're ready to smile."

"I bought a special whitening toothpaste."

Tyler looked at her. "You didn't."

"Of course I did. My job today is to look good," Kelsey said.

"I really should pay you. You take this way too seriously," Tyler said.

"You can pay me in sushi," Kelsey grinned.

As Tyler had predicted, there was media all over the event. Unlike the holiday party, the Tactec picnic was open to everyone in the corporation, not just upper management, and Lisa and Bob used it to announce new corporate initiatives. Tyler told that Lisa had been hoping to announce the finalization of the Taiwan purchase, but of course, it was still incomplete.

Lisa, as always, looked fashionably radiant. She was wearing another silk dress, this time a red-and-gold halter dress. Bob, who had been in Arizona working on a deal, looked newly tan. Dara and Ryan circulated, Dara absolutely stunning in her dress. And Kelsey escorted Tyler, keeping a sunny smile on her face all day. She knew her jaw would hurt tonight.

"Hello, Kelsey," Lisa Olsen said when Kelsey and Tyler finally spoke to her. When they had arrived, they had immediately been taken by the PR team to an area to greet picnic-goers that was far from Lisa, Bob, and the executive team.

"Hello, Ms. Olsen," Kelsey said.

"I'm glad you could make it today. Thank you for coming," Lisa said to her.

"My pleasure," Kelsey said in surprise. Lisa Olsen was usually simply tolerant of Kelsey's presence. Perhaps Tyler had told her to be nice.

Per usual, there were a significant number of beautifully-dressed young women giving the evil eye to Kelsey and Dara. Unlike at the first Tactec party, where she had been unnerved by the looks, today Kelsey calmly smiled and stood serenely at Tyler's side. She laughed when appropriate, shook hands with what seemed like hundreds of people, cooed at the fussy babies that had been brought by their Tactec employee parents and generally made herself useful. Although she knew Tyler didn't like to think about it, it was very possible that Kelsey was playing hostess for the next Tactec CEO and she wanted to do a good job.

After countless hours of smiling, the picnic turned into a concert which was open to the public, and she, Tyler, Ryan and Dara were finally free to leave. As they left, Kelsey could see Lisa and Bob, dancing off to the side of the stage with the executive team.

"How do they do it?" Tyler asked a while later as they sat in the bar of the Westin Hotel in Bellevue.

"I don't have a clue. Even I'm tired," Ryan said.

Dara had excused herself and gone up to her room to sleep. She would be flying back to L.A. early tomorrow. Kelsey had taken off her heels and was drinking sparkling water with the aspirin she was taking for the second time today. She wouldn't risk drinking her usual cranberry juice with this white dress.

"I'm going to have to increase my stamina if Lisa wants me to work for Tactec," Tyler said. "Otherwise, I'm going to pass out at my first event."

Ryan yawned. "It wouldn't be so bad, but there's so much thinking involved. The PR person stands there the entire time making sure you don't screw up and say something you aren't supposed to."

"Well, Lisa says whatever she wants. Maybe that makes the difference," Tyler commented.

"Kelsey was a star," Ryan said. "Dara said she had no idea how you managed with all the people that wanted to meet Tyler." Since everyone knew that Tyler, and not Ryan, was being groomed for the CEO position, the line to meet him had been twice as long.

"She's my Kelsey," Tyler grinned at her.

"Don't forget my sushi," Kelsey teased.

"You can have sushi for life," Tyler said seriously.

"I wouldn't volunteer for this," Ryan said. "Dara will get a little publicity out of it, though. By the way, Kelsey, Dara loved your dress. Who is it?"

"Valentino. I memorized the name for the reporters," Kelsey said. She was glad she had. Three of them had asked her about it. She had a feeling that if Jasmine Googled her name again, it would come up this time.

"This is like a career for you," Tyler said to her. "Thanks for being so diligent."

"You're welcome," Kelsey said.

"I hope Jess comes next year," Ryan said. "I really missed her today. Dara's kind of dull."

"She looked great," Kelsey said.

"She did, but she doesn't like kids, and she was complaining about the sun," Ryan commented. "I won't bring her again. If Jess won't go to the holiday party, I'll take Petra again."

"Jess will go," Kelsey said positively.

"I hope so," Ryan pouted.

"Come on," Tyler said, standing. "Let's get dinner."

Kelsey spent a second night at the condo, then returned to her own apartment on Sunday afternoon. Kelsey had had the misfortune of running into Brittany.

"You used the last of the dishwashing liquid. You're so thoughtless," Brittany complained as soon as Kelsey walked into the apartment.

"I did, but I bought a new bottle," Kelsey said mildly. She walked to the kitchen and opened the cabinet under the sink. She pulled out the new bottle.

"Why would I look there? Who keeps things under the sink?" Brittany asked nastily.

"Everyone?" Kelsey said.

"You're such an airhead. I don't understand why Collins Nicol thought you were worth hiring," Brittany said, turning on her heel and walking back to her room.

Back in the office on Monday, Kelsey felt like she was still recovering from her weekend. Happily, she hadn't seen Brittany again, but she really hated dealing with her. Her feet still hadn't fully recovered from the heels, which had looked beautiful, but were really painful, and despite her attempts to keep sunscreen on, her nose felt a little burnt from the sun.

"Miss North?" she heard. Kelsey looked up and smiled. A large vase of roses in a flurry of pink, yellow, and peach was in Ted's arms.

"Hi, Ted. Thanks," Kelsey said, standing.

"You get a lot of flowers," Ted said. Kelsey took the card out of the vase. It was in Tyler's handwriting, as she expected.

"I do a lot of favors," Kelsey replied.

"Well, these are very pretty. When I was walking them up here, everyone wanted to know who they were for."

"Thanks for bringing them to me, Ted," Kelsey said.

"No problem. See you later, Miss North," Ted said. He left the room.

Kelsey opened the envelope and pulled out the card. To her surprise, a Sephora gift card tumbled out of the envelope as well.

'Thank for your help this weekend, Kels. I owe you one. Love, Tyler,' read the card. Kelsey picked up the gift card which had fallen on the floor. She glanced at it, then picked up her phone and called Tyler.

"Hi, Princess," Tyler said.

"Thank you for the flowers." Kelsey said. "And the gift card."

"You're welcome. But the gift card isn't a gift. It's reimbursement."

"What?" Kelsey asked.

"I didn't realize that you had to buy things to go to these events with me."

"What?"

"Whitening toothpaste. Sunscreen. All that."

"Tyler, I need that stuff anyway," Kelsey protested.

"Fine, then you can buy it with the gift card."

"Tyler..."

"Kelsey, you have no idea how much I appreciated you coming on Saturday. I don't want you spending your own money in addition to so much time," Tyler said.

"It's not a big deal."

"It is to me," Tyler said. "Ryan was right, you were amazing. The First Lady herself couldn't have done a better job."

Kelsey smiled at the reference.

"Thanks, Tyler."

"No. Thank you," he replied.

On Friday, Collins Nicol held their summer open house. Kelsey had thought that it would be nice to invite Tyler and Ryan since she had done so many things with them this summer. As she was getting a drink, Alex walked up to her.

"Hi, Kelsey."

"Hi, Alex," Kelsey said. She picked up her drink and turned to him.

"So did you bring anyone today?" Alex asked Kelsey.

"Two of my classmates. They're talking to Mary White," Kelsey replied. Alex glanced over at Mary.

"You know Tyler Olsen? Of course, he goes to Darrow."

"How do you know Tyler?" Kelsey asked.

"I interviewed him, before he turned us down. Where is he working this year, anyway?"

"Simon and Associates," Kelsey replied.

"Bill Simon's a slave driver," Alex said.

"Tyler says he's a genius."

"A genius and a slave driver," Alex replied. Kelsey glanced at Tyler, who she was surprised to discover was looking at her. Tyler turned back to his conversation with Mary, who was talking animatedly. "Who's with Tyler?"

"Ryan Perkins."

"Ah, the troublemaker," Alex said.

Kelsey laughed. "Ryan's trying to be a better person."

"Really? Good luck with that. He's a tabloid fixture," Alex said doubtfully. "I can't believe how different they are when their parents founded a business together."

"Have you met Lisa Olsen?" Kelsey asked.

Alex shook his head. "I'm way too low on the org chart to be introduced to the royalty that is Lisa Olsen. I'm not sure Mary's met her, and we've been doing work for Tactec for at least seven years. Of course we do a lot more now, thanks to Richard Kinnon's screw-up."

Kelsey nodded as David Lim walked over and slapped Alex on the back.

"How's it going?" David asked cheerfully, joining their conversation.

Over the next hour, Kelsey continued to chat with Alex and David, then spoke to several other associates in the Intellectual Property group. Emily came over to discuss Kelsey's last brief, which had got good feedback from the partner who had assigned it to Kelsey. She also spoke to support-staff member Ted and a couple of attorneys from Trusts and Estates when Eliza came over to say hi. Every so often, she felt Tyler's eyes on her, but he and Ryan had found themselves largely cornered by the higher-ups at Collins Nicol, no doubt so Tyler and Ryan could report how excellent Collins Nicol was, and have Tactec send them more work. Lucas, thankfully, was nowhere to be seen.

Finally, having disentangled themselves from the partners, Tyler and Ryan joined Kelsey as she was talking to another summer associate, this one from Real Estate.

"Sorry," she said to them as they walked up.

"You didn't know. Right?" Ryan said.

"Of course, Ryan. I didn't realize that they would pounce on you two like that," Kelsey noted.

"See you, Kelsey," the summer associate said, heading off to get a drink.

"Bye, James," Kelsey replied.

"I should bill them for my time," Tyler said.

"What have they been talking about for so long?" Kelsey asked.

"How great Tactec is, how much Collins Nicol loves working for them, how Tyler should come work here next year, blah, blah, blah," Ryan said.

"If they only knew how little influence we have over Tactec corporate decisions," Tyler said.

"I'm so sorry. I thought it would be fun for you," Kelsey said.

"It's okay, Kels," Tyler said.

"The food's good," Ryan commented.

"Do you want to go?" Kelsey asked.

"Are you sure you're ready to leave?" Tyler replied.

"I want to go," Ryan said. "I'm going to make chicken marsala tonight."

"That sounds good," Kelsey said.

"You're invited," Ryan replied. "Anytime."

"Kelsey would rather go back to work with me," Tyler said.

"You have to go back?" Ryan asked.

"You know I do," Tyler said irritably.

"Ryan, I'll come over for dinner on Tuesday, if that's okay?" Kelsey said.

"Great! Maybe Tyler will manage to leave work early."

"Never going to happen," Tyler replied.

Saturday morning, Kelsey went running first thing in the morning, then went to the Queen Anne Pool for the day. Tyler had a filing on Monday, and since she had spent much of Friday evening hanging out in his office, she decided to let him have some time to work. She knew Bill Simon didn't mind, but Kelsey didn't want to be a burden.

She had been feeling like one because she was avoiding the apartment at all costs. She left early, then came in as late as possible to avoid Brittany, who was only getting worse. Kelsey had made the mistake of coming home early too many times this summer, and she was determined not to let it happen again. So Tyler's office had become a bit of a refuge.

Kelsey spent the day in Fremont and Ballard on Sunday, going to the Sunday markets and walking around the cool shops. Tyler was still working, and Ryan had mentioned that he was going to stay home and try a bunch of new bread recipes, so she decided to let them spend the weekend without her. She arrived back at her apartment at 8:45 p.m., having spent the entire day away.

Kelsey joined Ryan for dinner on Tuesday. To her surprise, Ryan had created a Moroccan feast. He had cooked lamb, saffron rice, and a salad that featured lemons and olives. Every bite was delicious and completely exotic.

"Do you like it?" Ryan asked her.

"I'm in heaven, it's wonderful, Ryan," Kelsey replied.

Ryan beamed.

They ate dinner, then Kelsey helped him wash dishes.

"Did you think about what we discussed?" Ryan asked her. "About Tyler?"

"No," Kelsey replied.

Ryan glanced at her and shook his head.

"What?" Kelsey challenged him.

"Nothing," Ryan said, returning to the dishes.

Kelsey saw Tyler again on Thursday. To her surprise, he was getting ready to leave work at six.

"I was just going to call you to go to dinner with me," Tyler said with pleasure when Kelsey walked in. "I can leave early today."

"Why?" Kelsey asked.

"Simon is going to some bar event in Vancouver, so we don't have a filing tonight or tomorrow. I'm getting the whole weekend off."

"That's fantastic," Kelsey said.

"Let's go before he comes back," Tyler said, grinning.

Tyler and Kelsey had dinner at a hip Italian restaurant on the top of

Queen Anne Hill. Ryan was having dinner with Bob downtown, so he wasn't cooking tonight. Tyler drove Kelsey back down the hill and to her building.

"Oh, I forgot to ask. Do you still have the IP book? I promised to bring it into work. One of Simon's paralegals wants to borrow it."

"Sure, it's inside. I'll bring it to your office," Kelsey said.

"Don't drag it across town for me. It's heavy. I can take it now," Tyler said.

Kelsey thought for the briefest of seconds. Brittany was probably asleep, but they would have to be quiet. Otherwise, she have to come up with a reason to explain to Tyler why he wasn't welcome in her apartment. She had never mentioned the difficulties that she had had with Brittany to anyone. She didn't want to complain.

"Okay," Kelsey said. They got out of the car and walked up the sidewalk.

"We need to be quiet," Kelsey said to Tyler. "Brittany's probably asleep."

Tyler looked at his phone. "At 8:15?" he asked. Kelsey put her keys in the door. They stepped into the living room and Kelsey turned on the light.

"Hang on," she said, leaving him in the living room and quietly walking over to her own room. Tyler sat on the sofa.

Kelsey walked into her room and flipped on the light. She took Tyler's book from her dresser and turned around.

Brittany stood at the door, frowning at her. "You woke me up, airhead," she said.

"Sorry," Kelsey replied, sighing.

"Honestly, I can't believe how irresponsible you are. Don't you have feelings for anyone else?" Brittany said loudly.

"I said I was sorry. I was trying to be quiet," Kelsey replied. She began to walk toward the door, but Brittany remained in the doorway.

"You are always doing this. You're so rude."

"Is something wrong?" Tyler asked from behind Brittany.

Britany whirled around, looked at him and yelled at Kelsey. "You brought a boy home? That's it, I'm telling the Collins Nicol coordinator," she said. She pushed past Tyler and walked out of the room.

"You don't have to put up with this. Pack your stuff. You can stay with me and Ryan," Tyler said to her.

"Tyler, it's okay," Kelsey said, but Tyler walked over to her closet and neatly removed all of her dresses with his arm.

"Pack up," he replied. "Let me have your key."

"Tyler…" Kelsey began.

"Kels, this is ridiculous. It's 8:15," Tyler replied. Kelsey thought for a moment. Tyler was right, she really couldn't live with this anymore. She handed him her key. Tyler took it and walked out of the room. Kelsey began gathering her things.

Brittany walked over to the doorway, phone in hand.

"I've left them a message," she said menacingly. "I'm sure they'll have plenty to say to you in the morning."

Kelsey didn't answer. Brittany walked away and a few moments later, Tyler returned, carrying three reuseable grocery bags.

"Here," he said, handing them to her. "Jeffrey thinks I should be more environmentally conscious." Kelsey smiled at him and began to place her things into the empty bags. She finished packing a few moments later.

"Done?" Tyler asked her. Kelsey nodded. "Then let's go home," he said, lifting the now-full grocery bags, and a duffel bag that Kelsey had stuffed her quilt into. Kelsey took her backpack, gym bag, and a tote bag Jessica had given her, dropped her keys on the living room table, and the two of them left the apartment, Brittany nowhere to be seen.

They walked to Tyler's car in silence, put Kelsey's things into the trunk, and got into the car. Kelsey noted that the clothes from her closet were in the back seat.

Tyler started the car and said, "Why didn't you tell us?"

"It wasn't a big deal," Kelsey replied.

"Are you kidding? She's insane," Tyler replied.

"I guess I had gotten used to it," Kelsey said honestly.

"Not while I'm around," Tyler said, as he accelerated.

Ten minutes later, Tyler parked his car in the basement of Ryan's condo.

"Did you tell Ryan I was coming?" Kelsey asked him, as he began pulling her clothes out of the back seat.

"No," Tyler replied. "He won't care." Tyler finished removing the clothes and walked around to the trunk. He placed five bags in his arms, over Kelsey's protests, and she took her backpack and the tote. They closed the car doors, walked into the elevator, and rode up to

Ryan's.

Tyler opened the door, and they walked in. Ryan was sitting on the sofa, reading a magazine.

"Kelsey's moving in," Tyler said, without preamble. He walked into the master bedroom.

"Cool," Ryan said happily. "I can get a second opinion on my cooking."

Kelsey smiled at him and followed Tyler into the master bedroom. Tyler placed the grocery bags on the desk, the other bags on the floor, and hung the clothes in the walk-in closet.

Kelsey placed her backpack and tote onto the bed, and looked out of the window. Her view overlooked Pike Place Market, with a small slice of Puget Sound.

"I'll give you a key," Tyler said, walking out. Kelsey followed him to the kitchen. Tyler opened a drawer and handed Kelsey a key attached to an access card.

"Bob, Jeffrey, Carol, and Tactec security all have keys," he said. "Mariel comes with Jeffrey to clean on Mondays and Thursdays. If you want something, just put it on the list on the refrigerator."

Kelsey glanced at the fridge door. There was a whiteboard on it, where Ryan had carelessly written "Raspberries!"

"That's it. I'll let security know that you're staying with us," Tyler said.

"Thank you," Kelsey said.

"Our pleasure," Tyler replied. "Make sure you aren't too loud. We go to bed at least by 3 a.m."

Kelsey stuck her tongue out at him. He grinned and left the room.

The next morning, Kelsey woke to sunlight streaming into the window. She stretched and got out of bed. After taking in the view, she took a hot bath, got dressed and walked out into the living room. To her surprise, Ryan was in the kitchen, wearing his suit, cooking. His tie sat on the corner of the breakfast bar.

"Good morning, Kelsey," he said, not removing his eyes from the stove.

"Hi, Ryan," Kelsey replied.

"Would you like breakfast? I'm making French toast," he asked her.

"Sure," Kelsey replied.

"Don't be afraid," Tyler said, leaving his bedroom and straightening his own tie. "Ryan's got French toast down to a science."

"Thanks, bro," Ryan said happily. He took a plate down from a shelf as Kelsey and Tyler sat at the bar.

"Did you sleep well?" Tyler asked Kelsey.

"Very well, thanks."

"Good. I'll drive you to work. Ryan walks to the office," Tyler said. Kelsey was about to protest, but she saw the look in Tyler's eye.

"Thanks," she said. Ryan put a plate of French toast in front of her with a flourish. It looked amazing, with a sprinkle of powdered sugar and a puddle of maple syrup. Ryan had even added a few cut strawberries to the side.

"Wow. Thank you, Ryan."

Ryan smiled at her as he returned to the stove.

"Eat," Tyler said. "Don't let it get cold." Kelsey picked up her fork and began to eat. It was delicious. Ryan placed a plate in front of Tyler, who picked up his own fork.

"Delicious, Ryan," Tyler said.

"I'd agree but I'm too busy eating," Kelsey added.

"Do you think Jess will like it?" Ryan asked.

"I'm sure. She loves French toast," Kelsey said in between bites.

Ryan nodded and returned to the stove. He took out the last slice of French toast, plated it, and turned off the stove. He shook powdered sugar over the piece and poured syrup next to it. He took a fork, placed the plate on the bar, and began to eat, standing in the kitchen.

"So your roommate is psycho?" Ryan said to her.

"Afraid so," Kelsey said.

"Is she like that in the office?" Tyler asked her.

"She hides it well," Kelsey said, swallowing another bite. The French toast was really spectacular.

"You should have said something," Ryan said to her. "The guest room's been sitting empty since Kim was here."

"And obviously, we would have preferred you in the room rather than Kim," Tyler commented.

Ryan glared at him. "Ha, ha," he said. Tyler smiled. "We should have the office turned into a bedroom," Ryan continued. "Maybe Jess can live with us next summer."

"Always hopeful, that's our Ryan," Tyler said.

"She doesn't like being away from me either," Ryan pouted.

"I know," Tyler said seriously. "Just tell Jeffrey you want to put in a bed. He'll arrange it. Carol will just turn it into another decorating fiasco."

"You're right. I don't want a new decorator coming in with more terrible ideas because we want another bedroom," Ryan commented. "It took forever to finish this condo, thanks to Carol and Charlotte. Kelsey, what color do you like?" Ryan asked her.

"For what?"

"The room next to Tyler's. You can have it next summer, so you might as well decide the color," Ryan said.

"Am I living here next summer?" Kelsey asked.

"Do you want to risk another roommate assigned by Collins Nicol?" Tyler asked her.

"I don't even know if I'll be there," Kelsey replied.

"Just pick a color," Ryan said.

"Fine. Ivory," Kelsey said.

Ryan picked up his phone and began to type a message.

"Ask Jeffrey how long it will take," Tyler suggested.

Ryan typed and waited for a response. "He said only a day, but he requested that I wait until the middle of the month for it to be done."

"That's fine, Zach can sleep on the sofa," Tyler said.

"Zach?" Kelsey asked.

"He'll be here next weekend," Tyler replied.

"He can have the master bedroom," Kelsey said.

"No, he can't," Tyler said. "That's yours." Ryan nodded in agreement.

"Thanks," Kelsey said.

The next morning, Kelsey woke up to sunlight streaming into her new bedroom window. After two nights, it was amazing how much more relaxed she was here than in the apartment with Brittany.

She stretched and walked out into the living room. In the middle of the floor, Ryan was sitting cross-legged on one of the large silk pillows. His eyes were closed and he was breathing deeply. Suddenly his eyes snapped open, startling Kelsey.

"Good morning," Ryan said.

"Hi," Kelsey said. "What are you doing?"

"Meditating. Would you like to join me? It's very calming," Ryan replied.

"That's okay," Kelsey said. "I was just getting a glass of water." She walked over to the kitchen and got a glass of water. She drank it as Ryan closed his eyes, and began to breathe slowly again. Kelsey rinsed out the glass, put it to the side of the sink and slowly walked across the living room so as not to disturb Ryan. As she passed him, Ryan, eyes still closed, said to her,

"Tyler and I were thinking about going to the beach today. Want to go?"

"Sure," Kelsey said. She took another glance at him, then walked into her room, closing the door.

An hour and a half later, Kelsey was sitting on the sofa reading her kindle, and Ryan was puttering around in the kitchen with his back to her.

"Good morning, Kels," Tyler said sleepily. Kelsey looked up in surprise.

Tyler was walking across the carpet, wearing his night-time wear of cotton pajama pants and a Darrow Law t-shirt. She had seen him tired, but unlike every other time Kelsey had seen him, Tyler had just woken up. His brown hair was tousled, he was unshaven, and as Sophia James might say, Tyler looked dead sexy.

"Morning," Kelsey managed to say.

Kelsey's eyes followed him as he crossed in front of her, reached into the linen closet, removed a towel, and walked into the bathroom. He shut the door behind him.

Kelsey unconsciously fanned herself with the Kindle. Perhaps she had been too hasty in refusing to get involved with Tyler on his own terms. Her vow not to kiss him until he committed to her was beginning to crumble.

A little while later, Tyler, Ryan, and Kelsey drove to Alki Beach. Tyler pulled over near a busy part of the beach and the trio unloaded the car.

"Do you need anything from the store? I'll walk past it on my way back," Tyler said, getting back behind the wheel.

"Get some more ice, and some ketchup," Ryan said.

"Yes, chef," Tyler said, winking at Kelsey.

Kelsey and Ryan walked down to the beach as Tyler drove off. Kelsey put down the towels and the mini-barbecue as Ryan placed the cooler in the sand. Kelsey took off the t-shirt dress she had worn over her old bathing suit, and folded it.

Ryan pulled his wallet out of his shorts pocket and threw it to Kelsey. She caught it in surprise.

"Go buy yourself a new suit," Ryan said.

"What?" Kelsey asked.

"Tyler's birthday gift," Ryan replied, grinning.

"Ryan, my bathing suit is fine," Kelsey said.

"Don't lie. You hate it too. Get two suits. Buy whatever you want," Ryan said, turning his back to her and opening the cooler.

Kelsey sighed. She knew from vast experience that no matter what she said, Ryan wouldn't take no for an answer, so she looked over at the strip of stores that fronted the beach, and holding his wallet, walked over to them.

A store with a lot of surfing decor caught her eye and she walked in. Kelsey looked at the racks of swimsuits and bikinis. After a couple of minutes, she found a bikini with a muted tribal print that she liked. It wasn't her normal style, but after she tried it on, she decided to throw caution to the wind and buy it. As she walked to the counter, Kelsey saw an off-white mesh cover-up and decided to get it as well. The clerk rang up the purchase, and Kelsey opened Ryan's wallet. Inside was a photo of Jessica, a half dozen debit and credit cards, and what seemed to Kelsey, over a thousand dollars in hundred-dollar bills.

"Forty-seven fifty," the clerk said. Kelsey handed over one of the bills and received the change, which she put back into the wallet.

"Do you mind if I change here?" Kelsey asked.

"No problem. Do you want me to take off the tags?" the clerk asked.

"Yes, thanks," Kelsey replied. The clerk snipped off the tags, and Kelsey walked back into the changing room. She put on the bikini and cover-up and looked at herself in the mirror. Even she had to admit she looked better. A lot better. Sexy, even. She glanced at her old suit lying in the corner of the room. Kelsey picked it up.

"Can I throw this away?" she asked the clerk as she walked out of the changing room.

He held out a small trash can. "Absolutely," he said. Kelsey threw the old suit away, said thanks and, carrying Ryan's wallet carefully, walked out of the store.

As she headed back down the beach slope, Ryan looked up. He smiled at her.

"Excellent choice. Tyler will love it," Ryan commented.

"I'm sure," Kelsey said, handing him his wallet. "But thank you."

"You're welcome. Thanks for not putting up a fight," Ryan said, replacing his wallet back into his pocket.

"I considered it," Kelsey smiled.

"Proud of you. Now you can teach Jess how to accept a gift gracefully," Ryan replied.

"We're not used to so much generosity," Kelsey commented.

"Kimmy should give you a lesson. She knows how to get what she wants."

"But I don't want anything."

"It doesn't matter. You should learn to want things," Ryan replied. "Don't just accept what you're given." He turned back to the barbecue, which was starting to get hot.

Kelsey sat on her towel and looked at the water. Ryan sometimes was surprisingly profound, Kelsey thought.

After her breakup with Lucas and the peaceful nights away from her roommate, Kelsey had to admit that maybe she did settle too often. Of course, the biggest situation that she was accepting without a fight, was her relationship with Tyler. But there, Kelsey had no idea where to begin.

Tyler walked up five minutes later. Kelsey was taking burgers out of the cooler for Ryan, who had got the barbecue ready for grilling. Tyler put the paper grocery bag he was carrying onto the sand. He glanced at Kelsey and Ryan looked at Tyler's face and smiled. Kelsey blushed and looked back at the cooler.

"Kelsey needed a new suit," Ryan said, taking a raw burger from Kelsey's hand.

"I see," Tyler said. "It's very pretty."

Kelsey felt herself getting red.

"I got ice and ketchup as per your request," Tyler said, changing the subject to Kelsey's relief.

"Thanks," Ryan said, placing a burger onto the grill. Tyler put the large canvas bag he was holding next to his towel and sat down. Kelsey finished handing burgers to Ryan, rinsed her hands with a bottle of water, and walked over to Tyler. She took off her cover-up, reached into the canvas bag and pulled out her own bag, which had sunscreen. She already felt like she was beginning to burn in the August sun. Kelsey retrieved the sunscreen and began to put it on.

"Tyler? Can you put sunscreen on my back?" Kelsey asked.

Tyler looked up from his iPad, where he had been reading *The Economist*. "Sure," he said. Kelsey lay face down onto her own towel and placed the sunscreen next to her. Tyler knelt beside her and put sunscreen on his hands.

"You should charge him for the privilege of putting sunscreen on you," Ryan commented.

"Right now, I'm trying to not to burn to death," Kelsey replied. She closed her eyes, and felt Tyler's gentle hands stroke her neck. As they did, Kelsey realized that it had been a long time since Tyler had touched her. After their discussion following the Law Review party, Tyler had been a man of his word and kept his distance physically. In fact, she could only remember one friendly hug since then. So this moment felt surprisingly intimate. Tyler spread the cool sunscreen over Kelsey's back, and on her shoulders.

"Done," Tyler said. Kelsey turned over as Tyler took off his t-shirt. "Can you do my back?" he asked. Kelsey nodded and picked up the sunscreen.

As she ran her hands over his taut back muscles, Kelsey noted that Tyler had seemingly managed to continue to exercise through his busy summer schedule. Although she hadn't noticed while he was wearing his suits, she realized that his body looked more fit than ever. Kelsey finished with the sunscreen, and Tyler looked at her.

"Thanks, Kels," Tyler said. He picked up his iPad and went back to reading. Kelsey leaned back on her towel and closed her eyes, basking in the sun.

After eating the delicious burgers and salads that Ryan had made, Tyler sat and worked on a brief, Ryan began building a sand castle, and Kelsey read her Kindle. A few times, a group of giggling girls passed by to ogle Tyler and Ryan, and more than once, Kelsey had seen guys checking her out. No one had approached them though, which was fine with Kelsey. She was enjoying the quiet and the summer sun.

"I want ice cream," Ryan announced, standing and brushing his hands on his board shorts.

Tyler looked up from his brief. "Bring some back for us," he said.

"Actually, I was hoping one of you would go. I want to finish my castle."

"Finish it, then go," Tyler replied.

"I'll go," Kelsey said, standing. "I could use the walk." And a moment of air conditioning wouldn't hurt either. She pulled on the cover-up, put on her sandals and took her wallet out of her bag. "What kind do you want?"

"Anything," Ryan said.

"Chocolate," Tyler said. "But you knew that."

"I did. I'll be back soon," Kelsey said. She walked down the beach for a few minutes, then crossed the street. She walked into the small convenience store, which was well air-conditioned, and looked at the selection of ice cream in the freezer.

"Hi," said a voice behind her.

Kelsey turned around. A guy with long curly brown hair and a big smile was standing there, in surf shorts.

"Hi," Kelsey said in return. She had seen him on the beach.

"I wanted to meet you but you're surrounded by your bodyguards today." He held out his hand. "I'm Jake."

Kelsey shook his hand. "Kelsey."

"So, Kelsey what do you do except look beautiful on the beach?" Jake asked.

"I'm a law student. And you?"

"Grad student."

"In what?"

"Library Science. At the UW. Do you go to the UW too?"

"Darrow," Kelsey replied. She looked back at the ice cream, and picked out two bars and a small carton.

"No way. A brainiac," Jake said admiringly. Kelsey looked at him.

"Not really," she said.

"If you got into Darrow, you must be smart. Are you going to eat all of that? Or did your bodyguards need a treat?"

"I'm the delivery girl," Kelsey said. She and Jake walked to the counter, and Kelsey paid for the ice cream.

"A cute one," Jake said. Kelsey blushed. They walked out of the store and back towards the beach.

"So which of the bodyguards is your boyfriend?" Jake asked her as they walked.

"They're my roommates," Kelsey replied.

"Seriously? You must be dating someone though." Jake looked at her with anticipation.

"I'm in a relationship," Kelsey said. It was true enough.

"I knew it," Jake said with disappointment. "Any chance of a breakup soon?" he asked hopefully.

Kelsey giggled. "I don't think so," she said.

"Too bad," Jake said. "Do you need any help delivering that ice cream?"

"I think I have it under control," Kelsey replied. "Thanks."

"It was nice meeting you, Kelsey," Jake said.

"You too," Kelsey said. Jake waved at her and walked away. A few steps later, Kelsey handed Tyler one of the ice cream bars. Ryan looked at her with interest.

"Going on another date, Miss North?" he asked.

"Not this time," Kelsey replied.

"Not random enough?" Ryan asked.

"You can have Ryan's ice cream," Kelsey said to Tyler, handing him the carton.

"Hey, I'm trying to help you," Ryan said to Tyler, as Kelsey sat on her towel between them.

"I know," Tyler replied. He tossed the carton to Ryan, who caught it.

"So why did you say no?" Ryan asked.

"Not my type," Kelsey replied.

"What does he do?" Ryan asked.

"Grad student at the UW. Library Science," Kelsey said, unwrapping her ice cream bar.

"At least you have some standards," Ryan said, opening the carton.

"What does that mean?" Kelsey asked.

"They must not be too high. She went out with you," Tyler commented.

Kelsey glared at him.

"I'm sorry, it was too good to pass up," Tyler apologized.

Kelsey giggled. "Look, I'm not accepting any dates right now, so you can stop harassing me," she said to Ryan. She took a bite from the ice cream bar.

"I'm simply concerned," Ryan said. "Like a big brother."

"I don't need a brother. I like being an only child," Kelsey replied.

"Who's going to look after you then?" Ryan asked.

"I will," Tyler said seriously. "Leave Kelsey alone. She knows what she's doing."

"When she marries someone else, will you still say that?" Ryan asked Tyler, eating some of his ice cream and looking directly at him. Tyler frowned.

"Ryan, it really isn't your business," Kelsey said.

"I just want the two of you to be happy. Like me and Jess," Ryan said. "What's wrong with that?"

"We are happy," Tyler replied.

"You certainly aren't," Ryan retorted.

"I'm not happy because I spend ninety percent of my day at the office," Tyler replied. "But I like when Kelsey comes to visit me." Tyler smiled at her. "Where's your girlfriend?" he asked Ryan.

Ryan frowned. "You know where Jess is."

"Stop analyzing my friendship with Kelsey, and I won't judge yours."

"What does that mean?" Ryan said.

"You know what it means," Tyler replied. Kelsey looked at Tyler. Clearly, there had been a prelude to this conversation, because she wasn't following what was going on.

"See if I help you again," Ryan said, taking another bite of ice cream.

"I hope you don't," Tyler replied.

"It's not my fault that Jessica went back to New York," Ryan said, putting the carton of ice cream on his towel.

"You really want to discuss this?" Tyler asked him.

"Why not? Kelsey's going to hear about it anyway," Ryan said.

"Fine. No, Ryan, it's not your fault. But clearly everything isn't as perfect as you want it to be. And as you claim that it is. So I think that you should refrain from telling me what to do with my life."

Ryan pouted. "I'm just trying to help."

"I don't need your help," Tyler said. "Work on your own relationship."

"My relationship is fine," Ryan said.

"Okay," Tyler said.

"Jess loves me."

"I know," Tyler replied.

Ryan sighed. "But she's not here." He lay back on his towel.

"No. She is not," Tyler said. "And you need to consider why."

Kelsey looked at both of them as she ate her ice cream. She knew why Jessica wasn't in Seattle, it was because Jessica was still unsure of the relationship. But obviously Tyler thought that something else was wrong, that Ryan had done something else. Kelsey wondered what it was.

"Maybe," Ryan pouted. Tyler took a bite of ice cream. "Kelsey?"

"Yes?" Kelsey asked.

"Does Jessica love me?" Ryan asked her. Kelsey didn't answer right away. She thought for a moment.

"Yes," Kelsey finally said. "I think so." She looked at Ryan for a moment. "What did you do?" she asked him.

Ryan closed his eyes and sighed. "I asked her to marry me," he said.

"You what?" Kelsey said in surprise.

"On the way to the airport," Ryan said. "She didn't tell you?"

"No," Kelsey said.

"I don't think she thought I was serious," Ryan said, looking at the sky. "But I think I might have scared her."

Kelsey thought for a moment. Then she spoke. "I don't think so, Ryan."

"Why?" Tyler asked in interest.

"Jessica isn't afraid of you getting close to her. She's afraid you're going to hurt her."

"I would never hurt Jess," Ryan said dismissively.

"She doesn't know that," Kelsey replied.

"She should. I love her," Ryan said. "What should I do?"

Kelsey shook her head. "I have no idea. I don't know what you can do."

"You don't think I'm pushing her too much?" Ryan asked.

"I don't think so. Ryan, I just think it's going to take some time. You're so different from each other."

"I know. That's what I love about Jess," Ryan said.

"Just give her some time," Kelsey said. But as she said it, she wondered if time would be enough, since what Jess really needed was trust.

They spent the rest of the afternoon in the sun, and let the sun set around them. They packed up and had dinner at the Mexican restaurant that Tyler had taken Kelsey to earlier in the year. The restaurant staff didn't recognize either Tyler or Ryan. As Kelsey had predicted, the media interest in them had diminished since the announcement about their trusts. However, she had a feeling that both of them were looking forward to the relative anonymity they enjoyed at Darrow.

They arrived home around eleven p.m. and Kelsey helped them put everything away.

"I had a great time," she said to them.

"I'm glad," Tyler replied. "It was nice having a day off."

"I'm going to bed. Good night," Kelsey said to them, heading for her bedroom.

"Night," Ryan said.

"Good night, Kels," Tyler said.

An hour later, Kelsey realized that she couldn't sleep. She had been lying in bed, eyes closed, but here she was, still awake. She was thinking about getting up for a glass of water when she heard Tyler's quiet voice from the living room.

"Stop torturing me," he said.

Ryan laughed.

"She needed a new bathing suit," Ryan replied.

"Right," Tyler commented. "And of course it had to be that one."

"I didn't pick it out, she did. Every girl wants to look pretty."

"Kelsey North doesn't need to look prettier. Kelsey needs to wear a paper bag over her head so I can get some work done."

"Of course if she did, you'd be looking at her legs," Ryan commented.

Tyler laughed. "That's true," he replied.

"And now of course, she's living with us," Ryan said.

"Stop it, Ryan."

"Just ask her out."

"You know why I haven't," Tyler replied.

"Yeah, and it's stupid," Ryan pointed out.

"I know," Tyler conceded.

"You're going to wait until we get back to Darrow, and there's a whole new group of guys ready to ask her out first," Ryan said.

"Probably," Tyler said. "Ryan, I don't have time."

"You've said that for a year. And Kelsey started dating Lucas. You might not be so lucky next time."

"I know," Tyler repeated.

"You're taking a big risk," Ryan said.

"I hope not. I hope this time she says no to everyone."

"Why should she? How long do you expect her to wait?" Ryan asked Tyler.

"I don't know."

"You don't know anything. I wonder why people think you're so smart," Ryan said.

"I wonder that myself sometimes," Tyler said.

"If you don't ask her out soon, I'm going to set her up," Ryan said.

"Considering your track record with Zachary, that might not be a bad thing for me," Tyler replied.

"What does that mean?"

"Ryan, let me deal with this," Tyler said.

"Don't you want to be happy?" Ryan asked.

"I am happy. I'm happy that's she here, and that's she's safe."

"And that's enough?"

"It's all I can have right now. Ryan, I'm not like you."

"Tyler, I know this is hard for you, but you can't keep stalling. Kelsey's not going to wait forever."

"I know."

"Stop saying I know. If you knew anything, you'd have been dating her for the past eleven months. I know that you love her."

Kelsey lay in bed, unmoving. She was wondering what Tyler would say next.

"I'm going to bed," Tyler said.

Kelsey sighed inwardly at the non-response. Zachary had said that Tyler loved her, but there was a part of her that wanted to hear it from him herself.

"You can't keep doing this. It's not fair to Kelsey, or to you," Ryan said.

"Good night, Ryan," Tyler said. A moment later, Kelsey heard his bedroom door close.

Now Kelsey really couldn't sleep.

The next morning, Kelsey woke up groggy and irritable. She had finally fallen asleep hours after she had gone to bed. She had gone over Tyler and Ryan's conversation in her mind over and over again. But there wasn't anything that was new.

Except for one thing. Ryan's comment that Tyler could have been dating Kelsey for eleven months. She had only known Tyler for eleven months. Did that mean that Tyler had expressed interest in her to Ryan at the beginning of their first year at Darrow?

Kelsey sighed to herself and pulled the covers over her head.

A half hour later, Kelsey walked out into the living room. She had taken a hot bath and reflected on last night's conversation once more. She came to the same conclusion that she had come to a hundred times before: that Tyler would continue to be Tyler, and that she should do whatever she wanted to do.

Of course, what she wanted to do was date Tyler. But for now, she would live with him and see him every day. Friendship without kissing.

"Good morning, Kelsey," Tyler said from the sofa as she walked out. He was sitting in jeans and a t-shirt, reading a brief.

"Good morning," Kelsey replied.

"Breakfast?" Ryan asked.

"Sure. Thanks," Kelsey said.

"Did you sleep well?" Tyler asked her.

"Not really," Kelsey replied, sitting next to him.

"No? Why?" Tyler asked.

Kelsey looked at him. There were a lot of things bothering her this weekend, and her relationship with Tyler was only one of them.

"I'm not looking forward to going to work on Monday," Kelsey replied. "I really don't want to deal with the fallout from Brittany."

"You'll be fine," Tyler said, returning his eyes to his iPad. "She's the one who's crazy."

Ryan walked over with two plates, and handed one to each of them. On each plate was a waffle, covered in fresh raspberry syrup.

"Wow," Kelsey said, taking her plate. Ryan walked back to the kitchen and returned with forks and knives for both of them.

"Thanks, Ryan," Tyler said, taking his utensils. Tyler set his iPad on the coffee table and began to eat. Kelsey took her utensils and began as well. The waffle was crisp and delicious, and the syrup was warm and sweet. Kelsey was in heaven.

"This is incredible, Ryan," Kelsey said. Ryan had returned to the kitchen to prepare a plate of his own.

"I'm glad you like it," Ryan replied. He poured syrup over his own waffle and joined Kelsey and Tyler on the sofa.

"You're getting as good as Margaret," Tyler said to him.

"That's a compliment," Ryan said.

"No, really. I'm impressed. Maybe you should be a chef," Tyler said.

"Only for my friends," Ryan said, taking a bite of waffle. He chewed, swallowed, then said, "So what do you guys want to do today?"

"Besides sleep?" Tyler asked.

"It's summer. You can sleep at Darrow," Ryan replied.

Tyler smiled. "Did you have something in mind, Mr. Perkins?" he asked.

"Actually, I did. I want to go blueberry picking."

"You?"

"I heard it was fun."

"From who?" Tyler asked.

"One of the support staff. She went with her sister last weekend, and brought blueberries into the office. They were delicious," Ryan replied.

"I'll go," Kelsey said. "I love fresh blueberries."

"Where can we pick them?"

"There's a place on the Eastside. It isn't far," Ryan replied.

"I'll go if you make blueberry muffins," Tyler said.

"I didn't know you liked blueberry muffins," Ryan said. "Actually, I thought I'd make blueberry scones."

"That sounds even better. I'm in," Tyler said, taking another bite of waffle.

The three of them sat in the living room, finishing their waffles. Then Tyler and Ryan had seconds while Kelsey went to change. She put on jeans and an old t-shirt. She walked back out into the living room.

"Why did you change? And what's with the shirt?" Ryan asked, licking syrup off of his fork.

"Blueberry picking is hard work. And I don't really want blueberry juice on my good clothes," Kelsey replied.

"Hard work. You sure you still want to go, Ryan?" Tyler teased.

"I'll pick more than you will," Ryan commented.

"You're on," Tyler said. "Loser buys dinner."

"Fine," Ryan stood. "I'm going to change. I need my working clothes on." He put his plate in the kitchen sink, then walked into his bedroom.

Tyler finished his waffle and went into the kitchen. He washed the breakfast plates, and Kelsey walked over to him and helped him dry them.

"So will this really be fun?" Tyler asked.

"You've never been?" Kelsey asked.

Tyler shook his head.

"We'll have a good time," Kelsey replied.

Tyler changed and the three of them piled into Tyler's car and drove to the blueberry farm, which it turned out was about 15 minutes away from Tyler and Ryan's Medina houses.

"I can't believe it's right here, and we've never been," Ryan said, as they took their plastic buckets and walked out into the blueberry patch.

"We're here now," Tyler said. "Don't forget our bet."

"I haven't forgotten. Kelsey, no helping Tyler," Ryan said.

"Okay," Kelsey smiled. "I'll keep my berries to myself."

"What do we do?" Ryan said.

Kelsey looked around.

"Let's find a good lane, with lots of berries. Follow me," she said. Kelsey led the two boys through the blueberry patch, to a quiet area which had plants drooping with blueberries.

Kelsey snapped a dark blue berry off of the bush. She showed it to them.

"That's what you want. Nice and ripe." She dropped it into her bucket.

Ryan took a blueberry off of the plant and ate it. "Delicious."

"If you eat them, they don't count," Tyler said. "Whoever has the highest weight back at the store wins."

"I won't eat any more," Ryan commented. "I'm not letting you beat me."

"Make sure they're ripe. Don't pick the green ones. They won't taste good," Kelsey said.

"Okay," Ryan said seriously. Kelsey smiled. He and Tyler looked like they were really going to compete to win.

"Go," Kelsey said, as a joke. But Tyler and Ryan both immediately began picking blueberries.

Kelsey giggled to herself, picked a blueberry and ate it.

Tyler and Ryan picked the blueberries diligently, only stopping to ask

Kelsey if a particular berry was ripe, or to move to a different part of the patch. Every so often one or the other would look at the level in the other's bucket to see who was winning. Then there would be a flurry of activity from the loser's side. Kelsey, who wasn't part of the bet, picked slowly. She was enjoying being out in the sun and away from everything else. Kelsey turned her face up to the sky and let the sunbeams warm her cheeks.

After about 45 minutes, they were done. And Kelsey was very surprised. Both boys had almost completely filled their buckets, while Kelsey's wasn't near the top.

"What are we going to do with all of these?" Tyler asked, as they began to walk back to the store.

"We could give some to Margaret. Lisa likes blueberries," Ryan replied.

"True. Let's drop by home," Tyler said.

"Does Zach like blueberries? We could give some to him," Ryan said.

"He can have some next weekend," Tyler said.

"Will they last?" Ryan asked Kelsey.

"We can freeze some," she replied.

They walked into the store and got in line for their berries to be weighed.

"You go first," Tyler said to Ryan.

"No, go ahead," Ryan replied.

"I'll go," Kelsey said, walking to the front. She handed her bucket to the clerk.

"Three pounds, seven ounces," the clerk said, transferring the berries into a container and handing them to Kelsey. Tyler opened his wallet and paid for Kelsey's berries. Kelsey thanked him.

"I'll go next," Tyler said, handing his bucket over.

"Five pounds, three ounces."

"Impressive, but not good enough," Ryan said.

"Just wait," Tyler said, paying for his berries and collecting his container.

Ryan confidently handed over his basket.

"Four pounds, fifteen ounces," the clerk said.

"Aw!" Ryan commented, as he paid for his berries.

"I'm sure you ate at least five ounces. Too bad. Where do you want to go for dinner, Kels?" Tyler gloated.

"We could just eat at your house," Ryan pouted.

"Forget it," Tyler said. "I want prime rib, since it's on you."

"Fine," Ryan said grumpily. They walked back to Tyler's car and got in. Tyler carefully put his berries on the back seat next to Ryan, while Kelsey put hers at her feet. Tyler drove out of the lot and towards Medina.

"So how many pounds of these do you want to keep?" Tyler asked as they drove toward downtown Bellevue.

"We'll give Lisa my bag. I'll tell her I picked them for her." Ryan said.

"Do you think she's going to give you less work because you gave her four pounds of blueberries?"

"Almost five pounds. Anyway, it can't hurt. I've still got three weeks left. Got to curry favor with the higher-ups."

"I wonder if she's home," Tyler mused.

"When did you last see her?" Kelsey asked.

"The Tactec picnic," Tyler said.

"She hasn't dropped by Simon's office?" Kelsey said.

"I'm not sure Ms. Olsen is welcome there," Tyler replied.

"Why not?" Kelsey asked.

"My mother's animosity with Bill Simon goes back to when she was practicing as a lawyer. I don't know why, but I think they were on opposite sides of a case, and it didn't go well," Tyler replied. He drove through downtown Bellevue and headed towards Medina.

"These are good," Ryan said.

"You should really wash them," Tyler commented.

"They're better with the dirt," Ryan replied.

Tyler reached his hand back. "Give me one." Ryan put a few berries into Tyler's palm and Tyler ate them.

"They are good," Tyler said.

"You didn't have any at the patch?" Kelsey asked in surprise.

"I was too focused on beating Ryan," Tyler replied. He turned the car and drove into Medina. A few minutes later, Tyler drove the car into his driveway, and the three of them got out.

"Ryan, I think you've eaten at least a pound," Kelsey said, eyeing

Ryan's container of blueberries.

"They're really good," Ryan commented.

"Here," Kelsey said, reaching into the car and taking out her own container. "Why don't we give her mine?" She handed it to Tyler, who smiled at her.

"Thanks, Kelsey. Ryan, you might want to wipe the blueberries off of your face," he said. Ryan put his blueberries back on the car seat and wiped his face. Then they walked to the front door, and Tyler let them in with his key.

"Is anyone home?" Tyler called as they walked into the foyer. Kelsey wondered if anyone could hear him, considering how large the house was.

"Tyler!" Lisa Olsen called out. Kelsey looked over, and Lisa Olsen glided into the hall. She was wearing a silk flowered halter sundress, different from the one she had worn at the picnic, and had sunglasses pushed to the top of her dark hair.

"Well, this is a nice surprise," Lisa said, kissing Tyler and Ryan. "Hello, Kelsey," she added.

"Hi, Ms. Olsen," Kelsey said politely.

"We brought you blueberries," Ryan said, pulling the container out of Tyler's hands and handing it to her. "I picked them myself."

Tyler rolled his eyes, and Kelsey stifled a giggle.

"Really? Ryan, you're such a sweetheart," Lisa said, taking the box from him. "Why don't you join me? I was having lemonade outside."

Tyler glanced at Kelsey, who nodded her assent. Lisa had been perfectly nice to her at the picnic, so she wasn't nervous. Yet.

"Sounds great," Tyler said.

"It's Margaret's day off," Lisa said as they walked into the kitchen. She pulled three glasses down from a cupboard, and handed one to each of them. Then they followed her outside.

She sat down at a table which had a stack of folders weighed down by a small rock. A pitcher of lemonade and her own glass stood to the side. They all sat down, and Tyler poured a glass of lemonade for Kelsey.

"You'll probably want sugar," Lisa said, standing and going back into the house.

Kelsey took a sip. It was completely sour.

"Lisa has weird eating habits," Tyler commented.

Lisa returned with a jar of sugar and three long stirring spoons. Tyler, Ryan, and Kelsey all added sugar to their own glasses.

"Ryan, I heard that you're doing really well at work," Lisa said. "Your father and I are quite pleased."

"Thanks," Ryan said modestly.

"How's Simon?" Lisa asked Tyler.

"Fine," Tyler said.

"I'm surprised that you have the day off," Lisa commented.

"I usually have Sundays off," Tyler replied.

"Only Sundays though?" Lisa asked.

"Yes," Tyler replied smiling.

"Will you be working for Tactec next summer?" Lisa asked.

"No. Simon again," Tyler replied.

"Seriously, bro?" Ryan said to him.

"Why not?" Tyler said.

"You really don't want to have a life, do you?" Ryan commented.

"It's fine, Ryan. I'm learning a lot."

"He does know how to structure a deal," Lisa said. "It's a skill you can use when you join Tactec."

"I guess," Tyler said noncommittally.

"Are you enjoying Collins Nicol?" Lisa asked Kelsey.

Kelsey was surprised that she knew where she worked. "It's great," Kelsey replied.

"Good," Lisa said. She turned back to Tyler. "Has Chris subpoenaed you yet?"

"What?" Tyler asked her.

"His lawyer notified us that he's planning on deposing you. You had mentioned that he might."

"I was hoping that he had forgotten," Tyler replied, frowning.

Lisa shook her head at her son. "No, he hasn't. Are you going to fight the subpoena?" she asked.

"Yes. I don't want to be deposed," Tyler said.

"I'm not sure how you're going to get out of it, but good luck," Lisa said. "Are you going to hire your own lawyer, or do you want to use Collins Nicol?"

"I'll ask Simon to help me for now. I'm sure he knows how to quash a subpoena," Tyler replied.

"I'm sure he does," Lisa commented.

"Did Chris's lawyer say what he wanted to depose me about?" Tyler asked.

"Your terrible childhood, I imagine," Lisa said with a smile.

"Interesting," Tyler replied. "I wish you had settled," he commented.

"Chris is going to wish I had too, once I'm done," Lisa replied. "But let's not discuss Chris on such a lovely day."

"How's the Taiwan purchase?" Tyler asked her.

Lisa's face fell. "Nothing has changed since the last board meeting," she commented.

"Nothing at all?" Tyler replied.

"I'm not sure what's going on," Lisa said thoughtfully. "I'm going to have to do something."

"Like what?" Ryan asked. Lisa glanced at him.

"My first instinct is to fire a bunch of people, but that's not going to fix the problem," Lisa commented.

"What does Bob think?" Tyler asked her.

"He's as lost as I am. It's not like the group isn't capable, and our go-betweens don't think it's a cultural problem. But the deal isn't getting done." She frowned. "I have no idea what to do."

"I'm not sure I've ever heard you say that before," Tyler said.

"I'm not sure I ever have," Lisa replied. "Never mind, I'm sure we'll have it done by fourth quarter. Ryan, what's going on with the Kinnon case?"

"The auditors are supposed to give us a preliminary report on Tuesday," Ryan said.

Lisa nodded.

"What were you working on?" Tyler asked Lisa.

"Nothing special," Lisa commented. She picked the rock off of the folders and handed them to Tyler. Tyler began looking through the folders.

"You seem very stressed," Ryan commented to LIsa.

"Do I?" she asked him. Ryan nodded.

Lisa sighed. "I suppose I am."

"You should enjoy the summer," Ryan said. "Hang on." He stood up and walked into the house. Tyler continued to look through the folders, and Lisa adjusted the Bulgari sunglasses in her hair. Kelsey looked out at the water, which was a vision of blue. Ryan returned with a bowl, full of blueberries.

"Try one," he said to her, placing the bowl on the table. Lisa took a blueberry and tasted it.

"Delicious. Where did you pick these?" she asked.

"There's a farm fifteen minutes away," Tyler said, not looking up from the paperwork.

"Really?" Lisa said, taking another blueberry. "Have you ever been blueberry picking before?"

"Never," Tyler replied.

"I wouldn't have thought to take you," Lisa commented.

"I bet Chris has been blueberry picking," Tyler said, handing the folders back to her.

"I bet he has. He's a country boy, and there's not much else to do in Idaho, is there?" Lisa said. "I'm sure that the kind of thing he's going to ask you about. All the wonderful, unimportant things you missed out on because he was in New York. Why fight the subpoena, Tyler? You seem to be on Chris's side."

"I said I wasn't taking sides, and I meant it," Tyler commented. "I don't have time to do the things I want to do now, and I really don't want to waste time on this."

"You should think about getting your own attorney," Lisa said. "Simon can help you try to quash the subpoena, but if you get deposed, you'll need your own counsel."

"Maybe," Tyler commented.

"Ryan, are you eating all of the blueberries you brought for me?" Lisa asked, amused.

"Sorry," Ryan said sheepishly.

"It's okay," Lisa said, pushing the bowl towards him. "Eat all you want."

"We should go," Tyler said, leaning back in his chair and looking up at the sky.

"What are you doing next?" Lisa asked.

"Ryan's going to buy me dinner since he picked fewer blueberries than I did. You can join us if you like," Tyler replied.

"Thanks, but Margaret left me dinner," Lisa commented. "I have a lot of work to do."

"You should get some rest," Ryan said, standing up. Tyler and Kelsey joined him.

"I'll try. Thanks for the blueberries."

"You're welcome."

"I understand from Margaret that you're becoming quite the chef. When will you make dinner for me?" Lisa asked Ryan.

"Whenever you want," Ryan said excitedly.

"Okay, wait until your father gets back. We can all have dinner together."

"I'd like that," Ryan said.

"Maybe I can see my son again as well?" Lisa asked.

Tyler shook his head. "I eat dinner in the office," he replied.

"Day after day," Ryan added.

"That's Bill Simon. Well, Tyler Davis, you wanted to work for him."

Tyler smiled. "That I did."

"Regret it?" Lisa asked.

"No," Tyler replied.

"Good. You should never regret the things you decide to do. I'll see you boys later. Goodbye, Kelsey."

"Goodbye, Ms. Olsen," Kelsey said. She and the boys left as Lisa slid her sunglasses down over her eyes and picked up a folder.

"Where should we eat?" Tyler asked as he started the car. "Here or back in Seattle?"

"Let's eat here. We always eat in Seattle," Ryan replied as Tyler pulled out of the drive.

"Kels, what are you in the mood for?"

"Steak sounded good," Kelsey replied.

"It's okay with me," Ryan said.

Tyler drove them back into downtown Bellevue and to the mall where Kelsey had had her Tactec party makeover more than a half year ago. As Tyler parked the car, Kelsey marveled at how much things had changed between them then.

The first time she had been in this mall, Kelsey hadn't heard of most of the designer stores lining the walkways. Now her closet held dresses and shoes from some of the most expensive ones here. When Tyler invited her to the Tactec holiday party, she had been hesitant to go. Now, she loved spending time with him, even though it was still on his own terms. They got out of the car and headed to dinner.

On Monday morning, Kelsey packed her gym bag and left her bedroom at 6 a.m. When she walked out into the living room, Tyler was standing in the kitchen, having coffee.

"Working out, Miss North?" he asked.

"I am. How about you?"

"Just about to leave. I'm glad I saw you. Do you want a ride?"

"Sure. Thanks," Kelsey said. Tyler took his keys off the kitchen counter and picked up his own gym bag. They walked out of the condo and to the elevator.

"Where do you work out?" Tyler asked her.

"There's a gym across the street from the office," Kelsey said.

"You can work out with me if you'd prefer. I go to the Athletic Club," Tyler replied.

"Thanks, but my gym is fine," Kelsey said.

"Do you go every day?"

"Monday through Thursday. How about you?"

"Whenever I can," Tyler said. They walked to Tyler's car and he put his gym bag in the trunk. Kelsey put hers in the back seat of the car. Tyler drove out of the lot.

"It looks like that's pretty often," Kelsey commented. "You've stayed in shape."

"Thanks," Tyler said. "It's been harder without my fitness coach around."

"You mean your eating coach," Kelsey commented.

"You're both," Tyler replied.

Kelsey looked out of the window as Seattle began to wake up.

"Is your gym on Fourth or Fifth Avenue?" Tyler asked.

"Fifth," Kelsey said. "Thanks for taking me in."

"It's my pleasure. Will you see your roommate at work?"

"It's not likely," Kelsey said. She was really hoping there was no call from the summer associate coordinator today.

"Good," Tyler said. He turned the car onto Fifth Avenue and drove south.

"Do you have a board meeting this week?" Kelsey asked.

"Tomorrow. Lisa will be yelling at the staff about the Taiwan deal again, I expect," Tyler commented.

"She didn't seem happy yesterday," Kelsey commented.

"There's no one to blame," Tyler replied. "Except herself."

"It must be difficult to be the CEO," Kelsey said.

"I hope not to find out," Tyler replied.

"It would be a loss to Tactec," Kelsey said. "You understand the business better than anyone."

"What makes you say that?"

"The way that you interact with your mother. I mean, she's sitting there with a bunch of confidential documents and she just hands them over to you. She obviously thinks a lot of your judgment," Kelsey said.

"Maybe. It doesn't make up for the fact that I don't want the job," Tyler replied, as he stopped at a light.

"No, I guess not," Kelsey replied. The light changed and Tyler drove on.

He was silent for a moment, then said, "By the way, Ryan asked me to tell you that if you want something special for dinner, just message him and he'll make it for you."

Kelsey smiled. "That's really nice. Actually, though, I thought I'd join you at work tonight. You still have a filing, don't you?"

"We do. We will probably file before midnight, though," Tyler said. "I'd love your company."

Kelsey nodded as Tyler pulled up to the Columbia Center. She reached into the back seat and took her gym bag.

"Thanks for the lift," she said to him. "I'll see you tonight."

"Okay," Tyler said, smiling. "Have a good day at work, Miss North."

"You too," Kelsey said, and she got out of the car.

That evening, Kelsey and Tyler entered the condo. Kelsey had had a great day at work. The summer coordinator had called her to apologize for putting her in an apartment with Brittany. She got two new assignments, both of which looked really interesting. And Alex Carsten had dropped by to compliment her on her work.

Afterward, she had gone to Tyler's office, where he was just finishing up his part of the filing. Instead of eating in the office, they had called Ryan to request dinner, but to all of their surprise, Ryan had to work late because of tomorrow's Tactec board meeting. So Tyler had treated Kelsey to dinner at Pike Place Market.

Tyler threw his gym bag next to the sofa and stretched out on the sofa pillows.

"I'm enjoying these days of getting home early," he said.

"I'm happy for you," Kelsey said, as she entered her room. She looked around startled, then quickly realized that Monday was Mariel's day to clean the condo.

There were fresh roses on the dresser, and all of Kelsey's things had been straightened up. The master bathroom sparkled, and there were cream-colored roses there as well. Kelsey opened a drawer and looked at it puzzled. She blinked and looked at it more closely. Half of her underwear was gone.

It wasn't exactly a loss. Like all things involving clothing, Kelsey felt that underwear was purely functional, and her mother had constantly complained about Kelsey's willingness to keep overstretched bras and torn undies well past their good days. But Kelsey was bewildered all the same.

She thought about asking Tyler, then immediately put the thought out of her mind. Besides the complete weirdness of asking a guy about the disappearance of her clothes, what would she say? "Mariel stole my worn-out bras?" Kelsey took one more look at the half-empty drawer and closed it.

Besides the mystery of her underwear, Kelsey discovered that things were quite normal at Ryan and Tyler's house. As she expected, Ryan spent most of his time at home cooking and Tyler was rarely home at all. Kelsey was surprised at the quiet, but realized as they were all only children, they were used to entertaining themselves. She spent her time helping Ryan in the kitchen when she was home, or joining Tyler in his office at night.

On Thursday afternoon, as Kelsey was letting herself back into the house, she felt a moment of apprehension. She wondered why, then she realized that Mariel had come to clean again. She wondered if anything else was missing. She walked into her room. The roses had been changed, this time to bold pink ones, and her desk had been straightened again. Kelsey put her bag down and opened her underwear drawer. She was surprised at what she saw.

Instead of the half-empty drawer, her drawer was now completely full of brand new underwear. It was in her size, in the muted colors and soft cottons she preferred, and as she discovered, exactly the same brand that she usually wore. It had all been washed and was ready for use. Kelsey gasped in surprise.

Holding a new bra in her hands, she realized what must have happened. One of Mariel's jobs must have been to rotate out worn clothing and replace it with new items. It was exactly the kind of detail that the billionaire Olsen household would have expected. Kelsey refolded the bra and put it back into the drawer. She heard keys in the door. Kelsey walked into the living room just as Ryan walked in.

"Hey, Kels," Ryan said.

"Hi, Ryan."

"Are you staying for dinner, or heading over to Tyler's?" he asked. It had become his normal question. It determined which recipes he would work on that night.

"I'll go to Tyler's in a bit," Kelsey bit her lip. "Ryan?"

"Yes?" he asked, taking off his jacket and tossing it carelessly on the sofa.

"Does Mariel buy new clothing for you?" she asked him.

"Clothing?" Ryan asked, unknotting his tie.

Kelsey took a deep breath. "Underwear," she said.

"Oh. Yes. Why?"

"Just curious," Kelsey said.

"Do you have new underwear, Miss North?" Ryan grinned.

"Go away, Ryan," Kelsey said blushing and turning to go back to her room.

The next evening, Kelsey stood outside on the Fifth Avenue side of the Columbia Center. She had changed out of her work clothes and was wearing jeans and a t-shirt. Her long blonde hair was in a ponytail, which stuck out of the back of a Mariners baseball cap. Kelsey's gym bag was slung over her shoulder.

Zach's Land Rover pulled in front of her. He beeped the horn, and Kelsey got in. She put on her seat belt and Zach drove off.

"Hi, Miss North," Zach said to her as they drove down 5th Avenue.

"Hey, Zach." Kelsey said. Zach was wearing a Mariners cap of his own. "How are you?"

"Very happy to be out of the Eastside," Zach replied. He drove out of downtown and into the International District. "How are you? How are your new roommates?"

"Great," Kelsey said.

"Great? Wow, your last roommate must have really sucked," Zach commented. He pulled the Land Rover into a parking lot and parked the car. Kelsey giggled.

"Give me your bag," Zach said as they got out of the car. She complied and Zach threw it in the trunk of the car. He locked the car and they walked toward the stadiums.

"Ryan said he'd meet us at the seats," Kelsey said.

"Ryan's not going to show," Zachary said confidently.

"Why do you say that?"

"I'm just guessing," Zach said. They crossed Fifth Avenue and walked toward the train overpass. "Tyler still can't come?"

"Another filing." Kelsey said.

"Tyler's insane. He'd be much better off working for Lisa."

"He says he sees enough of her at the board meetings."

"They've had a billion of them this summer. I thought Lisa was just making excuses to keep Tyler in town, but it seems like he and Ryan are going to one every week," Zach commented.

"I think it's the Taiwan purchase," Kelsey said.

Zach smiled knowingly. "Yeah, I need to ask Tyler about that this weekend."

"How has your summer been?"

"Misery," Zach said.

"Really?"

"My parents are always on my case," he sighed.

"I'm sorry to hear that," Kelsey said.

"Thanks. Ryan's grades didn't help matters either."

"Ryan's grades? They weren't on the internet this time."

"Ryan helpfully sent them to my parents' office," Zach said. "I hate him."

"He did better than you?" Kelsey guessed.

"By leaps and bounds. I can't believe he got an A in Schiavelli's class. I thought I would get a fail letter," Zach said.

"Well, first year is over now," Kelsey said in comfort.

"Tyler said you got straight A's. Congratulations."

"Thank you," Kelsey said. They were walking across the parking lot.

"How's work?"

"It's good. I like Collins Nicol a lot."

"Do they like you?" Zach asked her.

"I hope so. I really don't want to have to re-interview next fall," Kelsey said.

"You want to stay in Seattle, then?" Zachary asked her.

Kelsey glanced at him, and he was smiling. "I think so. Why?"

"No reason. Just wondering," Zachary said. "Do you want peanuts before we go in?"

Kelsey and Zach got peanuts, went into the stadium, and took their seats behind first base. They spent most of the game discussing the various things that they had done over the summer. As Zachary had predicted, Ryan was a no-show. She and Zachary ended the evening by stopping for Chinese at a restaurant in the International District, then drove home.

Kelsey walked out of the master bedroom the next morning. Zachary was sitting on the sofa reading, blanket over his feet, wearing a Princeton sweatshirt and pajama pants. Ryan was in the kitchen, cooking.

"Good morning," Kelsey said.

"Hi, Kels," Zach replied.

"Morning," Ryan said brightly. "Would you like breakfast?" he asked hopefully. Zach looked over at Ryan doubtfully, then looked back to his Kindle.

"Of course," Kelsey replied happily. She walked over to the kitchen. "What are you making today?"

"Scones," Ryan replied.

"Yum," Kelsey said. "Zach, do you want one?"

"You're willing to eat Ryan's cooking?" Zach asked in surprise.

"Ryan's an excellent chef," Kelsey replied.

"You're just saying that because you're living here," Zach said dismissively.

"It's your loss," Ryan snapped. Kelsey smiled, and took a plate and put two scones on it. They looked amazing, with bubbly red jam oozing out of the side, and crispy sugar crystals on top. She walked over to the sofa and sat next to Zach. Kelsey broke off a piece of a scone and offered it to Zach.

"You try it first," Zach replied.

"Fine," Kelsey said, popping the piece of scone into her mouth. It was delicious.

Zach looked at Kelsey for signs of dislike. Seeing none, he broke off a piece of scone and began to chew.

"Wow," he said in surprise. "Not bad, Ryan."

"Told you," Ryan said from the kitchen.

Zach broke off a larger piece of scone and ate it.

"So how are you this morning, Miss North?"

Kelsey, mouth full of scone, looked at Zach. Last night he had been wearing a Mariners baseball cap, so she hadn't noticed how short his jet black hair was. Unlike the slightly long look he had worn most of the school year, Zach's hair was now cut to a length appropriate for the military, or at least for a conservative corporate setting.

"I'm good," Kelsey managed to get out.

"Still breaking hearts?" Zachary teased.

"Hardly," Kelsey replied, finally finishing her mouthful.

"I heard you broke up with Lucas Anderson," Zach commented. Kelsey shrugged in response. Zach picked up the scone and said, "Tyler's completely jealous."

Then Zachary look a bite of the scone, and began to chew.

Kelsey laughed. "Not of Lucas. Tyler told me himself."

Zachary swallowed and grinned. "No, Tyler wasn't worried about Lucas. But there's someone interested in you at Collins Nicol, isn't there?" He looked at Kelsey for her response.

Kelsey looked back at Zach in confusion. "Is there?" she asked.

"You don't know. You're so cute," Zachary replied. "Yes, Miss North, there is."

Kelsey frowned for a moment and thought. She had no idea who it was. She mentally ran through the male summer associates. She shook her head.

"Not an summer associate," she concluded.

"Correct. Not an summer associate. An associate," Zachary said. He smiled at her. He seemed to be enjoying the game.

"One of the associates is interested in me? You must be kidding," Kelsey replied.

"I can't believe you haven't noticed. Tyler mentioned it to me. Tyler saw him at the party you took him and Ryan to."

Kelsey thought again. Almost every Collins Nicol associate had dropped by the party, mostly for the free food. And as a hopeful summer associate, she had talked to at least a dozen of them. She had no idea who Zachary was talking about.

"I'm clueless," Kelsey concluded.

"Well, you've managed to alarm Tyler. Good job."

"Tyler still isn't going to ask me out."

"Honestly, I'm not sure it matters. The two of you are devoted to each other, whether you'll admit it or not."

Kelsey took a piece of scone and ate it. She had to agree with Zachary about her devotion to Tyler. She wasn't as sure about Tyler's supposed dedication to her.

"Tyler will come around," Zachary said. "At the moment, between Bill Simon, Tactec, and Law Review, I'm surprised he has time to sleep."

"True," Kelsey agreed. It wasn't like Tyler had time to date anyone else.

"You and Tyler, Ryan and Jess. I'm the one who's jealous," Zachary commented. He took another bite of the scone.

"You have Kim," Kelsey said. Zachary glanced over at Ryan, who was putting something into the oven.

"It's not the same," Zach replied. "Anyway, Tyler's really glad you've been around this summer."

"It's been fun," Kelsey agreed. "We miss you and Jess though."

"Ryan's obviously been keeping busy. I didn't know he could boil water," Zach said.

Kelsey giggled. "He decided he needed a hobby. He didn't tell you?"

"Ryan and I don't talk a lot," Zach said matter-of-factly. Kelsey thought about this. She had realized since last night that Zachary and Ryan weren't as close as she had originally thought. She wondered if it had something to do with Zach's troubled relationship with Kim.

"Well, Ryan's working really hard. I think Jess will be impressed."

"How is Jess?"

"Good. She wishes she were here, though."

"I think Ryan has plans for Miss Hunter for next summer. There won't be a room for me next summer either, despite the renovation plans."

Kelsey smiled. "You can have mine."

"Jess won't stay here without you. And Tyler would throw me out anyway. He'd rather have you here."

"There's no guarantee I'll be in Seattle next summer. Collins Nicol hasn't made me an offer."

"I'm sure they will," Zach said.

"I hope so."

"Talk to your associate. I bet he'll want you to stay."

"I'm not sure I believe you," Kelsey said.

"Trust me. Don't tease Tyler with this one."

"Actually, it sounds like I should," Kelsey commented.

Zach smiled at her. "Like I said, you're a heartbreaker. Be nice. Tyler's working hard for you."

"For me?" Kelsey said in surprise.

"For your future. I've said enough," Zach said, biting into the scone and winking at her.

Kelsey frowned.

"I hate you, Zachary Payne," she said.

"Get in line," Zach grinned.

"For what?" Ryan asked. He had finished in the kitchen, and was wiping his hands on a dish towel.

"For your delicious baked goods, of course," Zach said.

"I shouldn't let you eat them."

"I'm sorry, Ryan, I really didn't know that you could cook," Zach said.

"I can now," Ryan replied.

"What else can you make?"

"Lots of things," Ryan said, sitting on floor in front of Kelsey. "You liked it, Kelsey?"

"They were wonderful, Ryan," Kelsey said. "Perfect."

Ryan smiled at her.

"Tyler's working all day, so do you want to go out with me?" Zach asked.

"Where are you going?" Ryan asked.

"I'm going to First Avenue. I want some new clothes."

"I'll go," Kelsey said.

"Nah," Ryan replied.

"When is Tyler usually done on Saturdays?" Zach asked them.

Kelsey and Ryan looked at each other.

"Two?" Ryan said.

"Five?" Kelsey commented.

"Seriously?" Zach asked in surprise.

"He doesn't usually work on Sunday," Ryan said.

"Simon's crazier than I thought."

"He's worse than Lisa," Ryan said. "I didn't think that was possible."

"I think Tyler likes it," Zach said.

"How can he like not having a life?" Ryan commented.

"Ask Tyler," Zach replied.

"I don't know how he can stay away from Kelsey all of the time," Ryan said thoughtfully.

Kelsey glanced at Ryan. And Zach smiled.

"So what has Tyler told you about her?" Zach asked Ryan.

Ryan looked at Zach, then at Kelsey, a bit alarmed.

"Nothing," he said. He stood up, and went back into the kitchen.

"Told you," Zach said.

"You've told me nothing. That's my point," Kelsey replied.

"Just be nice to Tyler and don't date your coworkers," Zachary said, smiling. "Things will work out."

Kelsey and Zach walked around the stores on First Avenue. Kelsey mostly shopped at the mall, so she was surprised to see the number of expensive specialty shops on the street. Zachary went into a store that carried the skater-boy/club wear that he often wore to class.

"Nothing you can wear to work here," Kelsey teased him.

"No," Zach said. "Are you coming out with us tonight?" he asked.

"I don't know. Where are you going?"

"Dua," Zach said.

Kelsey knew Dua was one of Seattle's hottest nightclubs, but she had never been. "I'll go."

"Will you dance with Tyler?" Zachary teased. Kelsey frowned. She didn't really want to be reminded of her dance floor behavior with Tyler.

"You weren't even there," she said.

"Ryan was happy to share that information with me," Zachary commented, as he picked up a pair of black pants.

"No, I won't be dancing with Tyler," Kelsey said.

"Aw. Too bad. I needed a post for Facebook. I was going to shoot video."

"You're hilarious," Kelsey said.

Zach laughed. "Actually, it's you and Tyler who are hilarious. I don't know who you think you're fooling," he said, replacing the pants on the rack.

Ourselves, Kelsey thought.

That evening, Kelsey walked into the living room. While she had been out with Zachary, she had bought a form-fitting beaded dress, and she was wearing it tonight. She had sent most of her non-work clothes back to Port Townsend before exams, figuring that she wouldn't be going out clubbing this summer. And she refused to wear the gold dress she had worn with Tyler to the Law Review party. It brought back way too many uncomfortable memories.

"Wow," Ryan said. For the first time during Zach's visit, Ryan would be joining them. "Kels, you look amazing."

"Thank you," Kelsey said.

"Is that a Missoni?" Ryan asked her, looking at the dress.

"I have no idea what that is," Kelsey said.

"Ignore Mr. Fashion," Tyler said, leaving his room and buttoning his cuffs. "You look beautiful, Kelsey."

"Thanks." Kelsey said.

"Ready?" Zachary asked, stepping out of the bathroom. He was also wearing the outfit he had purchased today: a pair of black jeans, a black t-shirt and a leather jacket. He had spent more than two thousand dollars on it. Kelsey's dress had cost twenty-nine dollars at a vintage store in Pike Place Market.

They took a cab across town to Dua. Tyler helped Kelsey out of the taxi, because once again she had worn high heels. Even after a summer in pumps, she still wasn't used to walking in anything higher than a sneaker. Kelsey felt Tyler's muscular arm around her waist as they walked to the door, and she strengthened her resolve to avoid dancing with him tonight.

"Ryan Perkins, for four," the bouncer was saying. Ryan nodded. "VIP section," he said to a woman wearing a very tight blouse and skirt combination next to him.

"Mr. Perkins," the woman said sexily, wrapping her arm around his and guiding the four of them through the crowd and to the VIP table.

Kelsey slid into the center, and Tyler sat next to her. Ryan took her other side and Zachary sat next to Tyler. Moments later, a tall waitress arrived with a large bottle of champagne and four glasses.

"Mr. Perkins? Compliments of the manager," she said.

"Thank you, but we don't drink," Ryan said.

"Sparkling water then?" the waitress said, without missing a beat.

"That would be great. Thanks," Ryan said.

"Since when do you not drink?" Zachary said as the waitress left.

"Jess doesn't drink," Ryan said.

"Neither does Kels," Tyler commented, glancing at Zachary.

"Just curious," Zachary said. He stood. "I'm going to check out the dance floor," he said, leaving the table.

A moment later, the waitress returned with the sparkling water. She poured it into their glasses and left the table. A few minutes later, a large cut fruit plate arrived. As Tyler handed her a strawberry, Kelsey asked, "How are we sitting in the VIP section and not having bottle service?" Every club Kelsey had been to required patrons to buy expensive bottles of alcohol to even go into the VIP section.

"Because you're with Ryan Perkins," Tyler said in amusement.

"I'm friends with the owner, Jordan. He'll drop by later," Ryan said.

"Jordan will get more than 500 dollars of publicity out of Ryan's visit, don't worry," Tyler said. "Do you want to dance?"

"Absolutely not," Kelsey said.

Tyler grinned at her.

A half hour later, Tyler was on the dance floor dancing with a pretty brunette who, from the looks of it, couldn't believe her luck. Kelsey had stuck to her promise, and was helping Ryan finish the fruit plate. As Tyler had predicted, Jordan had dropped by the table, and had taken a few photos of himself with Ryan, which Kelsey was sure were already on Twitter and Instagram. Zach was nowhere to be seen.

"Did you really do this all the time?" Kelsey asked Ryan. "Go out every night?"

"Pretty much," Ryan replied, eating a grape.

"Do you miss it?" Kelsey asked.

"No. I'd rather spend time with Jess," Ryan said. Kelsey smiled. If Jessica could only see Ryan's commitment to her even when she was three thousand miles away, she'd never worry about Ryan breaking her heart.

"Excuse me. Would you like to dance?" Kelsey and Ryan looked up. A handsome Italian was looking at Kelsey. Ryan lifted an eyebrow.

"I'd love to," Kelsey said, allowing herself to be pulled up.

"Traitor," Ryan hissed at her. Kelsey stuck her tongue out at Ryan, smiled at her dance partner, and walked to the dance floor.

Kelsey spent much of the next two hours dancing. Several men cut in, but never Tyler, who didn't leave the dance floor either. He did glance over at Kelsey in amusement several times. She discovered what had happened to Zachary, who she hadn't seen since the first five minutes they had arrived. He was talking to a stunning blonde girl, wearing a very short red satin dress. Ryan stayed at the VIP table, talking to various people, most of whom he seemed to know.

As she was dancing with a second-year medical student, Tyler walked up. He smiled at Kelsey and cut in. Kelsey glared at him.

"Don't worry, I don't want to dance. I saw you yawning, Do you want to go?"

Kelsey giggled at her annoyed reaction. She should have known that Tyler wouldn't push her to dance, when he knew she didn't want to. "Sure," she said.

"Okay," he said. He put his arm around her waist and led her off the dance floor and over to Zachary, who had been talking to the red dress girl for what seemed to Kelsey to be hours.

"Zach, we're getting Ryan and heading back," Tyler said to him.

"Okay. I'll see you back there," Zachary said. He looked at the blonde girl, who smiled at him.

"You're staying?"

"Yeah. Give me your key."

"No way. I'm not going to let Ryan throw me out of his condo because of you. Just call me later and I'll let you in," Tyler replied.

"Fine."

"I can't believe you're doing this in front of him," Tyler said.

"I'm a grown man," Zach replied.

"Suppose he tells Kim?" Tyler asked. Kelsey looked at him.

"He won't," Zachary said. "See you later," he said, walking off.

A few minutes later, Ryan walked up to Tyler and Kelsey. Ryan glanced across the room, where Zachary was standing with his new friend.

Ryan left Tyler and Kelsey, and walked over to Zach and the girl. Ryan said something to Zach, smiled at the girl, glared at Zach, and he and Zach walked over to Tyler.

"What are you doing?" Ryan said to Zach angrily.

"The same thing you used to do," Zach replied casually.

"No. Not the same," Ryan said.

"That's what you say," Zach commented.

"Don't you love her?" Ryan asked.

"Sure," Zach said, without enthusiasm.

"Then think about how she'd feel about this," Ryan said.

"She's not going to know," Zach replied.

"I'll tell her," Ryan warned.

"Go ahead," Zach replied.

"You don't care?" Ryan said.

"I'll accept the consequences if you do. I'm not afraid of Kim," Zach said. "I'll see you later." Zach walked back over to the girl.

"Let's go, Ryan," Tyler said. Without a glance at Zach, Ryan headed toward the exit.

"How can you excuse this?" Ryan snapped at Tyler once they were in the cab. Kelsey sat in the middle of the back seat, between the two.

"I have nothing to do with this," Tyler replied calmly.

"You don't think he's doing anything wrong," Ryan replied.

"Incorrect. Zachary is doing what Zachary does. I'm not judging him, just like I don't judge you."

"It's because it's Kim, isn't it? I wish I knew why you hated her so much," Ryan said..

"I don't hate Kim, but I told you that if you cared about her, you should keep her away from Zach. In fact, I said it in front of Zachary."

"He thought it was funny," Ryan commented

"Because he knew it was true," Tyler replied.

"I never should have trusted him with her."

"But you did, and now you have to live with that decision. So don't blame me."

"You could stop him."

"That's not my job. I don't want him meddling in my life, so I stay out of his," Tyler said.

"I'm going to tell her," Ryan mused.

"No, you aren't. You would break her heart," Tyler replied.

"It's going to be broken anyway."

"Stay out of it, Ryan. She'll never believe you."

"It's true."

"Where's your proof?"

"We aren't in court," Ryan replied.

"Of course we are. Kim's the judge and you're going up against Zach. Who do you think she'll believe?"

"Me," Ryan said.

"She still loves him, so no," Tyler commented.

"I can't just sit by, and watch him do this to her," Ryan said.

Tyler looked out of the window. "We're here," he said to the cabbie. The cab pulled over, Tyler paid the cab driver, and they piled out of the back seat. The cab drove off, and they entered the lobby of Ryan's building. Ryan jabbed the elevator button violently, and the elevator arrived. The three of them went up to Ryan's and Tyler opened the door. Kelsey went into her room to change.

When she came out five minutes later, Tyler was sitting on the sofa, and Ryan was pacing in front of the window. Tyler smiled gently at Kelsey and patted the seat next to him. Kelsey walked over, a bit timidly. She wasn't sure she wanted to watch the rest of this discussion. Kelsey knew she would hate to be in Ryan's position with a friend.

"What do you think, Kelsey?" Ryan asked, his back to her. He had stopped pacing and was looking out of the window. Elliott Bay shone in the moonlight.

Tyler shook his head at her to be quiet. Kelsey decided to take his advice. After a moment of silence, Ryan turned around.

"Keep Kelsey out of this. This isn't her battle," Tyler said to him.

"I just want her opinion."

"Kelsey is friends with Zach. You don't need it."

"Why not?"

"Because I don't want you telling Zachary later that Kelsey was on Kim's side."

"Are you?" Ryan said directly to Kelsey.

"I'm taking the Fifth," Kelsey replied.

Tyler and Ryan laughed, and the tension in the room broke.

"Only you could make us laugh in this situation," Tyler commented.

Ryan leaned against a wall. "I hate him for doing this to her," he said.

"Because it's Kim," Tyler mused.

"She doesn't deserve this. Even you know that," Ryan said.

"I know."

"I can't tell her," Ryan said. "She'll never forgive me."

"No, she won't. Let her find out on her own."

"I won't let her marry him," Ryan said with determination.

"He's not going to ask her," Tyler replied with confidence.

"I wish I understood Zach as well as you do."

"Just drop it, Ryan. Let Zach and Kim work things out on their own."

"She knows he's here this weekend. What am I going to tell her?"

"Don't pick up your phone. If you do, tell her about your scones."

Ryan laughed. "I'm going to bed," he said.

"Good call."

"He better not wake me up when he gets in."

"He won't," Tyler said.

"Good night, Kelsey," Ryan said, and he went into his bedroom.

Tyler turned to Kelsey. "It's like a really bad soap opera, isn't it?" he said.

"Why doesn't Zach just break up with Kim?" Kelsey asked him quietly.

"I think he likes the drama," Tyler replied.

"Why is Ryan so upset?"

"Ryan feels responsible for bringing them together. Which of course, he is."

"He didn't realize it wasn't a good idea?"

"Ryan isn't a good long-term thinker," Tyler replied.

"I suppose that's true," Kelsey commented.

"So did you miss dancing with me?" Tyler asked her.

"I'm taking the Fifth for all questions, Tyler Olsen," Kelsey replied, smiling at him.

"Smart girl," Tyler replied.

Hours later, Kelsey stirred as she heard the front door open and quietly close. She glanced at the alarm clock. It was seven a.m.

At 9:30 a.m., Kelsey peeked out of her room, showered, and dressed. Zachary was sleeping soundly on the sofa.

An hour later, Kelsey heard noises from the living room. She looked back out. Zachary and Tyler were sitting on the sofa talking.

"Good morning, Kelsey," Tyler said to her.

Zachary rubbed his eyes and smiled at her. "Want to go to brunch?" he asked her.

"Sure," Kelsey replied.

"I'll get dressed," Zach said. He stood up and walked to Tyler's room.

"What are you in the mood for?" Tyler asked Kelsey.

"Anything," she replied.

"There's a place on Capitol Hill I've been wanting to try," Tyler commented. He pulled out his phone. "I'll get us a table," he said, typing into it.

"What else will you do with your one day off?" Kelsey asked.

"I should sleep," Tyler said, thoughtfully. "But there's another meeting about the Taiwan purchase next week, so I'll read the memos about that today."

"Why are there so many meetings about that one deal?"

"Lisa really wants it to happen, and her team isn't up to the task. They're completely out-matched, and Lisa's not happy about it. So she's gathering them together regularly to yell at them."

"Sounds like fun," Kelsey said doubtfully.

"Since I'm not the one on the hot seat, it's fine. It's better than sitting in a lecture with Eliot," Tyler commented.

"Does she yell at her staff a lot?"

"No, that's what makes it interesting to me. It's not her normal management style. I think she's really frustrated and that's why she's lashing out."

"Why is the deal so important?"

"The company that she wants to buy is a major supplier of hardware to Tactec. It's family-owned, and they want to sell, so it's not clear why the deal still isn't finished yet. Tactec's negotiators are being supported by a local team in Taipei, and obviously Tactec has the money. But something isn't going right, and Lisa's trying to figure out what it is."

"Why do you have to go to all these meetings? The deal will get done eventually."

"Once they buy the company, it will have to be integrated into Tactec. It's going to take a while to do that, and Lisa wants Ryan and me to know what's going on from the start. Once we join Tactec in a few years, it will still probably be one of our top agenda items as board members."

"When's the meeting?"

"Tuesday. Simon's already on my case about it because there's a filing Tuesday night. I'm not expecting a lot of sleep over the next few days, so I might as well enjoy my Sunday."

Ryan walked out of his bedroom. "Morning, Kels," he said, as Zachary walked out of Tyler's room.

"Hi, Ryan," she replied.

"We're going to brunch, Ryan. Do you want to come?" Tyler asked.

"No," Ryan replied curtly.

"Thanks for the hospitality, bro," Zach said to him with sarcasm. Ryan gave him a withering look and walked back into his bedroom. He shut the door firmly.

"Come on, let's go," Zach said. He picked up the bag that had been sitting by the arm of the sofa, and he, Kelsey, and Tyler left the condo.

Both Zach and Tyler drove their respective cars. Zachary was going to drive directly back to the Eastside after brunch. They met up in front of the restaurant and went inside. They were seated and looked over the contemporary-Southern-cuisine menu.

They ordered and Zach sat back in his chair.

"So is Ryan going to speak to me again?" Zachary said in amusement.

"You shouldn't aggravate him," Tyler commented.

"He'll get over it," Zachary said. "I'll do what I choose."

"Clearly."

"Don't you start," Zach said.

"I'm done," Tyler said.

"Good. How's Lisa's Asian adventure?"

"A disaster."

"She should give up."

"Lisa never, ever gives up," Tyler replied.

"I know."

"Why do you think she should give up?" Kelsey asked Zach.

"Because she's willing to pay twice as much as the company is worth in order to run it herself," Zachary said.

"She must have a reason," Tyler said.

"That's true. No one ever made money underestimating Lisa. My parents certainly discovered that the hard way."

"What do you mean?" Kelsey asked. "I thought your parents were some of Tactec's first investors."

"They were. About five years after their initial investment, Tyler's mom decided to fire the CFO. There were a few other issues, and my parents decided to sell a good chunk of their Tactec stock. Lisa called them to ask them not to do it, but they went ahead, and the stock dropped. Lisa and Bob got second mortgages on their houses and bought every share they could get their hands on. The stock went up tenfold within three years. My Dad says Tactec was the best and the worst investment they ever made," Zach explained.

"Don't bet against an Olsen," Tyler said.

"Interesting," Kelsey replied.

"So basically your parents are second-guessing Lisa again," Tyler said.

"She doesn't know everything," Zach said.

"That's true."

"So why is she willing to pay so much?" Kelsey asked.

"There's a lot of reasons, but the one that she's given the press is that she expects to have some major cost savings after the merger," Tyler said.

"But of course that isn't the real reason," Zach commented, grinning at Tyler.

"Of course not," Tyler replied. "But I obviously can't tell you."

"I don't see why not. I can't afford to buy Tactec stock," Zach said.

"I'm guessing that your parents still can," Tyler replied. "I'm not in the mood to go to jail for insider trading."

"Oh, come on. We're friends."

"Forget it. We aren't that close," Tyler replied. Zach laughed.

Kelsey was back at the office on Monday, working on a new, less annoying project for David Lim. On Tuesday, she helped Ryan cook green curry chicken, which they wrapped up and took over to Simon and Associates.

"Thanks," Tyler said, tucking into a plate of the Thai curry with rice. Ryan and Kelsey had plates of their own.

Kelsey looked around Tyler's desk. As the summer had gone on, it had slowly become more disorderly, as Tyler had been given more and more responsibilities. The last summer associate — since Simon had fired a third one after he had fallen asleep in a client meeting — Tyler was working on three projects at once.

"Ryan, this is great," Tyler said. "You'll have to cook this one for Jessica."

Ryan beamed. "Thanks. I'm glad that you like it."

"What cuisine are you trying next? It seems that you have Thai down," Kelsey asked him. Tyler was right. The curry was delicious.

"I was thinking Greek," Ryan said, eating a bite of curry. "It isn't too hot?"

"It's perfect," Kelsey said. "Just spicy enough."

"What did you think about the board meeting today, Ryan?" Tyler asked.

"Mostly I was trying not to sleep. Why was Lisa so angry at Roger Eastman, though?"

"That's what I've been trying to figure out. His group isn't really involved in the Taiwan purchase, but she seems to be blaming him for the holdup."

"Whatever," Ryan said. "Why don't you ask her?"

"I will, later. I just wanted to get out of there today," Tyler commented.

"I'm thinking that Bob decided to do so much traveling this summer on purpose."

"He's a smart guy," Tyler said.

Wednesday, Kelsey received what she expected would be her final project for the summer from Emily, a revision of a licensing agreement. After Emily left, Kelsey walked over to Alex's office to get some guidance.

"Hi, Kelsey," Alex said to her.

"Do you have a minute?"

"I always have a minute for you, Miss North. Sit," Alex said.

"I just got a licensing agreement from Emily and I wasn't exactly sure where to start."

"What did Emily say?" Alex asked her.

"To revise it," Kelsey said.

"That's our Em. Always helpful. Let me see it," Alex said. Kelsey handed the contract to him, and he leaned back in his chair to skim through it.

"Did she say what her concerns were?" Alex asked her.

"To make sure the client was protected," Kelsey said.

"We really need to explain to associates how to give assignments to summer associates," Alex said. "Do you have a pen?"

"Yes," Kelsey said, ready to take notes.

"Examine clauses 21 and 22 in particular. They aren't typical clauses in a licensing contract, so try to figure out why opposing counsel wants them in. I wouldn't strip them out, unless you have a clear explanation as to why they shouldn't be in the contract. What Emily should have told you, is that the client wants to be able to license this software to more than one company, so make sure there's nothing in the contract that gets in the way of them being able to do that. Also, make sure there's nothing that grants more than limited rights to the company that is licensing the software."

"Limited rights?" Kelsey asked.

"They can use the software, but not copy and sell it," Alex smiled. "Make sure that's clear. The company is going to insist that they need to be able to copy it, take the source code, and use the software in any way they please. Don't let them." He handed her back the folder.

Kelsey nodded. "Thanks for the help," she said, standing.

"Next week is your last one, right?" Alex asked her.

"It is," Kelsey replied.

"Then you go back to the joy that is Darrow Law School."

"Two more years."

"Are you coming back to us next year?"

"If I'm invited," Kelsey said.

"I'll see what I can do," Alex said to her. "Let me know if you need any more help." He looked back at his computer screen and Kelsey walked out and back to her office.

On Thursday, Kelsey ate with Tyler at his office and helped him do some IP research, while he worked on an M&A brief that was due the following morning. Bill Simon glanced in on them around 9 p.m.

"Making Miss North work again?" Bill Simon said to Tyler.

"I'm thinking about hiring her myself," Tyler commented.

"Are you having trouble keeping up with the workload?" Simon said in amusement.

"A dozen lawyers working on one project would have trouble keeping up with the workload here," Tyler said.

"You're only doing the work of four summer associates," Simon commented. "If you plan on coming back next year, you should learn to become more efficient."

"This is what passes for humor in this office," Tyler said to Kelsey, who giggled.

"I'm sure your mother's legal department has a place for you any time, Mr. Olsen," Simon said.

"The brief will be finished in a timely fashion, Mr. Simon," Tyler replied.

"Glad to hear it, Tyler. It's nice to see you, Kelsey," Simon said, and he left.

"The ultimate threat. Working in my mother's office," Tyler said.

"Is it that bad? Ryan seems okay," Kelsey said.

"Ryan's busy collecting recipes and flirting with support staff. Despite what he's said, I bet he's done twenty minutes of work this summer.

My mother lets him get away with anything." Tyler stretched his arms up. "I'm so tired."

"At least it's Thursday," Kelsey said.

"Yes, I can look forward to my one day off this week," Tyler replied.

"I think someone's looking forward to a relaxing second year of law school," Kelsey said.

"I really don't think I realized how much worse things could get," Tyler commented. "It makes my time with Sophia seem like a day in the park." He sighed. "It isn't like I wasn't warned."

"Collins Nicol would love to have you," Kelsey teased.

"I know. You seem to have had a relaxing summer," Tyler groused.

"You would have too."

"That's what I was afraid of. I could do nothing at Collins, be worked to death here, or deal with my mother's office all summer. Talk about a choice. Maybe next year, I'll go work in Portland."

Kelsey giggled. "Could you?"

Tyler smiled at her. "Not if you're here."

"Hmm," Kelsey said.

The next evening, Kelsey put her key into the lock at Ryan's condo. It was her birthday, and she had had a really nice one. Collins Nicol had given her a specially decorated cupcake, Tyler had sent her pink roses, and Jessica, Morgan, Jasmine, Ben, her parents and grandparents had all called her at work. Every time someone passed by her office today, she had been on the phone. Kelsey wasn't sure if it made her look busy or like she was slacking off. She opened the door.

"Surprise!" Ryan and Tyler said. Kelsey blinked in surprise. The living room was covered in bright yellow-and-pink balloons. And there was a big banner that said, 'Happy Birthday, Kelsey' hanging over the windows.

"Thank you," Kelsey said, walking in and closing the door behind her. She put her bag next to the sofa, and both Ryan and Tyler gave her hugs.

"Happy birthday," Tyler whispered in her ear as he hugged her.

Tyler had taken the evening off, although he was expected back in the office on Saturday. To Kelsey's delight, Ryan and Tyler had prepared dinner for her at home. They tucked into an Italian feast of spaghetti carbonara, garlic bread, and an arugula-and-pear salad.

"That was amazing," Kelsey said to them. "Thank you."

"Now it's time for presents!" Ryan said brightly. He and Tyler both left the table. Tyler returned first, carrying a beautifully-wrapped package. Ryan returned next, carrying a clearly homemade cake.

"Ryan, did you make this?" Kelsey asked in surprise.

"I did," Ryan said proudly.

Kelsey looked at the cake with interest. As far as she knew, Ryan hadn't made any cakes this summer, and the novelty showed. The layers were uneven and the frosting was as well, but Ryan had not only put lit candles on the cake, but had also attempted to pipe 'Happy Birthday Kelsey' on top.

"Wow. Thank you, Ryan," Kelsey said.

Ryan beamed. "It's chocolate with raspberry filling," Ryan said.

"Those are your favorite flavors," Tyler said.

"Kelsey likes them too," Ryan pouted.

"I do," Kelsey said. She blew out the candles.

"Did you make a wish?" Tyler asked her. She smiled mysteriously at him, and he grinned back at her.

"Here," Tyler said, handing her the package. Kelsey weighed it in her hands. It felt a little light to be a book. She opened it and her eyes widened in surprise. It was a brand new iPad.

"Open it. Look on the back." Tyler prompted her. Kelsey opened the box and removed the iPad. She flipped it over. On the back, it had been engraved with the words *Justitia et Lux*. Justice and light, the motto of Darrow Law School.

"Tyler, thank you," Kelsey said in awe.

"You're welcome," Tyler said to her.

"Open mine," Ryan pouted, handing her a small box. Kelsey took the box and unwrapped it. The box inside read Cartier, which Kelsey knew was a very expensive jewelry brand. Nestled inside the box were a pair of small hoop earrings, made out of tri-colored gold.

"Ryan, these are beautiful," Kelsey said. "Thank you."

"You're welcome, Kelsey," Ryan said. "I gave her two presents," he said to Tyler.

"Two?"

"The cake and the earrings," Ryan said.

"I sent her flowers this morning," Tyler replied.

"I made the cake. Everyone knows that homemade things are better. Kelsey said so," Ryan said.

Kelsey looked up from the earrings.

"Are you two competitive about everything?" she asked.

The boys looked at each other.

"Yes, except for grades," Tyler said.

"And partying," Ryan added.

"I see," Kelsey said in amusement.

"Let's have cake," Ryan said, standing up to get plates.

"Do you want ice cream?" Tyler asked.

"Is there still peanut butter ice cream?" Kelsey asked him.

"Of course," Tyler replied with a grin.

Late that night, Kelsey lay in bed, trying out the iPad. She had discovered to her surprise, that in addition to the iPad itself, she had a $1000 credit in the Apple Store. Tyler had smiled when she asked him about it.

"Apple doesn't give refunds on gift cards. Enjoy it."

Kelsey sighed as she dragged her finger across the touchscreen. She had really lived a life of luxury this summer. Ryan had rebuffed her offer to pay rent by pointing out that Tyler wasn't paying anything to stay with him, that he was a guest, just as she was. Tyler had fed her food from some of Seattle's most expensive restaurants when she spent evenings at his office, and she couldn't remember the last time she pulled out her wallet outside of the hours of work, during the rare times she paid for a lunch or went to Starbucks. She had even got free underwear, courtesy of Mariel.

Kelsey knew that she could live without these luxuries, but they seemed to come with the territory of hanging out with Tyler and Ryan. She knew what her mother would think. At least at Darrow, she would pay for her own room and would eat at the dining hall again. In the meantime, Kelsey had to admit that she had had a very special birthday.

As expected, Tyler headed back to work first thing on Saturday morning. Margaret came over to teach Ryan how to bake bread. Kelsey found Margaret delightful. She was like Tyler's sweet Norwegian grandmother, with wise sayings to match.

"Ryan," she scolded in her softly accented voice, "You have to use warm water when you're preparing the yeast. You're trying to wake them up, not freeze them."

"Sorry," Ryan said, frowning. "Maybe I'll just buy bread."

"Ryan Alexander. There is no taste better than fresh-baked bread," Margaret said.

"I can think of other things I prefer," Ryan commented.

"You aren't learning to cook for yourself," Margaret replied.

"I guess."

"Stir," Margaret commanded him.

Ryan stirred.

"Kelsey?"

"Yes, Ma'am?" Kelsey replied.

"Measure out two-thirds of a cup of brown sugar," Margaret said.

"Okay," Kelsey said. She retrieved a measuring cup and carefully measured out the brown sugar.

"And four tablespoons of cinnamon," Margaret added.

Kelsey measured out the cinnamon.

"Are you listening, Ryan?" Margaret asked him.

"To what?" Ryan asked.

"The yeast. It's speaking to you," Margaret said. Ryan looked at Margaret as if she were crazy.

"What is it saying?" he asked.

"That it's almost done," she replied. "Look at your bowl." Ryan looked at the bowl. The yeast was slowly beginning to foam.

"Kelsey, please chop enough pecans to fill a cup." Kelsey retrieved the pecans and began to chop them with a knife.

"Why are we using pecans?" Ryan asked Margaret. "The recipe calls for walnuts."

"Tyler doesn't like walnuts," Margaret said to him.

"I'm not making this for Tyler."

"You aren't making it. I am," Margaret corrected him. "So we will make it the way that Tyler prefers."

"This is why Tyler is so spoiled," Ryan commented.

"You should talk, Ryan Alexander," Margaret replied, smiling at him.

"Fine," Ryan pouted. "Now that the yeast is talking, what do I do with it?"

"Pour it into the bowl with the flour."

"This one?" Ryan asked, pulling over a bowl he had prepared earlier with flour and several other ingredients.

"Yes," Margaret said. "Kelsey, are the pecans chopped?"

"Yes, Margaret," Kelsey replied.

"Excellent. Ryan, stir the yeast in, and I'll chop the apples."

"Stir or mix, Margaret?"

"Stir with the mixer, Ryan," Margaret said.

Ryan turned on the mixer and blended the yeast into the bowl, while Margaret deftly chopped up the apples. Ryan turned off the mixer and took a piece of apple.

"Are we using this kind of apple because Tyler prefers them?" Ryan asked.

"No, because they are perfect for baking with," Margaret said, sliding the chopped apples into a bowl. "But Ryan, one of the benefits of cooking for others is that you can tailor your choices to their tastes. If they don't like a certain spice or flavor, you can just substitute a different ingredient."

"How do you know what they like?" Ryan asked her, as she turned the bread dough into an oiled bowl and turned it.

"Of course you can ask them. But if you cook for someone for a long time, you will learn their preferences. You, for example, like berries. Lisa prefers citrus." Margaret said as she covered the bowl.

"And Tyler?" Kelsey asked.

"Chocolate."

"Not a fruit?" Kelsey asked.

"Not unless it's with chocolate," Margaret said. She took some previously prepared dough and began to roll it out.

"What about Bob?" Kelsey asked.

"Ryan's father doesn't like sweets," Margaret commented. She handed the rolling pin to Ryan, who rolled it over the dough.

"Crazy, right?" Ryan said to Kelsey.

"Kelsey, let me have the cinnamon and sugar please," Margaret said. Kelsey handed her both bowls. Margaret dumped the cinnamon into the sugar, and began to stir them with a spoon.

"Am I done? This hurts my arms," Ryan said.

"You really need to work out," Kelsey commented. She took the rolling pin and finished rolling out the dough.

Margaret took a pastry brush and brushed melted butter over the dough. She handed Ryan the sugar mixture.

"Take half and sprinkle it over the dough."

"It sticks together," Ryan complained.

"It's supposed to," Margaret said. "Do the best you can."

Ryan sprinkled the dough with the sugar. Margaret followed him, by sprinkling the pecans and apples over the dough. She ran a knife over the pieces, pushing the nuts and fruit deeper into the dough. Then she rolled up the dough, as Ryan watched carefully, and placed it into a prepared loaf pan.

"Now what do we do?" Ryan asked impatiently.

"Now, Ryan Alexander, we wait," Margaret replied.

Later that evening, Ryan, Tyler and Kelsey sat on the sofa and watched movies. Kelsey and Ryan ate the bread that they had made with

Margaret, while Tyler ate the chocolate chip cookies she had made for him while she was in the apartment.

"You don't want any more?" Kelsey asked, holding out a piece of bread to him. It was absolutely delicious.

Tyler shook his head no. "There's no chocolate in it," he said.

On Sunday, at Ryan's insistence, they returned to Alki Beach. Kelsey felt particularly strange wearing her new bikini in front of Tyler after his late-night conversation with Ryan, but he didn't seem to notice.

When Kelsey returned to the condo on Monday night, she was surprised to see Jeffrey standing in the living room, holding a clipboard. The door to the office was open, and she could glimpse workmen inside.

"Hello, Miss North," Jeffrey said.

"Hi, Jeffrey."

"Hi, Kels," Ryan said to her. "I'm not cooking tonight."

"Do you want me to?" she asked him.

"No, thanks," Ryan replied.

"I'll go over to Tyler's later, then," Kelsey said. It was her last week at Collins Nicol, and she didn't have a lot to do. Alex had helped her a lot with Emily's licensing contract, having dropped off one of the standard contracts he had drafted, and she was almost done. "How's the renovation?" she asked. Ryan had taken Tyler's advice and had asked Jeffrey to transform the office into a bedroom.

"Almost done," Ryan said, walking into his own room.

"Really?" Kelsey craned her neck to look into the spare room. Ryan was right — the room had been repainted, carpet laid down, and the workmen were currently assembling a bed.

"Jeffrey? May I ask you a question?" Kelsey asked him.

Jeffrey looked up at her in interest. "Of course, Miss North," he replied.

Kelsey took a deep breath. "What would Tyler like for his birthday?"

she asked. She was completely clueless what to get for him. Ryan had been less than useless when she had asked him, and she had already asked Tyler. She had decided that Jeffrey might have an idea. He seemed to know all of Tyler's preferences, much like Margaret.

Jeffrey smiled at her. "What have you considered?" he asked her.

"Everything," Kelsey said. And she had. Books, music, but as Ryan had pointed out, if Tyler had wanted it, he probably would have already bought it.

Jeffrey nodded thoughtfully. "Well, Miss North, buying a gift for a billionaire is quite difficult."

Don't I know it, Kelsey thought grumpily.

"I would suggest that you consider purchasing something rare," Jeffrey said.

Kelsey frowned. Rare meant expensive in her view.

"It doesn't need to be expensive, but it should show creativity," Jeffrey said, as if reading her thoughts. "Some of the most appreciated gifts that Ms. Olsen has been given are things like first-edition books, one-of-a-kind clothing items, and art. Tyler is quite an avid reader, so you might want to start there."

Kelsey nodded. "Thank you, Jeffrey."

"Happy to help, Miss North," he said to her. Kelsey turned and walked to her room. Talking to Jeffrey had given her an idea, and now she just needed to find out whether she could afford it.

On Tuesday, Kelsey attended the final summer associate luncheon. Unlike the first one, she stayed far away from Lucas, and of course she made sure there was a lot of distance from Brittany. Alex Carsten sat down next to her.

"Leaving us, Miss North?" he asked.

"I can't believe it's already the end of summer," Kelsey said.

"How's Emily's contract going?"

"I sent a draft to her this morning," Kelsey said. "She said she would let me know if there were any changes."

"Great. I'm sure you did a good job."

"Thanks, Alex," Kelsey said.

On Wednesday afternoon, Tyler and Ryan were called to a special meeting on the Taiwan purchase, so Kelsey was surprised when they were both at home when she arrived after work.

"Don't worry, I'm going back to work," Tyler said, seeing the look on her face.

"I thought maybe Simon had fired you," Kelsey said seriously.

"No such luck," Tyler replied. "I just decided to take advantage of the fact that I was already out of the office. We have a filing on Friday."

"Again?" Ryan asked. He was making tea.

"Always," Tyler said. He took a chocolate-chip cookie and broke it in half. He handed a piece to Kelsey, who took it. "Want to go back with me?"

Kelsey smiled. "I'd love to," she replied. "What's for dinner?"

At 4:55 on Friday afternoon, Kelsey was looking around her office, making sure she hadn't forgot to pack anything. It was the end of her summer internship. Alex knocked on her open door.

"Hi, Alex," Kelsey said.

"Hi," he said, coming into her office and closing the door behind him. He sat casually in one of the client chairs.

"I'm not your official mentor."

"I know," Kelsey replied.

"Because if I was, I couldn't ask you out," Alex said to her.

Kelsey blinked in surprise. Alex was the associate that was interested in her?

"Ask me out?"

"Sure. Now that you're heading back to Darrow, would you like to go to dinner with me?" Alex asked.

Kelsey thought for the briefest of moments. Alex must have been the associate that Zachary had been hinting about. He had said that she shouldn't tease Tyler about him, because Tyler saw him as a threat to starting a relationship with Kelsey.

But she didn't see Alex that way. She saw him as a friend. Tyler had girl friends as well, Sophia being a perfect example of that.

"I'd love to," Kelsey replied.

Tyler worked his usual half-day on Saturday, then the three of them hung out at the pool at Ryan's condo.

"I'm going to miss this," Kelsey said.

"Live with us next summer," Tyler said. "We know we'll be in Seattle."

"I don't."

"They'll want you back, Miss North," Tyler said.

"Maybe," Kelsey said. Alex had told her that the firm would make summer offers on Monday, and that he had put in a good word for her.

"Work for Tactec," Ryan said, pulling his sunglasses down over his eyes.

"No. Don't do that," Tyler said. "There's no reason you should suffer."

Kelsey giggled.

On Sunday, Tyler drove them to Ballard and the trio rented bikes and rode on the bike trail between Ballard and Fremont. Kelsey was able to visit the two Sunday markets that she had gone to earlier in the summer. They ended the evening sitting on the canal, eating take-out from an organic health food grocery, watching boats float past them.

Monday, Ryan was back in the kitchen. Kelsey lay on the sofa reading a book that she had checked out of the library.

Kelsey glanced at her phone. She had got a message from Jessica.

Ryan didn't disappoint.

Kelsey wondered what the message meant, but Jessica wrote nothing else.

What do you mean? Kelsey replied.

Later, Jessica replied, logging out.

Kelsey shrugged and returned her mind to her book.

"Jess isn't returning my messages," Ryan said to Kelsey at dinner that evening. They were sitting outside at a restaurant on the Harbor Steps along with Tyler, who was reading a brief. "Is she okay?"

"I think so," Kelsey said. "She messaged me today, and said she'd talk later."

Ryan nodded thoughtfully. "Well, she'll be back on Wednesday. I can't believe the summer's finally over."

"Finally?" Tyler asked. "You used to love summer."

"I missed Jess," Ryan said. "She can't go back to New York next summer. I'll die."

Tyler laughed. "It's up to her, you know."

"You don't understand. Kelsey was here in Seattle. You didn't have anyone to miss."

Tyler glanced at Kelsey. "True. Well, I'm personally looking forward to the relaxing quiet of Darrow Law School. Bill Simon is insane."

"It was good though, wasn't it?" Kelsey said.

"He's brilliant. But I'm so tired. I didn't know I could work so many hours in one day," Tyler said.

"What are you reading?" Ryan asked him.

"A brief that's due tomorrow. One more day. Seriously, I'm sleeping all day Wednesday."

"Why are you working tomorrow? Why did you work today?" Ryan asked. "School starts this week."

"Bill Simon knows how to read the Darrow Law School calendar," Tyler replied. "He figured one day off was enough."

"Are you seriously going to work for him next summer?" Ryan asked.

"I am," Tyler said. "I learned more in two weeks with him than I learned last semester at Darrow."

Kelsey sipped her drink. She was excited that she had been offered a job at Collins Nicol for the next summer. She had got the call this morning.

"I guess we all know what next summer will look like. I'm glad to avoid the drama of job interviews next year," Tyler said.

"You could have avoided it this year," Ryan said.

"Your summer wasn't that much better than mine. I told you Lisa would work you to death."

"I didn't have anything to do anyway," Ryan said.

"I know. I had a busier social calendar than you did," Tyler said. "And that's just pathetic."

Ryan laughed. "I'm a changed man," he said. He smiled broadly. "I can't wait to see Jess." Ryan's phone rang, and he put it on speaker.

"Yes?" he said.

"Hello, Mr. Perkins. This is Susan in PR. I'm sorry to bother you, but we've been asked numerous times to make a comment about Dara Smith."

"Dara? What about her?" Ryan asked. Tyler looked up from his brief.

"The media outlets are reporting that you are about to get engaged to Ms. Smith."

Ryan laughed. "That's ridiculous."

"So we should say no comment?"

"No, you should tell them it's ridiculous. I've been on one date with her," Ryan replied.

"Mr. Perkins, Ms. Smith is claiming in her social media feed that you're in a relationship with her."

"What?" Ryan said. "You must be joking." Tyler put his brief to the side and pulled out his iPad.

"At least two news weeklies have featured Ms. Smith's claims and a third is publishing this weekend," Susan said.

Tyler placed his iPad under Ryan's nose and Ryan looked down.

"I'll, I'll call you back," Ryan said in dismay. He hung up the phone and took the iPad.

On the iPad was a story from a celebrity news website. The headline was *Wedding bells for Ryan Perkins and Dara Smith?*

Kelsey looked over Ryan's shoulder as he scrolled down the page.

For weeks, new model Dara Smith has been teasing us with her snaps of her relationship with bad boy billionaire Ryan Perkins on Instagram.

Following the text was a photo of Dara with Ryan at the Tactec party, along with some of the selfies Kelsey had seen Ryan take with Dara. Additionally, there were several photos that Dara seemingly had taken herself the day she was in Ryan's apartment.

The selfie of Ryan freshly out of the shower.

One of her holding his bare chest before he put on his shirt.

A photo of Dara wearing his robe.

And one of her lying seductively in his bed.

Each had been captioned and dated in a way to imply that Dara and Ryan were in a relationship that had evolved over the weeks since the Tactec party.

"Oh, no," Ryan whispered, handing the iPad back to Tyler.

"Don't panic," Tyler said to him. "Call Jessica."

"This is why she's not returning my messages," Ryan said. "Kelsey, did she mention this to you?"

Kelsey thought for a moment about the message she had received this morning. *Ryan didn't disappoint.*

"I think she was going to," Kelsey replied. Ryan covered his eyes with the palm of his hand and ran his fingers through his hair. Abruptly, he picked up his phone and dialed a number.

"What are you doing?" he demanded.

"Ryan? So nice to hear from you," Dara's voice said.

"I am not in a relationship with you," he said.

"I know, silly. Those nasty tabloids," Dara said.

"Deny it," Ryan said.

"Of course not. I've never gotten so many bookings," Dara said. "You're well known for dating the next hot supermodel. You dated Kimberly Chan and now everyone thinks you're dating me."

"You are ruining my life," Ryan said softly.

"You're Ryan Perkins. I couldn't ruin your life. Everyone knows what you're like," Dara said. Then she disconnected.

Ryan sat frozen. Tyler and Kelsey looked at him, both unsure of what to say.

"She's never going to believe me. I've lost her," Ryan finally said. Tyler put his hand on Ryan's shoulder.

"We'll tell Jessica the truth. Right, Kels?"

"Of course, Ryan. We know Dara's lying about you," Kelsey said. "Jess will understand."

Ryan put his head on the table and sat there unmoving. He said nothing else all night.

Ryan spent most of Tuesday sitting in front of the television. But Kelsey had the feeling that he wasn't watching anything that was on. She wanted to comfort him about Jessica, but she had no idea what to say. Jessica wasn't responding to her messages either.

At 6 p.m., Kelsey walked over to Tyler's office, carrying take-out from Pike Place Market. She had bought it herself, her first purchase in a while. When she arrived at Simon's office, she walked into Bill Simon.

"Hello, Kelsey," he said. "Did you enjoy your summer?"

"I did," Kelsey replied.

"Did they make you an offer for next year?" he asked.

"They did."

"And you accepted?" Bill Simon asked.

"I did," Kelsey replied.

"My loss. Let me know if you change your mind. I know you did half of Tyler's work for him." Simon winked at her, and headed to the outer doors. Kelsey giggled and walked back to Tyler's office. He was typing, per usual.

He looked up. "Hi, Kels."

"Your last night," she said.

"That it is. What did you bring me?"

"Mexican."

"Thanks, I'm starving. Did you eat?"

"I brought some for me too. I can eat with you."

"Even better," Tyler said. He cleared a space on his side table and they set up the food. He and Kelsey pulled up the client chairs and began to eat.

"How's Ryan?" Tyler asked.

"He hasn't said a word all day." Kelsey said.

"What is he doing? Cooking?"

"Watching TV," Kelsey said.

Tyler sighed.

"Did you read the articles?" Kelsey asked. She knew that Tyler didn't usually read stories about Ryan, but she had a feeling that this might be different.

"I did. It doesn't look good," Tyler said. "The media is convinced that it's true, and Dara's not telling them otherwise."

"What about Ryan?"

"He hasn't let them put out a statement."

"Why hasn't he denied it?"

"I don't think he sees the point. No one would believe Ryan anyway," Tyler said.

Kelsey took a bite of her food. Of course Tyler was right. Dara had said it — Ryan's reputation preceded him. No matter how much he had changed over the last year, there weren't a lot of people who would believe Ryan. And Kelsey was afraid that would include Jessica.

Wednesday morning, Kelsey, Ryan and Tyler left the condo and drove to Bellevue to have lunch and to stop by the mall so Ryan could buy jeans. Almost the only words Ryan spoke were to the staff at the store.

At the mall, Ryan stopped to look at the cookbooks. Kelsey slipped away to look at the newsstand. As she looked through the celebrity section, to her dismay, she saw photos of Ryan and Dara on at least two magazine covers.

By the time they arrived at their new home next to Darrow, all of their things had been moved from Ryan's condo and into their respective apartments. Even all of Ryan's cookbooks had been neatly replaced in a brand new bookshelf next to the small kitchen. Kelsey hadn't packed anything, not even a sweater.

After a quick tour of the boys' new apartment, Kelsey went to her own. She assumed Jessica would be back soon. Jessica hadn't told anyone the time of her return flight.

A few hours later, Kelsey opened the door of her new apartment. Jessica wheeled her bag in.

"Jess," Kelsey said hugging her.

"Kelsey," Jessica said, hugging Kelsey back. She broke away. Jessica looked tired.

She sat on the edge of the sofa. "I knew he'd break my heart," she said softly.

"Jess, he's not dating Dara. I've lived with him for the past month. Don't you think I would have noticed if something was going on?

"You're in denial about Tyler. I can't imagine you'd do any better figuring out Ryan."

"Jess..."

"I don't want to talk about it."

"He didn't do it," Kelsey said.

Jessica looked at her in disdain.

"Ha," Jessica scoffed. "I've seen her. Of course he did. I don't want to talk about Ryan," she said. There was a knock on the door.

Jessica stood up and opened it. Ryan and Tyler stood in the doorway.

"I saw you arrive," Ryan said. "Can I come in?"

"No," Jessica said. "You can't."

"Jess, I didn't do it."

"How many times have you said that in your life?"

"It's true," Ryan insisted.

"Right. Stop this, Ryan," Jessica said. "Let me move on with my life."

"Jessica…" Tyler began, but she cut him off.

"I know whose side you're on, Tyler. So you can stop too," She began to shut the door, but Ryan pushed it back open.

"Jessica, don't do this. Listen to me," he said.

"I'm done hearing your excuses," Jessica said. "We're over." She pushed the door hard, and closed it.

"Jessica!" Ryan wailed outside the door.

Jessica leaned against the door. Kelsey looked at her as Jessica burst into tears.

Want my unreleased 5000-word story

Introducing the Billionaire Boys Club

and other free gifts from time to time?

Then join my mailing list at

http://www.caramillerbooks.com/inner-circle/

Subscribe now and read it now!

You can also follow me on Twitter and Facebook